B

T. Edwards-Barks

Enduring Love Series – Book One

Never Unloved

Enduring Love Series – Book Two

Sealed with a Kiss

Never Unloved

Enduring Love Series — Book One

T. Edwards-Barks

Prepared for publication by 40DayPublishing.com

Cover design by 40DayGraphics.com

Printed in the United States of America

Chapter 1

Forty years later, Tessa could still taste his kiss, still feel his lips on her neck, inching lower. She still flushed at the memory of his warm breath on her cheeks. And she could still hear his sexy voice whispering in her ear, as his hands moved behind her, pulling her close. Her memories of him never waned, but they'd also never taken hold of her like this until recently. Where the hell did that come from? Why, after forty years, did he suddenly flood her thoughts this way? She rarely saw him; they almost never talked. Oh sure, over the years she ran into him a few times, and they were always glad to see each other. They shared quick chats peppered with small talk about what was going on in each other's lives, how many years it had been, and how the families were doing. They always parted with a smile, carrying with them fond memories of days gone by. But they hadn't seen each other in years.

Tessa was caught off guard by the force of these memories of him, so pure and clear. She would never forget the details of his handsome face or the way it felt to be held in his arms. She felt protected, loved, cherished. She always considered him the one who got away and still wondered what prompted him to break it off. She remembered the heartbreak, the desperation of wanting nothing more than to find out why. After almost a year and a half, why did his feelings change overnight? To say it came out of the blue would be an understatement. They were so young, she finally chalked it up to her fear of taking their relationship to the next level, going "all the way." She had definitely been scared—of what, she wasn't sure. But Dylan, ever the gentleman never pressured her. For that, she would always be grateful, but sometimes she wished she would have summoned the courage to ask

1

him what changed instead of tearfully walking away with a broken heart. Now, suddenly Dylan was all she thought about. Her mind sifted back through the memories. Their relationship felt like a dream, almost like a Romeo and Juliet romance. Well, almost—but without the whole suicide thing. She drifted back further, to where it all began.

May 1978

One evening, when Tessa was fifteen, her parents loaded the family up in the car, announcing they were all going to visit an old friend. Her dad had run into Donny, a previous next-door neighbor they hadn't seen in years. They pulled up to the house, and everyone piled out and headed inside. The house was nothing fancy, but it was nice and clean. Making small talk, they learned that Donny's ex-wife had become a home health nurse and was attending to a patient who was sadly nearing the end of his life. Donny's three sons sat silently in the living room, along with Tessa and her siblings, listening to the adults catch up. As they sat and listened to the "old folks" reminisce about old times and what they had been doing since they last saw each other, she found she couldn't take her eyes off Donny's oldest son, Dylan. Dylan was handsome, with green eyes and a mysterious expression. The adults droned on for what seemed like forever, talking about people she didn't know and places that she could only vaguely remember. She couldn't have kept up with the conversation even if she'd wanted to because she so was focused on Dylan. She noticed him looking at her, too, catching her off-guard. She blushed. She couldn't remember any other time a boy made her blush. Then he spoke to her, and suddenly the visit didn't seem so intolerable anymore.

He asked her all the usual questions: how old she was, what grade was she in, if she liked school. Then, he suddenly asked her if she was dating anyone. After she told him no, the questions just stopped. She wasn't sure what to make of his sudden silence. She felt confused— a little disappointed, yet still hopeful. Every time she glanced his way, he was looking at her, and he was not shy about it either. His smile when she caught him staring was amazing; his whole face lit up. Then he would abruptly look away. Feeling awkward, she took an envelope from her back pocket that held a letter from her best friend. She already knew what it said, but it gave her something to do other than just sit there. She read it twice, then put it back in her pocket. When she lifted her eyes again, he was watching her, smiling, eyes sparkling. The odd feeling that he could read her mind washed over her, which was a bit uncomfortable because she had just been daydreaming about being his girl, thinking about where they would go and what they would do. She told herself she was just being silly.

Suddenly, her older brother, Jaime's voice broke through her thoughts, announcing he was going outside. After getting her mom's permission to go with him, she stood to follow Jamie out. Dylan rose and led the way. The three of them milled around out front as Jamie lit a cigarette and asked Dylan about his car. Tessa knew nothing about cars. She stood a few feet away, watching them. She was entirely focused on Dylan, fascinated at the excitement and passion he showed while telling Jamie about the condition of the car when he bought it and all of the improvements he had made. He showed so much pride talking about "her." She smirked. Why did guys always refer to their cars that way?

Jamie finished his cigarette, and they all moved to the porch where they sat, making small talk. Dylan kept looking at her and smiling. Completely unaware of what they were talking about, she concentrated on trying not to stare at him, reminding herself to look away. But each time she glanced back, his eyes were on her, and he was smiling. Conversation trickled to a stop, and they were finally just staring at each other in the quiet. Jamie rolled his eyes and walked back into the house. Instinctively, Tessa got up to follow him.

"Wait," Dylan said, just as she walked past him. She stopped and looked at him, waiting.

"What?" she asked. He reached behind her, pulled out the letter that was peeking out of her pocket, and took off running. What the hell, she thought. That's not cool. And she took off after him. He ran out into the yard and around the house with her hot on his tail. He finally stopped in the back yard behind a tree. They bolted back and forth, from one side of the tree to the other, for several minutes.

Finally, he stopped and held the letter at full arm's length above his head. As soon as her reaching fingers touched his hand to grab the note, she felt a spark that made her jump back. At first, she didn't know what to make of it. His gaze was leveled on her, left eyebrow raised. The smirk on his face taunted her, clearly asking what she was going to do now. She pleaded for him to give the letter back, explaining that it was a letter from her best friend. His smirk faded into a genuine smile, and she melted right then and there. She could still feel that spark where their hands touched, and she was pretty sure it was going to burn her from the inside out. She softly asked him to give the letter back, and this time he agreed—if she promised to go out with him.

Her heart leapt but came crashing back to reality as she suddenly remembered the rule. "My parents don't allow me to date. I have to wait until I'm sixteen, which won't be until December."

Dylan didn't miss a beat. "Of this year?"

"Yes, New Year's Eve of all days."

"That sounds like a fun birthday," he said.

Tessa's forehead furrowed. "Not really. I'm always stuck at home babysitting."

"Well, not this year, little lady. I will make sure of that!" he promised with a wink.

She couldn't help but smile. "You're a bit cocky, aren't you?"

"I have a way with parents," he assured her. "We will be going out soon, you'll see. Before you leave here tonight, we will have a date set for this weekend. Follow me inside and watch me work my parental magic."

"You really are full of yourself," Tessa said dryly.

"I have heard that before. And while I would love to argue with you about it because you are really cute when you are frustrated, I have work to do if we are going to make this a date. We better get inside before your mama comes looking for you." She started to move but couldn't seem to get anywhere. Both stood frozen for a few seconds.

Dylan smirked. "Thought we were going inside?"

"I am, as soon as you give me back my letter," Tessa insisted.

"You still have to promise to go out with me when I get your mama to agree."

She still couldn't believe this was happening. Her mouth went dry. "Okay, I promise," she said, barely above a whisper.

"That didn't sound too convincing," he teased.

Tessa cleared her throat and found her voice. "A proper young lady keeps her word. You get Mama to agree, and I will go out with you."

Dylan grinned and quickly bent down as if to kiss her, but at the last moment turned to whisper in her ear, "You owe me." At the same time, he slid the letter back into her pocket, letting his hand linger on top. She pulled back, blushing, and turned to walk into the house with a dreamy grin on her face. Dylan opened the door, placing his hand on her lower back to guide her into the house, causing her whole body to heat up like never before.

"Please, Mama, say yes!" she said under her breath as she walked into the living room where the story of Dylan and Tessa began.

Chapter 2

ylan picked her up the following Friday, right on time. She was blissfully happy and excited for her first date but nervous at the same time. Butterflies danced in her stomach. Mama had fallen for Dylan's charms and agreed to this date, but not without giving her "the talk" about behaving like a lady. Mama also scared her with dire warnings about how some guys would force themselves on young girls, but she reassured Tessa that Dylan would most likely be a gentleman because that's how his mama and daddy raised him. But sitting beside him, all of Mama's warnings kept running through her mind, and she couldn't help but be nervous about what to expect. Mama made every boy sound like a heathen who could barely keep his hands to himself.

Dylan headed to the local drive-thru to get something to drink, as the two chatted, getting to know each other on the way to his house. After saying hello to his father and little brother, they headed to his room. As Tessa stepped through the door, she noted it was a typical boy's room with a bed, nightstand, and dresser. Posters of cars with women in bikinis draped across them covered his walls. She was surprised the room was clean and not a complete mess like Jamie's room always seemed to be. Sitting on the edge of the bed, they talked, eager to find out more about each other. His brother, Cal, came in holding hands with his girlfriend, Shelly. Tessa and Shelly became instant friends. The four of them visited for a while, then Dylan announced it was time to take Tessa home. The perfect gentleman, Dylan opened the car door for her. As they approached her house, all Tessa could think about was whether he would try to kiss her or not.

He didn't disappoint. Sitting in his car in the driveway of her parents' house, Dylan leaned in and gently kissed her on the lips. That first kiss was quick and sweet, sending shivers of desire racing through her. The second was even more magical. Parting her lips with his tongue, Dylan deepened the kiss for a few short seconds. Tessa had never been kissed like that. She melted right on the spot. Dylan pulled back and softly asked if she was disappointed in her first date. She quickly reassured him that she actually felt relieved after hearing horror stories from her mom. She thanked him for the evening and for being a gentleman.

Dylan looked her in the eyes and promised, "I will always treat you like a lady. I would never push you into something you don't want. I had a great time tonight, and I can't wait to go out again, if you are up for it?"

Tessa's heart skipped a beat as she replied, "I would like that."

As he walked her to the door, they decided he should pop inside to say hello to her parents. Still feeling the magic of Dylan's kisses, Tessa found the small talk boring. At least until she realized that it wasn't just their parents that had once been neighbors. As her parents droned on, they discovered that when Tessa was a baby and Dylan a toddler, they lived next door to each other. Tessa walked Dylan back outside. They stood out on the porch, sharing their disbelief that technically, they'd known each other all their lives. As they ran out of things to say, Dylan leaned in and kissed her gently on the cheek, then climbed reluctantly into the driver's seat. She waited on the porch, watching until his car disappeared, then walked inside, straight to her room with a silly grin on her face.

Shaking her thoughts free from the past, Tessa found herself wondering again where these memories were coming from. Forty years and three kids later, Tessa felt very content with her life. As far as she was concerned, life turned out how it was supposed to. Her relationship with her husband, Tom, had been happy until she lost him twenty-five years ago in a car accident on his way home from work. Since then, she had dated a few guys over the years but never came close to remarrying. Her children came first. Now, they were all grown, living their own lives. Tessa was very proud of them all.

So why did Dylan flood her thoughts now? Maybe she was having a mid-life crisis. Or she could have mad housewife's disease. Did that even really exist? She'd heard talk about it, usually followed by stories of ugly divorce and more unhappiness. Perhaps she simply craved having a companion. Whenever she and Tom had explored the hypothetical "what if's" life can throw your way, he always told her to embrace love. He didn't want her to be unhappy, to be alone, but of course, she never really believed it would happen to her. Once it did, and the waves of grief steadied, she found ways to fill her time, to enrich her life. Tessa spent time in her garden, craving the feeling of warm soil under her hands. She loved to travel, and she went on adventures with friends from time to time. Mainly with Laura, whose carpe diem wild side usually got them into trouble. Tessa always took control of the crazy situations they found themselves in, getting Laura safely back to their hotel room or the cabin on whatever cruise ship they were on. The kids came to visit often, and she spent time with them at their houses, too, especially during the holidays. Tessa would describe her life as full. But still, she missed her husband. And she had to admit that sometimes, she still craved the warm touch of a man on long, lonely nights.

Tessa tried to busy herself with her daily routine but couldn't get Dylan off her mind. And each time he invaded her thoughts, she smiled.

May 1978

Tessa spent the entire school day in a trance. With summer vacation only a few weeks away, her classes couldn't capture her attention. Bored and restless, she penned a letter to her best friend, Laura. The two became pen pals when Laura's family moved away several years ago, still exchanging at least one letter each week. And this week Tessa had big news to share. She had found "the one."

Laura,

Hey girl, how are things in hell? Ha, just kidding. I can't tell you how much I miss you. I need my bestie right now. I have so much to tell you and don't know where to start. Remember when we were talking the other night, and I told you I had a date? Well... we went out last night. And it was an awesome first date! We talked and talked. He asked a lot of questions. Oh, and I met his brother's girlfriend, Shelly. Really cool, you would like her. And she has gorgeous, long, wavy hair. UGH, it's all natural. You know, the hair we've always wanted but will never have?

Anyway, hopefully we can get together this summer. It seems like it has been forever. And I really want to meet Clayton. Gotta see if he's good enough to be with my bestie, ya know!

I bet you would like Dylan. He's sweet, and good looking, and he has a car! And guess what... He kissed me! It was sooo nice. Not at all like what Mama said. Maybe she grew up with pigs, but Dylan is nothing like that. It's almost like he can see right through me and knows how I'm feeling. We are going out again tonight! Oh, and when he got home after dropping me off, he called and said he already missed me. Isn't that sweet? Laura, I think I found the one!

I haven't been able to focus on anything today. I'm so glad school is almost out. Thankfully my grades are decent enough to get me through these next few weeks or I would flunk for sure! But I still have to study for tests in math and science tomorrow so I will close for now. Write back soon! I miss you so much.

LYLAS,

Tessa + Dylan

Laura + Clayton

All the way home from school, she thought about nothing but Dylan. But of course, that's all she thought about anyway. She walked faster, obsessed about getting home quickly so she could do her chores and study for those tests. Bad grades would get her grounded for sure and then she wouldn't be able to spend more time with him. She couldn't let that happen! He called around 6:00 that evening, outlining the plan to shower and head that way. Giddy, she hurried through her chores, promising herself she would study when she got back from their date. Afterall, she couldn't focus on schoolwork now, even if she wanted to. Walking on air, she turned her attention to getting ready to go.

He arrived within the hour looking dashing in his blue jeans and t-shirt, hair still damp from his shower, and that irresistible smile on his face. Mama warned them both to be home before 10:00 pm and not one minute later. Dylan held open the passenger side door and she climbed in, sliding to the middle on the bench seat. He jumped in, turned the key, then rested his arm on her knee before pulling away from the house. The feel of his closeness wrapped her in a silky cocoon of euphoria. Just like before, they ended up at his house. After watching a show in the living room, they moved to his bedroom and began talking about random things. Out of the blue, Dylan leaned over and kissed her, leaving her speechless. As she relaxed into the kiss, his tongue eased into her mouth, sending shivers of desire racing through her. A moment of doubt tried to pierce the moment. She wasn't used to kissing like this. She knew she was winging it, but then he deepened the kiss, and she surrendered to it. As she melted into him, his arms tightened around her. The timing seemed perfect because she suddenly wasn't sure she could hold herself up anymore. He gazed into her eyes, and she felt as if she was floating.

"I'm afraid someone is going to come and snatch you away from me. What would I do if I couldn't look into those deep, blue, need-you eyes?" The emotion in his words rushed through her. She was blown away. Tessa hadn't realized that words could send shivers through you like this. She stared back into his eyes, speechless.

Dylan lowered his mouth to hers again. This time he wasted no time slipping his tongue into her mouth, burning her with desire. The kiss ended too soon, as Dylan pulled back. His gaze followed his movements as he softly tucked a piece of her hair behind her ear, then swept over her, making its way slowly back to her eyes. He smiled.

"Tessa, we need to get out of here if I'm going to remain a gentleman." His voice, deep and sensual, sent a ripple of awareness through her. Taking her by the hand, Dylan pulled Tessa to her feet, kissing her once more. Her pulse beat wildly in her throat as they walked, hand in hand, to his car. He leaned against the hood and pulled her into his arms again, simply holding her close. It felt so good. The unrecognizable scent of soap and cologne washed over her, imprinting memory. Silently, they watched the sun sink into gorgeous color. They continued to watch contentedly as the sky darkened and the stars blinked awake in the night sky.

Just as she thought to herself that the night couldn't possibly get any better, it did. Dylan tilted her face up to his, whispering, "I don't know what it is, but I think I'm in trouble with you around."

Then he smiled again and kissed her on the tip of her nose. Still holding hands, they filled the rest of the time Mama allotted to them with conversation, talking about her day at school and what they wanted to do this upcoming weekend. As she stood on the front porch, watching his taillights disappear into the darkness, she thought to herself that it was a good thing she didn't mail that letter yet. She had so much more to tell Laura.

Hey, me again. I meant to mail this letter this morning but it's a good thing I didn't. Man, can he kiss! Wow. Literally took my breath away. Dylan picked me up for our date tonight, and we went back to his house. At first, we watched tv with his little brother, but I couldn't even tell you what show was playing. I was too busy wondering when he was going to kiss me again. And when he did, Girl, I kid you not—I melted. He's perfect, Laura. Remember when you told me with Clayton, you just knew? I feel the same way with Dylan. I'm still a little nervous. I'm pretty sure he has more experience than me. He is older. I still want to save myself for marriage. This boy is either going to marry me or kill me!

Ha-ha!

I sure wish you still lived here. Don't get me wrong, I made new friends at school, but they don't know me like you do. There is one girl I talk to named Candy. She's really sweet, and I feel like I can trust her and tell her anything, but she's not you. I tried calling Twilla, but they moved, and I don't have their new number. I guess when you wait six months to call your friends after moving, you take a chance on losing touch. Donna still has the same number, but her mom is going through a divorce, and well… you know Donna. She's always playing Mama to her brother and sister. But she always was the responsible one of the bunch.

Anyway, it's getting late, and I want to get this finished so I can mail it in the morning. Write back soon. I'm dying to hear more about Clayton and your new friends.

LYLAS,

Tessa

Chapter 3

Pulling herself back from the memory, she couldn't help but smile. She wondered again about why he'd broken up with her. She just knew her friend, Darla, must have had something to do with it. Afterall, she'd eventually married him. She knew that Darla and Dylan eventually divorced, but she wasn't sure why, and it never came up during the few times she'd bumped into her. Or maybe her brother, Jamie, had gotten to him. Jamie played everything tough, and even though they weren't close, he used her as an excuse to act out aggressively. Jamie wasn't fond of Dylan, but Jamie was never fond of anyone unless there was something in it for him. Once, when she and Dylan were standing in her driveway, Jamie barreled out of the house threatening to "whip Dylan's ass" because he was disrespecting his sister by not coming in the house. In a blink, Dylan pushed Jamie up against his car, warning him to think twice before swinging on him. That was the last time Jamie acted tough with Dylan, but it certainly didn't endear them to one another. She laughed out loud. She simply couldn't stop thinking about him, reminiscing about the past. Maybe the universe was sending her a message. Maybe she should look Dylan up.

June 1978

Almost a month into their relationship, Dylan and Tessa's dates fell into a normal routine. Dylan would pick Tessa up and take them to his house. They hung out there, usually in his room. Sometimes they would socialize in his brother's room. They enjoyed their time with Cal and Shelly. In fact, the two girls became fast friends, spending time together even without the boys. She felt welcome at Dylan's house, almost a part of the family. She was sure if anyone did anything to hurt her, they would all be there in a New York minute to defend her. She enjoyed spending time with them. Dylan's dad owned a muscle car that he loved taking to car shows. His boys would polish the car alongside him and join him at the shows. Sometimes she went; sometimes she didn't. She still didn't know anything about cars and would feel a little lost in their world sometimes. But she loved seeing them work together and watching Dylan's passion. And she had to admit, that car was nice.

This night started like every other, sitting in his room, casual conversation leading to making out. They were on his bed, kissing, when suddenly his hands began to roam. He nibbled her neck and shoulders as his hands worked their way down her torso. This new development took her by surprise but she didn't want him to stop. Mesmerized by his kisses, she found herself floating again. She wanted to see where this led. Dylan's hands found her waist and quickly slipped under her shirt, electrifying her body. The kiss grew deeper, and he moaned into it as he discovered the warmth of her stomach. He inched his hand up to her bra and fondled her through it. His uneven breathing felt hot on her neck as she squirmed under his touch. He slid his hand under the final barrier and pinched her, sending a thrill throughout her entire being.

She almost came undone at the unfamiliar touch. Carried away on the excitement, she moaned into his mouth, craving more. He squeezed and fondled her until she could scarcely catch her breath. He lifted his head to look into her eyes. Finding an answer there to his unspoken question, he pulled her clothing away. Her breathing grew more jagged as she held her breath, waiting. He lowered his mouth and tasted her. His hand moved again, working its way down to her waist where it lingered, as his tongue and teeth continued to torture her. She bucked in his arms, begging for more. He undid the button on her jeans, then lowered the zipper. Her eyes grew big as his hand slipped below, fingers exploring. Gentle and slow, his fingers did wicked, intoxicating things to her. She moaned, her body responding.

Suddenly, he lifted his head, grinning. "Easy Tessa, we're not in any rush." His hand retreated, her skin burning at the void. He gently kissed her on the forehead. "It's almost time to get you home, and if I don't stop now, I'm not sure I will be able to." He caught the dagger in her eyes and laughed. "Wow, if looks could kill, I would be dead right now."

She took a deep breath and responded the only way she could, "Are you serious right now? You are going to tease me, get me all worked up, then just stop like that," she sputtered, snapping her fingers.

"Tessa, if I don't stop now, I can't promise I will not stop ever. You are so dang sweet and irresistible." He explained, looking like a panther ready to pounce.

Tessa lowered her clothing back into place and made her way to the bathroom. It took her a few minutes to compose herself. She emerged from the bathroom, still feeling the heat and frustration. As they headed to the car, Tessa didn't wait long to tell Dylan how she felt, obviously still worked up. "So, did you plan to tease me for some reason?"

"No, Tessa. I didn't intend on that happening at all. Of course, now that I know how sweet you are, you can go ahead and prepare yourself for it to happen more often." He flashed that grin she couldn't resist.

Her cheeks heated as she blushed. Dylan snickered. She didn't utter another word on the short drive. They arrived at her house fifteen minutes early. They spent the time sitting out in his car, talking and kissing, of course. With five minutes left to curfew, Dylan walked her to the door. After one last peck on the cheek and a promise to call her tomorrow, he climbed back in his car and drove away.

The next day was agony. Tessa drug herself through the day, after a sleepless night. Dylan made her feel things she didn't even know were possible. It was heavenly, but it also felt a little wrong. She shook her head. She honestly didn't care. What she shared with Dylan was amazing. Now she just had to worry about how to slow things down a bit. Stepping into the sunlight to trudge home, she congratulated herself on barely making it through the day. Dylan had to work so maybe she could catch up on some sleep tonight.

After dinner, Tessa cleaned the kitchen with Mama. At 9:00 the phone rang, and her heart began to pound. It was Dylan. They chatted idly about their day. Then she admitted to having trouble sleeping the night before because of the things he had done to her. His teasing reply took her breath away. "You think that was exciting? Just wait 'til tomorrow." Relieved that he couldn't see her blush, she stammered out a goodnight and disconnected the call. Heavy with fatigue, she found sleep almost before her head even hit the pillow.

Morning brought a free day from school, thanks to the scheduled parent/teacher conferences. Tessa dressed, mowed the lawn, and started the laundry. Mama worked as a waitress and came home exhausted. Tessa wanted to surprise her by taking care of some of the housework. Fridays were Dad's paydays, so they always went out to eat for dinner. Often, they would drop her off at the skating rink with her brother, Nelson. Jamie always opted to go to a friend's house. But tonight, Tessa had a date. After dropping off her brothers, they turned onto her street. When she saw Dylan parked in front of her house, she smiled. With a shake of her head, Mama reminded her to be in by 11:00.

Dylan hadn't eaten yet, so they went to the drive-thru where he ordered a burger and fries. As they talked about a little of everything, Tessa nibbled on a few of his fries. One of Dylan's friends pulled into another bay, and Dylan headed over to talk to him. While they visited, Tessa pulled out the latest letter from Laura and started to read. Laura reported that things were going well for her and Clayton. Her stepdad didn't like him, but that just made her like him more. Tessa shook her head. That one always was a rebel. Laura was on the drill team squad at her new school and was sore from working out so much. Clayton started a new job, saving to buy a car that wouldn't fall apart every time they used it. Laura was worried, though, because Clayton planned to buy it from his shady brother. Laura was clearly in love. These last few years had been hard on her. Her parents divorced three years ago, and she was uprooted when her mom accepted a job in another town teaching nursing students. Laura felt overshadowed by her brother, a major pain in the ass who was clearly the favored child. Laura knew her mom didn't want the divorce. Don was so much like their dad. And Laura had always been a wild child. Her mom didn't seem to know how to approach her. They mixed like oil and water.

Tessa wrote back as soon as she got home.

Laura,

I got your letter today. Glad to hear you and Clayton are doing well. I think it's hilarious that your stepdad doesn't like him. Hopefully, I will be able to talk mom into taking me to see you before school starts. I miss you so much.

Things with Dylan are good, too. He's just dreamy. I know you told me you have to approve of him, but you'd better hurry and visit then!

I'm not surprised to hear that your mom never misses Don's ball games. I'm sure once school starts, she will try to make it to one of your games to watch you. If only the drill team performed at baseball games, too... You know, I think she just still loves your dad and that's why she is so attached to Don. He looks just like him. Hopefully, he will be a better husband and not cheat like your daddy did. Sorry, I hope that didn't sound too hateful. I know you miss him.

Are you coming down before school to visit him? Is he flying a lot now that he doesn't have to be home? I always thought it was cool that your dad is a pilot. Maybe someday he will fly us to Hawaii for free. That would be so cool.

Jamie is starting his crap at home. He doesn't like Dylan and won't say why. Like I really care what he thinks, anyway. All he does is hang out with his hood friends and get high. He stinks when he comes home.

Thanks for sending me Twilla's new number. I will try to call her this weekend. I gotta get for now. It's late and Dylan just dropped me off. Miss you!

LYLAS,

Tessa

Chapter 4

Tessa blinked. What was wrong with her? She had to stop with these memories. Given, two years was really a long time to go without. Her battery-operated boyfriend hadn't been delivering what she needed, but wow—she didn't realize it was failing this bad. Okay Tessa, she coached herself, get it together! And get your mind out of the past and out of the gutter. There was so much to do since she had decided a little beach therapy was in order. Some last-minute packing, a mid-day flight, and she would be in Pensacola in no time. Then she'd take a quick shuttle to the hotel, and her toes would be buried in the sand before she knew it.

But tonight, it was girl's night. She and Candy got together with three other ladies every few months for dinner and to catch up. Sometimes, while getting ready for these dinners, she wondered what she might change if she could go back and do it all again. She had a good life. She'd even kept in touch with most of her friends, with semi-regular outings and the occasional cruise. She had a great relationship with her children, and had enjoyed a happy marriage, even if it was cut short. No, she wouldn't change her life for anything.

But still she wondered what Dylan was doing now. She determined she would see if she could find him on social media later. What would she do if she found him? Oh, so many steamy things, her mind decided—including finding out if he was still as hot as she remembered. It was settled. She would look him up as soon as she got home.

Dinner with the girls relaxed her. They traded stories of grandkids and travel. They reminisced about the fun times they'd shared with

Laura and the lingering disbelief over losing her to a rare disease five years ago. Each offered love-laced battle stories of significant others. Tessa, the only widow among all five, still laughed at their stories. It felt so good to get out of the house; she hated to say goodnight. She hugged each of them, promising to do it again soon. Driving home, memories of Dylan overcame her again.

July 1978

Tessa's family celebrated the fourth of July in a big way. Her mom's family hosted a cookout, and no one ever missed it. All of her cousins, aunts, uncles, and grandparents came, grilling fish, burgers, and hot dogs. The women always brought a favorite side dish. They topped the night off with homemade ice cream and, of course, fireworks. Dylan arrived just after 3:00 that afternoon, coming straight from work to pick her up. She couldn't believe her mom was letting her go.

When they made it to his house, Tessa sat in the living room, visiting with his brothers and dad while he showered. Then Tessa followed a still-damp Dylan back to his room. They kissed, but as things quickly heated, Dylan pulled away and suggested they head to a firework's show in the next town. She couldn't help being a little disappointed, but watching the colors explode around them with her head on his shoulder was the first time she truly felt the show instead of just watching it. Afterward, they returned to his house, finding it dark and empty. Deciding that everyone must still be out celebrating, they turned on a few lights and waited for Cal and Shelly to come back. Gathered in Cal's room, all four sat visiting and listening to the radio until it was time for Dylan to take Tessa home.

Pulling up to her house, they realized her parents weren't home yet. Dylan turned to her, smiling. "Looks like we have a little more time. Want to neck?" he asked, wiggling his eyebrows up and down, comically. She giggled and leaned into him. The kisses started innocently enough, but soon morphed into much more. As he assaulted her with kisses, Tessa reached down, rubbing him to attention. She couldn't get enough of him. Aroused and moaning, Dylan begged her to stop before she went too far, and he couldn't control himself. That didn't deter her at all. Unbuttoning his jeans, she reached in to touch him. She felt his sharp intake of breath, and it only encouraged her more. Dylan's hands moved under her shirt and bra. Tessa found herself rethinking the whole saving herself for marriage thing. And she wasn't going to lie to herself, she enjoyed holding that kind of power over him.

But Tessa reminded herself to be ladylike, and that her parents would be coming home any minute and might catch them making out in the front seat of his car. She was right. Just then, headlights cut across the car, coming toward them from down the street. She panicked, struggling to get her shirt and bra righted. Dylan worked frantically to compose himself and get his wardrobe back in order, too. She sprang out of the car, attempting to cut her parents off from an obviously still-heated Dylan. Passing her daughter by, Mama stalked up to the driver's window, scolding them. "Midnight means she is to be inside the house, not sitting in your car kissing and doing other things a fifteen-year-old shouldn't be doing."

Tessa was mortified. She helplessly looked on, silently mouthing "I'm sorry" as her mother whirled away from the window. Her father chimed in, grounding her for two weeks. Dylan apologized, looking stressed. Tessa announced loudly that there was nothing to be sorry about. It was totally worth it. She leaned in to give him a quick peck on the cheek to punctuate her point. As she did, Dylan grabbed her for a long, hot kiss. She didn't resist the urge to caress his jeans again. "Tessa," he groaned, "you're going to drive me mad if you keep doing that."

"These two weeks are going to be hell," she muttered, as if in physical pain. Giving him one last quick kiss, she walked reluctantly to the porch and stood watching as his car disappeared down the road.

Her mother caught her as she entered the house, chewing her out about her behavior. As soon as the words "proper young lady" made their way to her ears, Tessa exploded. "How would you know?" she retorted. "From what I've gathered, you were not a proper young lady at all." That earned her a stinging slap across her right cheek. But damn, it felt good.

Laura,

Hope you had a good 4th of July. I did—at least until the parents got home. Dylan and I were sitting in the driveway not ten minutes ago when they caught me out a little past midnight. Apparently, curfew means "IN the house," but suffice it to say we were just getting started when they drove up. Luckily, I saw them coming down the road, so they didn't really see anything. A few more minutes, and I wouldn't have cared. My mom and I got into a shouting match, and I'm currently grounded from seeing him for two weeks. But I think I have that figured out.

Shelly works at the pool. I'll tell them I'm going to the pool, then Dylan can pick me up! Good plan, huh? Shelly understands. Her parents don't approve of Cal, so she sneaks around to see him, too. I'm calling her tomorrow.

Girl, he is so hot! He has Roman hands and Russian fingers, and talented ones at that. If I wasn't such a chicken, I would have put that talent to better use by now. I want to sooo bad. With my luck, I'd get knocked up, though. But I am a chicken. Does it hurt? You know I'm a wimp about pain.

Hey, it's been a few weeks since I got a letter from you. I just hope everything is okay. Too bad your mom had to work extra shifts at the hospital. I was looking forward to you coming to visit.

Oh, I called Twilla. She's getting a little weird. And what's up with her brother? What a creep! When I called, he answered and seriously asked me what bra size I wore! No wonder she never wants anyone to stay at her house. She lives with a pervert! I feel sorry for her. She said he drilled a hole in her closet to watch her and she has to make sure her closet is closed any time she's getting dressed. She's afraid to tell her mom because of the divorce. She said her mom just gets drunk and cries all the time. Did you know her parents split and that's why they moved?

Well, I'm gonna close for now. Write back soon. I miss you!

LYLAS,

Tessa

Chapter 5

Tessa pulled up her social media account, feeling excited. Finding Dylan after all these years! What if he was married? What if he didn't remember her? Please, oh please don't let that be the case, she thought as she logged in. She clicked the search bar and typed in his name. Wow. How many Dylan Wilsons could there be? Seven, apparently. Seven Dylan Wilsons and one memory page. She panicked as she clicked on the memory page. Quickly scanning posts and pictures, she breathed a sigh of relief. It wasn't him. Navigating back to the list of accounts, Tessa kept scrolling. She stopped on one from her area. The profile picture showed a car. This one had potential. She decided to send a request and see if she got a response. She took a breath and clicked the button, then headed off to bed. She had a busy day tomorrow, packing and getting ready for her trip. Tessa snuggled into her pillow, her thoughts drifting back as her eyes grew heavy.

July 1978

Today was the day. Tessa had talked to Shelly the day before, ironing out the plan. Mama agreed to let Tessa go to the pool since she'd cleaned the house without being asked, but she had to take Nelson along. Shelly relayed the message to Dylan so he could pick her up. Mama was going to drop them off when the pool opened at 10:00, then pick them up around 6:00. Adding in a buffer to avoid being caught, that would give them seven glorious hours together!

In the car, Mama gave Tessa and Nelson $5 each for admission and snacks. She told them to be careful, then pulled away. At the entrance, Shelly let them in for free. Tessa handed over her share to Nelson for hush-money, then counted the minutes until Dylan arrived. Thirty minutes later, he arrived. Laughing, they ran, holding hands, to his car. After climbing in, he grabbed her face with both hands and laid a long, hot kiss on her. Breathless and sweating in the shade, Tessa rubbed the front of his jeans. He moaned into her mouth, encouraging her. Pulling his mouth from hers, Dylan groaned. "If we are going to leave this parking lot, you are going to have to remove your hand. Otherwise, you should just hop into the back seat now." She moved her hand. Winking, he tweaked her nose and said, "You have the cutest little button nose I have ever seen." Then he turned and drove out of the lot. As Dylan ran a few errands, Tessa spent the entire time trying to catch her breath without being obvious. But as they finally entered Dylan's house, she was surprised. The house was empty.

"Where is everyone?" she asked, glancing around.

"Work. And out with friends," he replied with that signature, irresistible cocky look on his face.

"So, we're completely alone?" she asked, hearing the shake in her voice. "Do you plan on ravaging me? "

He paused, looking at her intently, as if trying to figure out what she was thinking. His voice was low, almost a broken whisper, "Not unless you want me to." He stepped back, then added, voice stronger, "We're not all pigs, you know." He looked stung.

Tessa was quick to object. "No, that's not what I meant! Not at all! I'm just... nervous." She looked down at her hands, fidgeting a moment before continuing. "I have a habit of saying stupid stuff when I'm nervous. I know I shouldn't be nervous around you, but I get so worked up around you. I'm just scared. You know, I'm a virgin, and well..." She could feel her face turning red as she finished in a whisper, "I don't think I'm ready to take it that far."

Dylan flashed a quick grin. "Don't worry about it," he soothed, moving back in close and gathering her into his arms. "I promise not to push you into anything you don't want to do."

She didn't know what to say. Hell, she didn't even know what to think. Shyly, she looked up. Mama had told her so many stories. But this was Dylan, and she knew in her heart that she could trust him.

He grabbed a can of soda from the fridge, and they headed to his room. They settled in, sitting on his bed across from each other, when he leaned in and kissed her. A simple, gentle kiss. Then he smiled, pulling his lips into his teeth, and kissed her again, laughing. Confused, she waited for him to explain. Once he stopped laughing, he wrapped her in his arms and fell back, pulling her on top of him. Pulling his lips in again, he repeated the silly kiss then explained, "That's how we will kiss when we get old!"

She had to smile. He was so cute. She didn't want him to think her hesitancy had anything to do with him. "By the way, I'm not saying no. Just… not now." Again, she blushed.

He reassured her again. "I'm not going to force anything on you, but we can keep having fun, if you're up for it?"

With the house to themselves she was a little braver. Taking charge this time, she led him to his room and started kissing him. She could see the fire in his eyes as they explored each other. Seeing how it affected him gave her courage. She unbuttoned his jeans and lowered his zipper while staring into his eyes. "You don't have to do that," he protested.

"I want to," Tessa said, breathlessly.

Giving her hands free-reign, Tessa traversed beyond the denim barrier that stopped her before. Dylan growled. Then, unable to stop himself, he did the same. Nibbling her neck, he moved south, kissing her belly. Then lower again. She had both hands deep in his hair, moaning and calling out his name until she came completely undone. Dylan stood before her as Tessa caught her breath and tried to regain her composure. Her eyes gravitated to the waistband of his jeans, still undone and barely concealing his still obvious desire. She reached for him, biting her lip. Urged on by his questioning gaze, she allowed her tongue to follow the path her hands had carved before. Dylan, too, reached his crest. Feeling shaken, Tessa made her way to the bathroom. When she returned, he was sitting on his bed with his head in his hands.

Tessa was concerned. "What's wrong?" she asked.

As Dylan looked up, she could see the bewildered smile etched on his face. "Not a damn thing," he assured her, rising, and taking her into his arms. "My baby girl just surprised me is all." She blushed.

Spent, they went to their favorite drive through and got a drink. Dylan announced he was hungry and ordered a burger and fries. Tessa said she wasn't hungry but ate most of his fries. Dylan grinned, obviously not bothered in the least. Tessa couldn't wait to tell Laura all about their stolen date.

Laura,

I know I just wrote to you, but I have to tell you what happened. You remember I told you I was grounded, but I would find a way to see him? Well, I did! I had to pay Nelson to keep his mouth shut, but girl, I would do it over again in a heartbeat. I haven't figured out how to see him again before the grounding is up, but I'm working on it. At least they are letting us talk on the phone.

Anyway, we tried something new. I was a nervous wreck, but I guess I did it right. He said I blew more than his mind! Ha-ha. I still can't believe I did that, though. My mother would freak if she knew. The look on his face was priceless.

Shelly said she would help me see him again anytime, just let her know. I got back to the pool about an hour before Mama came to get us, so I did get to swim for a little while. Oh, Andy was there. Remember all the fun the three of us had when you were here? He said to tell you hi, and we talked about my new house. He said school is boring without us there to keep him entertained. I guess he's not fond of high school. I still love it. Miss you, though!

Write back soon and tell me about all of your new adventures. Gotta go for now.

LYLAS,

Tessa

Chapter 6

Tessa awoke and started brewing her coffee. She had a lot to do this morning and the beach was calling. She glanced through her closet, trying to decide what to pack. Abandoning the thought for the moment, she stepped into the shower. As the warm water ran down her body, her thoughts returned to Dylan. She wondered what he was like now, what he was doing, if he had remarried. Who knows, she thought with a shrug and stepped out of the shower. Wrapping her hair in a towel, she went through the mental list of what she needed to pack. Even though it was chilly outside, she slipped into a favorite pair of Capri leggings. Lacing up her tennis shoes, she reminded herself to pack flip flops in her carry-on bag so she could change into them before landing in Pensacola. The chilly temps just outside her door would be quickly forgotten when she stepped into the sunny 82-degree weather that would be waiting for her as she disembarked.

After getting all of her toiletries packed, Tessa turned back to her closet. As she selected each item, she folded and placed in in her suitcase. She decided to bring slacks for dinner and a couple of her favorite sundresses. She planned on doing some shopping once she got there, too. She decided to pick up sunscreen after she arrived. Tessa did a twirl as she snapped the suitcase closed. She couldn't wait! She would have two days to herself, spend one with her niece and family, then finish her vacation alone—just sand, spa, and relaxation. She'd never really enjoyed being alone, but she had gotten used to it. She was going to enjoy every minute of this trip.

All that was left was the carry-on. Grabbing her tablet and charger, she stuffed them inside with her phone charger. She added two books, one she was almost finished reading and a new one to take to the beach. Tessa scanned every room, making sure she had everything and turning off lights and appliances. Then she grabbed her bags and headed for the door.

As the car took Tessa toward the airport, her mind returned to 1978 again, where Dylan waited.

November 1978

The summer had passed quickly. Dylan and Tessa spent every evening together, except when Dylan was working at the local service station. When they weren't together, they were on the phone, talking for what seemed like forever about absolutely nothing. Tension at home deepened. Her parents grew increasingly unhappy with the amount of time she spent with him, and both of her brothers believed Dylan had taken advantage of her.

The letters she exchanged with Laura slowed with their return to school. Drill team kept Laura busy, and Tessa filled her time hanging out with Shelly whenever she wasn't with Dylan. He was working extra hours whenever he could, but he always called in the evening. She missed the time they had spent together.

One evening Shelly called, inviting her to go cruising. When Shelly picked her up, she headed to Dylan and Cal's house instead. Surprised, but pleased to see her, Dylan gave her a hug before they escaped into his room and each other's arms. After setting each other aflame again, they talked comfortably in the stillness, wrapped in their still-growing love.

Chapter 1

Tessa pulled herself back to the present as she approached the airport. She'd arrived early enough to check in and relax before they called passengers to board. While waiting near her terminal, she took out her tablet and powered it on. She didn't trust airport Wi-Fi, opting instead to enable her phone's hotspot. As she waited for her tablet to connect, she observed the other passengers. Her gaze first settled on a young mom with her toddler. Guiltily, she hoped they would be seated toward the back of the plane, a reasonable distance from the first-class seating she had splurged on. She noticed several people dressed in business attire and figured they would be in first-class as well. Another group of adults sat huddled behind her, all intently scrolling on their phones.

She glanced back at her tablet and found it waiting for a command. Navigating to her social media app, she discovered three notifications causing her heart to flutter. Nervously, she clicked the notification to view the requests. The first opened to a connection request from someone she didn't know. She deleted it, moving to the second one. A note from Candy wished her a comfortable flight and fun trip. She responded, thanking Candy and instructing her to keep everyone out of jail and stay out of trouble until she got back. The final notification confirmed approval of her connection request. She started shaking. What if it wasn't really him? Determined, she decided to send a quick hello and see what happened.

Hi! How are you?

The immediate response caught her off-guard.

I'm good. You?

Short but sweet, she thought.

*I'm fine. Just sitting at the airport, waiting
for a flight to Florida.*

Tessa couldn't take her eyes off the tablet as she waited for a response. Minutes ticked by, seeming like hours before she heard the responding beep.

*Sorry about that. I had to take a call. But I
was surprised to see a message from you.*

Tessa felt stalled. She decided to go sit at the bar and have a drink while waiting for her flight. A glance at her watch told her she had at least 45 minutes. Tucking the tablet back in her carry on, she gathered her sweater and purse, then walked the short distance to the bar. Selecting a seat that gave her a view of the flights coming in, she ordered a White Russian. She pulled the tablet back out and placed it on the table in front of her. How should she respond? Was this even her Dylan?

The bartender delivered her drink, politely informing her of the two-drink maximum. Tessa assured her she was only having the one to help her relax for the two-hour flight. She hoped to catch a little shut eye on the flight and took the moment to check on the headphones she planned to use to listen to the new music loaded to her phone. Finding them in the carry-on, she turned her attention back to the waiting tablet. She decided to respond.

*I'm curious. It's hard to tell from your
profile. Are you the Dylan Wilson I think
you are? If so, tell me a memory I would
know.*

And she waited. Taking a drink of her White Russian, she watched the indicator spin, letting her know he was typing a response. Trying to calm her nerves, she tried people watching again. A woman wandered slowly, scanning signs as she walked. A man in a business suit practically flew past her, probably scrambling to catch a connecting flight. She peeked back down at the tablet. Still spinning. It seemed like forever before the message appeared on her screen. Taking the rest of her White Russian in a single gulp, she started reading.

*I remember the most beautiful blue eyes that
lit up every time I kissed you. And I
remember a HOT afternoon you spent with
me when you were supposed to be swimming.
Oh, and I remember a spectacular 4th of July
that was getting pretty exciting until your
parents came home… Is that enough?*

OMG. It was him!!! She signaled the bartender and ordered another drink. Her mind was reeling. How to respond? How to respond? she thought numbly as her excitement built. It was him. Her Dylan. She didn't have a chance to decide on a response before her tablet chimed again. As her second drink arrived, she checked her watch. She had 30 minutes. She took a deep breath and clicked open the message.

Were you expecting someone else?

*No, not expecting someone else. Honestly, I
was hoping it was you. I have thought about
you a lot over the years. Tell me what's going
on in your world.*

Taking a long sip of her second drink, Tessa was starting to feel a bit more relaxed.

*Not a lot. I divorced Darla. Remarried and
lost my second wife 3 years ago. Now I'm
just working a lot. I have 2 kids, all grown
up and spend most of time working in my
shop. What about you?*

Tessa thought about what to say. She didn't want to come off as an idiot but chatting with him made her feel fifteen again. She decided to just plunge in.

*Sorry to hear about the loss of your wife. I
lost my husband, too, years ago. Sometimes it
seems like an eternity and other times like it
was just yesterday. I have 3 grown children
and they are doing well and happy. I still*

31

*hang out with Candy. Not sure if you
remember her or not. And I like to travel.*

Tessa looked at the time, then glanced over and saw her flight had arrived. She needed to get back to the terminal. She signaled for the check, then allowed herself a memory while she waited for it to arrive.

December 1978

Thank goodness Christmas break had arrived. School was brutal this time of year with so many tests and so little will to concentrate. Tessa had worked extra hard to keep up and was sure she passed them all. More than anything, she hated the cold. And waking up the first morning of break was always boring. As much as she wanted a break from the stresses of school, at least that gave her something other than Dylan to focus on. She hoped she could stay out of trouble so she could spend time with Dylan over the next two weeks. She pulled out fresh stationary and her new pen.

Laura,

Hey girl, what's up in your world? Same ol' same ol' here. I'm so glad Christmas break is finally here. Maybe I can catch up on some sleep. Dylan works during the day so that should help me get some naps in.

How are things with Clayton? Is your mom getting off your back? Mothers!! Mine hasn't been too bad lately, but it is December and with all the parties and down time, we'll see...

Anyway, things with Dylan are good. We spend time together whenever we can. Of course, Dylan is working a lot of extra hours again. He's supposed to get off early tomorrow, though, so we plan on spending some time together. I haven't gotten his Christmas present yet.

I have been babysitting for Aunt Nancy on Mondays. I cook dinner and watch the kids while they go bowling with my parents. I'm making a little bit of cash and I get out of the house, so it's a pretty good gig. And Dylan works on Monday nights anyway, so he calls me there when he can. Aunt Nancy's daughter cracks me up! She's six years younger than us, but she's a lot of fun.

Kind of like the little sister I never had. She has double beds in her room, so I sleep in there. The two boys aren't bad. They are easy to watch, watching TV mostly. Then I just gotta make them take their baths and go to bed.

Head to school from there on Tuesday morning. Her house is pretty big. She keeps it clean, but I do the dusting, clean the stove and fridge, mop floors and clean the sinks and tubs while I'm there. It's not really that bad. And like I said, the money is nice. Sometimes she takes me shopping with her on Saturday and we grab lunch out.

Anyway, I have stuff to do if I'm going to see Dylan tonight! Write back soon. Let me know how things are going with Clayton and all your crazy drill team stories.

LYLAS,

Tessa & Dylan = TLA

Laura & Clayton = TLA

Tessa & Laura = BFF's 4 Ever

Chapter 8

As she settled the check and moved to the terminal, her mind was going in a thousand different directions. A little buzzed, she decided to tell Dylan she was boarding before she made an idiot of herself. She quickly sat down and fired off a message.

I'm getting ready to board the plane.
Hopefully, we can reconnect later today. It
was great chatting with you.

She turned off her tablet and stood to board. She couldn't quite believe she was able to find him so fast. She wasn't expecting it to be that easy. Maybe one day they could meet for dinner and catch up. She wondered if he still had that amazing smile she remembered. And that sexy voice she would never forget. Making her way to seat B-2, she slid in next to the window. As the passengers loaded, she booted her tablet back up, wanting to see if he'd responded. She busied herself watching people file by. The toddler she'd spotted earlier wasn't too happy. She sighed in relief as the sound of the grumpy toddler grew fainter as they moved toward the back of the plane. Hearing a ding, she looked at her tablet and saw she had a message.

Have a good flight. Let me know when you
land. I can't wait to catch up. So glad you
found me and sent a request. You made my
day!

Settling in for her flight, Tessa positioned her headphones and pressed play. Quickly, the music and memories overtook her again.

Christmas Eve, 1978

Tessa rose early and did her chores. Dylan was picking her up at 2:00, and she wanted to make sure nothing kept them apart. It was their first Christmas together! She had struggled, deciding on a gift for him, before settling on a simple ball cap and t-shirt that were just his style. After she finished two loads of laundry, she cleaned the kitchen and her room. Mama checked her work, then gave her the thumbs up to go to Dylan's house. She had to be home by 9:00 pm. She took a quick shower, then wrapped herself in a towel and surveyed her closet. She decided to wear a simple long-sleeve shirt, her favorite jeans, and tennis shoes. She had just finished drying and styling her new Farrah Fawcett hairdo when she heard the doorbell. She ran to her room to grab Dylan's gift while Jamie answered the door. She strained to hear them talking, wondering if Jamie was going to smart off as usual, but to her surprise, Jamie wished him a Merry Christmas, then yelled, "Tessa! Dylan's here. Don't keep him waiting!"

When she saw him standing in the entryway, she was taken aback by how handsome he looked. She obviously hadn't forgotten, but there did seem to be a kind of magic in the air today. Christmas Eve had always been one of her favorite days. Dylan smiled, lighting his eyes and her spirits. They practically floated past the porch to Dylan's car. He opened the passenger-side door for her, just like he always did. She climbed in, automatically scooting to the middle of the seat. Dylan jumped into the driver's seat, leaned in for a kiss, and started the car, automatically resting his right arm on her knee. It was routine by now.

They talked a little about their Christmas traditions, and before she knew it, they were pulling into his drive. She held out his gifts. He paused, looking into her eyes. "You didn't have to get me anything."

Tessa kept the packages extended. "I wanted to. It's nothing big."

He grinned, took the gifts in one hand and held hers with the other, as he led her into the house. They stopped in the living room to visit his dad and little brother. Then, wishing them both a Merry Christmas, they headed to Dylan's room.

As she sat on the bed, Tessa noticed he had moved the furniture around and cleaned. She grinned at the mental picture of him wielding a duster and broom. But Dylan kept things neat, so she probably shouldn't have found it so surprising. He eagerly asked if he could open his gifts, and she nodded, smiling. She wasn't sure who was the more excited between them. He opened the hat first, immediately putting it on his head. He bobbed his head around comically, then he took the hat back off, adjusting the band until it fit the way he liked it and posed with a grin. Snatching up the second package, he opened the t-shirt and held it up, beaming. "I love it! Does my baby girl know me or what?"

Her heart was thundering. He stood up and placed a tender kiss on her lips that made her knees go weak. Dylan quickly pivoted, pulling a tiny box from the top drawer of his dresser. He turned to her, explaining in a nervous voice, "I have been excited all day waiting for this moment. I got you something that I have never gotten another girl."

He held it out between them, lifting the hinged lid of the box. The light glinted on the star-shaped diamond set in a white-silver band. Her breath caught as she stared at the ring. She lifted her head to look at him, then glanced back at the ring. In the silence, she did it again. She could feel the tears starting to form in her eyes. "I know you are only fifteen, soon to be sixteen. This is a promise ring. Tessa, I promise to love you and protect you as long as you wear it. One day, we will trade this in for an engagement ring and wedding set. If you will have me that long."

She smiled at the cheesy grin on his face. "Of course, I will wear that promise ring! And I promise to always be by your side, for as long as you will have me." Happy tears fell as he slipped the ring on her finger. It fit perfectly. "How did you know my size?" she wondered, aloud.

"I have a good jeweler," he teased with a wicked grin. Tessa was so excited, she jumped into his arms, and he fell back on the bed, taking her with him.

She spent the rest of the evening staring at her ring. He spent it holding and kissing her. They discussed their future together between long pauses of companionable silence. Tessa sighed. "I will not get a moment's rest tonight with this on. I'll be up all night, just looking at it."

Dylan chuckled. "That's fine with me, but I would actually love to look at those beautiful eyes, if you could just look my way for a little while." She laughed and planted a big kiss on his lips. "You might want to be careful. I'm in a pretty giving mood right now," he drawled.

Tessa's eyes were sparkling as she looked at him. "You have already given me enough for a lifetime!"

With a shake of his head, Dylan smiled. "Ah, Tessa. The best is yet to come."

Her parents were still up when she arrived home ten minutes early. They shared kisses in the car before Dylan walked her inside. They visited with her parents for a while before Dylan announced that he needed to head home, promising to call her in the morning. She walked him to his car, and he embraced her, holding her close until he insisted that he needed to go. She agreed, but not until she kissed him breathless. "We will just have to finish this another day," she whispered, chuckling. Then, she turned, leaving him hot and bothered, and sauntered away.

Christmas morning, Tessa woke up smiling. She lifted her hand, admiring how the morning light burst into sparkles that danced on her ring. This was going to be the best Christmas ever. She stretched, hopped out of bed, and pulled her hair back. After going to the bathroom and brushing her teeth, she ventured into the living room. It appeared that everyone was up and waiting on her. "Sorry for keeping you guys waiting. Guess I slept good for a change."

Mama stood and walked into the kitchen to refill her coffee cup. As she came back into the living room, she assured her, "Well, we haven't been up that long. And you were home early last night. So, there's nothing to be sorry for." Tessa smiled contentedly as she sat on the couch watching her dad pass out presents. Everyone tore into the wrappings. Tessa got some new jeans, two new shirts, and a necklace with her name engraved on it.

Once all the gifts had been opened, Tessa and her mother went into the kitchen to cook breakfast. Tessa set to work breaking eggs for scrambling. As she cracked the third egg, Mama asked, "Is that a new ring on your finger?"

Tessa looked down and smiled. In a rush of words, she answered, "Yes, Mama, it is. Dylan gave me this promise ring last night."

Her mother took a closer look. "Very pretty. I guess things are getting serious?"

Tessa thought for a second. "I'm not sure I'd say serious. Exclusive. Are you surprised? We have been dating since May."

Mama replied, "No, not really. But please tell me you are still a virgin?"

Tessa was irritated. "Oh my God, Mama, yes. He hasn't even tried. I wouldn't let him if he did try. You talked to me about this. I'm saving myself for marriage, and he knows that." Tessa's face was beet red.

Relieved, Mama dropped it, and they went on to finish breakfast. After they ate, Tessa loaded the dishwasher and went to shower. Her family headed to her grandparents' house, spending the rest of the day with all the extended family.

Chapter 9

Tessa finally landed in Pensacola. As she stepped off the plane, she was really glad she had packed her flip flops, and even more happy that she put them on mid-flight. The joy of traveling first class was definitely the extra space. Heading to baggage claim, Tessa tried to figure out what she should say to Dylan next. There were still so many questions. It had been over forty years since they had dated. She had no idea if he had a current girlfriend. She was going to have to keep her cool when talking to him. He made her feel fifteen again, but she didn't want to act like it.

While waiting for her bags to be unloaded, she pulled her phone from her pocket and opened the social media app. Immediately, a message popped up from Dylan, sent 45 minutes ago. She clicked it and read the message.

So, do you still have those pretty eyes?

She blushed. About that time, the luggage conveyor began to move. She fired off a reply.

*I sure do. Waiting on my luggage, then
headed to the hotel. Talk later?*

She slipped her phone back into her pocket and waited for her luggage to appear. She heard a chime and couldn't resist checking her messages.

*Of course. I still have a few things I need to
get finished anyway. I'm almost done with
this job. You know, when I think of you, I*

*always remember you the way you were when
I saw you last.*

She smiled and put the phone back in her pocket as her luggage headed her way. She stepped up to the belt, pulled her suitcase free and headed outside to look for the shuttle to the hotel. She didn't have to wander far to find it. The driver was loading luggage at the back. She gave him her name, then climbed aboard as he finished loading. She was pleased to note that the shuttle wasn't crowed. Tessa took a seat and pulled her phone out again. No new messages. She slid the phone into her purse and turned to look out the shuttle window as they rolled forward.

Tessa settled into her hotel room, changed into her swimsuit, then eagerly headed out to check out the beach. An empty lounge chair with an umbrella beckoned, and she happily obliged. Not long after she opened her book, hoping to finish reading the last three chapters, a waiter arrived to take her drink order. Feeling free, Tessa asked for something fruity with a little paper umbrella. She tried to dive back into her reading, but her mind quickly wandered back to her messages. She wondered if she should respond, what he really thought about her hunting him down the way she did. With a sigh, she realized her book was a lost cause and the only way she'd ever know what Dylan was thinking was to respond.

*I don't remember too much about young me.
I'm not really that little girl anymore. I don't
exactly look like her, either. I suppose some
things have changed more than others.*

*Your profile pictures say you are still pretty
as ever. Same dimples, same smile.*

Tessa wasn't sure how to react. It had been so long since she'd had to respond to such glowing complements. Even when she was married, Tom just didn't show love that way. Dating since he had passed away hadn't helped her brush up on gracefully accepting complements, either. She'd gone on one blind date with a total ass. The others were simply bland.

Thank you, you are too kind!

Just telling it as I see it.

*So, tell me about you. Where are you living
now? How are your brothers? Give me all
the basics.*

About that time, the cabana boy showed up with her drink, a Pineapple Upside-Down Paradise. She took one sip of the heavenly concoction of pineapple juice, vanilla vodka, and amaretto topped off with a pineapple slice and cherry juice and knew what she would be drinking the rest of the week. Her phone chimed, pulling her away from her newest obsession back to Dylan. She punched in her code, clicked the notification, hoping it was from Dylan. She was not disappointed.

> *I'm doing well. The kids are great. I'm very
> proud of them. I have 3 grandkids who I
> enjoy very much but I must admit—they wear
> me out! But in a good way, of course. I'm
> living just a few miles from where dad lived.
> It's hard to leave an area you grew up in.
> But there have been so many changes the last
> few years. My brother is doing well with a
> family of his own. We lost Cal several years
> ago. We try to get together at least once a
> month and do a family dinner. Life is pretty
> good right now. I'm enjoying helping people
> design their dream homes. I love seeing their
> reactions to the finished product. I'm an
> architect now. I got out of the building part
> and went into drafting and design. What
> about you?*

*I'm haven't moved far either. Next town
over, maybe 10-15 miles. Jamie passed away
not long after my husband. Nelson lives in
Texas with his wife and 5 kids AND a
house full of grandkids. I see them a few
times a year. I don't have any grandkids yet
but hoping to have some one day. I go out*

with friends every once in a while. I have
thought about getting a job to get out of the
house, but it's not really needed. I garden and
read a lot. Life hasn't been bad. I'm luckier
than most I guess.

Well, since we're almost neighbors, how do
you feel about getting together for dinner one
night after you get back?

Sounds like a plan! I would love to catch up
and visit with you.

It's a date!

Tessa's pulse quickened. Her mind raced. Date? He's calling it a date? She thought about what she'd wear and decided she might be doing some serious shopping Wednesday.

What are you thinking? I could really go for
burgers where we use to go. Or pizza? We
can talk about old times and catch up on
what's new!

I was thinking the same thing. Can't wait!
Now go enjoy the beach. We can talk later
this evening?

Works for me. I can't wait either. Enjoy the
rest of your day.

Smiling, Tessa tossed her phone onto the lounger beside her and lowered her sunglasses. Glancing around her, she felt at peace. She sighed, gazing at the water as it surged and receded. The sound of the waves whispered to her as she sipped the delicious drink in her hand and drifted back in time.

Chapter 10

New Year's Eve, 1978

Tessa couldn't believe how fast the time had flown by since Christmas. She looked down at the ring on her left hand for the millionth time since Dylan had slid it onto her finger, promising her forever. She hadn't stopped smiling since that night. And today was her birthday. Sweet 16!

Since her birthday fell on New Year's Eve, Tessa normally spent the evening babysitting while Mama watched Daddy's band play at whatever gig they'd lined up. But not this year! Just as Dylan had promised, she was going out with him. And she didn't have to be home until 1:00 am! Excited, she danced down the hall. The sound of the morning news droning from the tv told her that her parents were up already. She was quickly greeting by the scent of coffee coming from the kitchen. Tessa headed straight to the bathroom. With teeth brushed and hair pulled her back in a ponytail, Tessa bounded back into the hallway, almost bumping into Jamie as he passed by the doorway.

"Hey there, birthday girl! Better watch where you're going," he warned with a grin, "or I will just have to add a few swats to that spanking you have coming later."

Tessa smirked and shot back, "When you feel froggy, jump! But remember, I'm mean as all get out if you try to hold me down. Don't forget last year when you ended up with a busted lip."

Laughing, Tessa continued through the living room and into the kitchen where she found Mama sitting at the table drinking a cup of coffee. Tessa headed to the fridge, poured herself some juice, and sat down beside her. For several moments, they both stared out the window at nothing. It looked like it was going to be a nice day. Chilly, maybe, but the sun was out, so that counted for something. Mama broke the silence by asking her what her plans were for the day. "Well, I'm going to clean my room and get my laundry done. Then, Dylan is picking me up at five this evening, if that's ok with you?"

Her mom just looked at her for a long moment, then asked, "How serious are things with you and Dylan?"

Tessa was a bit surprised and wasn't sure what to say. "Well, you know he gave me the promise ring for Christmas. We promised we would not see anyone else, and when the time is right, we plan to get engaged." She paused. "I love him, Mama. He loves me, too. I know he's a bit older than me, but he's good for me. He's good to me."

Her mother just looked at her. Then she asked the question Tessa had come to expect, "Are you still a virgin?"

Tessa calmly replied, "Yes, Mama, I am. I told you, Dylan respects me. He knows and understands that I will be a virgin until my wedding night. I made that clear a long time ago." Her mom just stared at her, making Tessa grow uncomfortable.

"What, Mama? What are you thinking?" Tessa prodded.

"I was thinking that maybe I should take you to the doctor and get you on birth control," her mother said evenly.

Tessa's mouth fell open. This, she did not expect. Embarrassment hit her first, but then Tessa was angry. "Seriously, Mother? You think I'm lying to you?"

"No, I believe you," her mother assured her, hesitantly, "I just know things can get.... heated. Things happen."

Tessa couldn't believe what she was hearing. Her mother had given her "the talk" when she was fourteen and had never missed an opportunity to remind her of the highlights since. She knew and understood what could happen. "Mama, I don't need to be on the pill. Dylan and I kiss and touch each other, but that's as far as it goes. I promise. Besides, I want to finish school and become a nurse. Babies will have to wait."

Her mom smiled. "Good to know. Do you have any questions? Anything at all? I know I'm just your mom, but I'll answer the best I can. Don't think I don't know what goes on when you two are sitting in his car at night."

Tessa turned beet red and looked away. "I don't have any questions right now, Mama. But I might someday, so please keep that option open for me." She stood up, putting her glass in the sink, and headed to her room.

Dylan showed up at 4:30 with a dozen roses artfully arranged in a vase and a birthday card. She was so surprised, she almost cried. She had never gotten flowers from a boy before. She proudly carried them into the kitchen and placed them in the center of the table while Dylan visited with her parents. She joined them in the living room just in time to hear Daddy ask what the plans were for the evening. Dylan said he was taking her for a birthday dinner at her favorite pizza place, then they were going to ring in the New Year with Cal and Shelly back at his house. Mama reminded them all how much she liked Shelly while Daddy told them to have a good time.

As they stepped outside, Dylan grabbed her, giving her an earth-shattering kiss. When he pulled back and released her, she almost fell over. They laughed as she caught her balance. "Happy Birthday, baby girl," he drawled.

Tessa blushed. "Thank you, Handsome," she answered with a wink. And off they went, walking hand-in-hand, to his car.

Tessa glanced at the drink in her hand, then at the two empty glasses sitting on the small table beside her. She really must have gotten carried away remembering that night. Looking around, she noticed the beach was much more deserted than when she arrived. She decided to head back up to her room. As the elevator rose, she pulled her phone out to check the time, almost choking on the last of her drink. It was after 6:00. She noticed then that she had missed messages from both her niece and Dylan. She responded to her niece first.

*Hey, Liz. Yes, I made it in just fine. Sorry
it took me so long to get back to you. I blame
the beach! These waves lulled me into
daydreams.*

> *LOL, that's ok! It happens more than you
> think. I'm looking forward to seeing you
> Wednesday. Wish I could get off work
> tomorrow.*

*Don't worry about it. I have a full day
planned for tomorrow anyway. I am really
looking forward to seeing you, too! Do you
mind if we do a little shopping Wednesday?*

> *Are you kidding? That's my favorite thing to
> do! See you Wednesday. Around noon?*

*Can't wait! you guys have a good evening.
I'm going to catch up on my reading.*

Tessa stepped off the elevator, putting her phone in her pocket so she could unlock the door. As she entered the room, the coolness from the air conditioning soothed her. She hadn't realized how warm it was outside until now. She went into the bathroom and took a quick shower. Throwing on a sundress, Tessa decided to let her hair dry naturally. Sitting on the bed, Tessa opened her conversation with Dylan.

> *Hey, quick question. You ok with going to
> that pizza place we went to on your 16th
> birthday? It's not the same name, but it's
> still good pizza.*

*Believe it or not, I was just sitting on the
beach thinking about that night. While
polishing off three drinks, apparently.*

> *Oh, so you're tipsy right now? Dang, I
> always miss all the fun. LOL*

*No, Goober. I'm not tipsy. Not feeling too
bad… but not tipsy. Maybe the salt water*

*and sun make alcohol less potent because they
tasted pretty strong. I didn't even realize how
many I had until I came out of my trance.
Going back there would be fun. Great idea!*

> *Great, now answer my previous question.*

Puzzled, Tessa scrolled back up and found the message he'd sent just before.

> *You want me to fly out in the morning and
> come hang out with you?"*

She sat there for a second not sure how to answer. It could be fun, but sunburnt and tipsy with Dylan might not be the best idea.

Funny, but:

#1- I already have a full day tomorrow.

*#2- you're not getting away with not taking
me back to that pizza place!*

*#3- I'm not sure you wouldn't take one look
at me and run. Could be a wasted trip.*

> *#1- Plans change every day.*

> *#2- I'm not about to change my mind about
> dinner.*

> *#3- Tessa, I have been looking at your
> pictures online. You are still as pretty now as
> you were then. And no way do those pictures
> do your eyes any justice. But I can't, anyway.
> I wish I could.*

Tessa almost melted on the spot. Suddenly she had irrational doubts about the sun and alcohol, so she read the message again to make sure she wasn't dreaming. She wasn't dreaming. Tessa melted again.

*You really shouldn't say such sweet things.
You could cause heart failure.*

Oh, but I can't make any promises. I call 'em as I see 'em. Besides, it wouldn't be a wasted trip if I got to spend time with you.

I see you still have that wicked sense of humor. That is one of the things I have missed about you.

One of the things, huh? Does that mean there are more?

You could say that. I have thought about you many times over the years. You were the one that got away, you know.

I've thought about you a lot, too. When I opened that message from you earlier, I couldn't believe my luck.

Luck? Don't go thinking its good luck just yet. Wait until we meet up. I'm a bit crazy now. Just ask anyone who knows me.

I ain't scared.

Yeah, you say that now… LOL

So, what's your plan for the rest of the evening?

Oh, I will probably go down to the burger place next door and grab something to eat. Maybe walk the beach. Catch up on my reading. I have a massage scheduled for 9 tomorrow morning and some sightseeing later in the day. Liz and I are going to lunch and to do some shopping on Wednesday.

You should let me send you some money for your shopping trip. A pretty lady like you deserves pretty things.

Awe, that's awful sweet of you. But I think I'm fine in that area.

*Let me know if you change your mind. You
should be able to get what your heart desires.
I can send it to your account through an app
my kids showed me.*

*You're a mess. We haven't seen each other or
even talked in twenty years and now you
want to spoil me?*

*Like I said. Pretty ladies deserve pretty
things.*

You are too much...

Nah, I'm just me. Nothing special.

*Right... LOL. I'm going to go grab
something to eat. Catch you later?*

Alright then. Later it is.

As Tessa waited for the elevator that would take her the seven floors down to the lobby, she pulled her phone out of her purse to re-read her last conversation with Dylan. But as the doors opened to her floor, a family with two small children waited inside. The dad was holding the hand of a little dark-haired girl, while the mom tried valiantly to calm the small boy she was holding. He looked like he was fighting sleep, and putting up a good fight, too. The dad noticed her watching and spoke up, "You sure you want to brave a ride with us? His fussing might be more than you bargained for."

Tessa just smiled and reassured them as she stepped inside, "Oh, I've been there, don't worry. Mine are grown now, but I remember how fussy they can get." As the door closed behind her, she saw the little girl gazing at her. Tessa gave her wink, which seemed to encourage her. "What's your name?" she asked, "My name is Marie."

Tessa smiled and bent down to look her in the eye. Reaching out her hand for a handshake, she replied, "How do you do Marie? My name is Tessa. I'm pleased to meet you." Marie's little brother had stopped fussing and was watching the exchange.

Suddenly, the door slid open, and they all stepped out. The family of four went on their way to the hotel restaurant as the baby resumed his fussing. Tessa turned the opposite direction, heading outside. A sea-salted breeze swept over her, keeping her cool as she walked the short distance to the restaurant next door. People were everywhere, perfect for people-watching. She decided to enjoy her burger outside on the patio as opposed to taking it to her room and eating alone. She'd had enough of that.

She placed her order with the waitress, ordering another Pineapple Upside-Down Paradise. Lulled by the sound of the waves caressing the beach, she watched as people strolled by, hand-in-hand. She couldn't help but wonder how it would feel to be there with Dylan. The chime of her phone broke her reverie.

Do you remember why we broke up?

Not really, I've been wondering that myself.

Another question, why did you look me up?
I'm not complaining, trust me. Just curious.

Hmmm… Should I tell you? Probably not,
don't want you getting a big head. Ha-ha.

I already have a big head, so no harm done.
LOL. At least according to my kids, I do.

Tessa thought for a minute Should I tell him the truth? Should I tell him that I can't get him off my mind? What the hell, she decided. She'd already made the first leap…

Well, honestly, you've been on my mind
lately. It seems like every time I turn around,
thoughts of you just pop into my head.

That's good for me, right?

Maybe…

I can't wait until you get back. I'm excited to
see you again. I promise to be a gentleman.

You always were. I doubt that has changed.

You have crossed my mind so many times.

*I know that feeling. I have always wondered
if you are happy.*

                       I was, for a while.

That's better than not at all I guess.

                I guess. What about you, were you happy?

*Yes and no, you know how it goes in a
marriage. Some days are amazing, some a
disaster.*

                Please tell me you were never abused?

*No, never. But I do suspect he cheated on me.
Sometimes I think he just wanted to keep his
"family man" reputation. But he never hurt
me like that.*

                *I heard about his passing, I'm sorry about
                your loss. I thought about reaching out, but I
                was in a relationship. Didn't want it to be
                awkward.*

*I know. I remember running into you around
that time. You told me about the divorce and
that you were seeing someone else. I was so
focused on my grief and the kids at the time.
It was a tough time. I had to move us out of
the family home into something smaller.
Seems like our worlds were always moving in
different directions.*

                *I'm so sorry you went through all that. I feel
                like I should have stepped up and taken care
                of you.*

Why? I wasn't your responsibility.

                *I know, but my heart hurt for you. I knew
                you needed time, but then life kind of got
                away from us. Life just kept going. How did
                time pass so fast?*

*I wish I knew. Seems like just yesterday we
were dating and being goofy together.*

> *By goofy, do you mean doing everything but
> what we both wanted?*

*LOL, yes exactly. You made it so hard to be
a good girl, Dylan Wilson. But I'm not
complaining.*

> *You always did like making it hard.*

*LOL That I did. My burger was just
delivered. I'll message you after I eat, if that's
alright?*

> *That works for me. Enjoy.*

Tessa read over their messages while enjoying her burger. She was
excited, but still nervous about seeing him again. What if she didn't
meet his expectations? What if he didn't meet hers? Did she have
expectations? She thought about it and decided she really didn't.
Regardless, she still got chills just thinking about him.

As she finished her meal, she looked out over the beach. The sun
was setting, setting the sky ablaze with color. She snapped a picture
and sent it to Dylan. He responded immediately with a thumb-up
emoji.

*Just finished my burger. Think I'll take a
walk down the beach, then head back up to
my room.*

> *Enjoy. But be careful. There's a lotta weirdos
> out there. A pretty gal like you is hard to
> find.*

*Stop, lol. With all of the hot, young people
here to choose from, I'm really not worried.*

> *I wouldn't be too sure about that. Just be
> aware of your surroundings and let me know
> when you get back to your room. You can
> never be too careful.*

Don't worry about me, I'm a big girl.

> *Not too big if I remember right. I will still worry until I hear from you.*

Alright. I will let you know when I am safe in my room.

> *Good, enjoy your walk. Don't get too far from your hotel. Maybe that hot cabana boy who was trying to get you drunk will walk with you.*

LOL, I never said he was hot, and he wasn't trying to get me drunk. You are tripping.

> *Any man in his right mind would try to get you drunk and take advantage of you. You still look as purty as you did 40 years ago. Now GO. Just don't forget to let me know when you make it back safe.*

Yes sir!

Chapter 11

essa headed for the beach. As she was walking, she remembered a steamy, rainy night at the lake.

Valentine's Day, 1979

Dylan picked Tessa up around noon on Saturday. He surprised her with a teddy bear and a heart shaped necklace. It was overcast, but not cold. They drove out to the lake and parked. They sat, talking, for what seemed like hours when the sky suddenly opened and started to pour. As the sound of the rain whispered to them, Dylan and Tessa started to kiss. Before long, the windows fogged, and Dylan teased her, saying anyone who saw the car would know they were making out. Tessa blushed, threatening to die of embarrassment while they shared a laugh.

Talk turned to school. Dylan asked her if any of the boys at school showed any interest in her. Shaking her head, she said she didn't think so. Not that she'd notice any boy but him anyway. Dylan quickly corrected her. He wasn't a schoolboy; he was a man. Tessa managed not to giggle. It was so funny how calling him a boy seemed to set him off.

Changing the subject, Tessa asked him questions about the future. They dreamed together about the kind of house they would live in and how many kids they wanted. He promised to build her the biggest house in the world while she was content with a simple farmhouse with high ceilings and a big porch. They agreed it didn't matter where they lived or what kind of house they had, as long as they were together.

Tessa looked up, finding herself back at the hotel. She didn't remember anything about the walk except the sound of the waves, which probably prompted the memory of that day in the rain at the lake. That was definitely the best and most memorable Valentine's Day she had ever celebrated. Entering her room, she closed the door behind her. Kicking off her shoes, Tessa changed into a pair of shorts and a tank top to sleep in. She looked at the clock. 10:22. Quickly doing the math, she realized it was 9:22 where Dylan was. He should still be up.

I'm back from my walk.

Two minutes passed before he responded.

> *Well, It's about time. You were gone over an hour. I thought for sure some hot surfer dude swept you off your flip flops and I'd lost you again.*

You're so funny. Like any hot surfer dude would be interested in an old lady like me.

> *You are not old. And you ARE hot. Don't argue with me, or I will fly to Florida, find you, and turn you over my knee.*

Promise?

> *Yes, it is a promise. I see you are still feisty as ever. Besides, you're the one who said no. I'll still drop everything and jump on a plane.*

No, you won't. Besides, I really do have plans for most of the day tomorrow and Wednesday I'm going shopping with my niece, remember? Thursday I'm on my own but then I'm flying back Friday.

> *Are you saying you don't have time for me?*

No, silly. I'm saying most of my time is
already planned out. I hunted you down,
didn't I?"

          Plans can change, you know. Is that what
          you call this? Hunting me down?

Ok, plans can change, but I have been saving
and planning this relaxing trip for months. I
have no doubt I wouldn't be able to relax
with you around. And you are NOT getting
off the hook to take me to that pizza place
no matter how hard you try!

          Alright fine. I can take a hint. But I have
          never been to Florida, and I just wanted an
          excuse to go. Meanie.

LOL, Whatever. You don't need an excuse
to come to Florida. Do it just because.

          Good point! See ya tomorrow!

Don't you dare! I told you I have this all
planned out. I will be back Friday afternoon.
My plane lands at 2:00

          Fine. Do you need me to pick you up from
          the airport?

No, my car is in long term parking. But
thanks for the offer.

          You know I would do anything for a certain
          pretty gal.

You are too sweet. But enough about me.
How was your day?

          Long. I'm currently working on designing
          houses for three different customers. Should be
          finished up with one tomorrow. Plus, keeping
          up with the lawn and house here. It gets old
          sometimes, doing the same thing day in and
          day out.

*Yeah, but at least you have something to
keep you occupied. I wander around the house
looking for something to do. I do have my
garden during the spring and summer.
Speaking of which, it feels like the best of
summer here. The highs tomorrow are in the
low 80's. After my massage, I will probably
just relax in the sun.*

Maybe you could get a part time job?

*I could. I have a little bit of office experience.
I did some clerical work for the military.*

*You were in the military? Are you a bad ass
now?*

*LOL. Not really. I worked FOR the
military. In an office. Why, do you know
someone looking for part time office help?*

No, but I can keep my ears open.

That's not a bad idea.

*Actually, I'm considering hiring someone to
help me organize and keep up with
paperwork and payroll.*

*Hmmm, I would have to think about that.
Working with you could be dangerous. You
already stole my heart 40+ years ago. Not
sure I have much left to give.*

*Funny. We can discuss it when we go for
pizza. You still like pineapple and ham?
That's still gross.*

*I do, but I like other kinds, too. My
tastebuds have matured over the years.*

*That's good. I never understood how you
could eat pineapple on pizza to begin with.*

*If I remember right, your tastebuds could've
done with some maturing. You didn't like
anything. Way too picky. You are missing
out! Just saying…*

> *What-EVER!*

LOL You're still weird.

> *I'm not weird, I'm unique.*

You can say that again!

> *Well, as much as I hate to say this, I need to
> go. It's past my bedtime.*

*I'm pretty tired myself. Talk soon. Good
night and sweet dreams.*

> *Good night to you, too. Anytime I dream
> about you, it's sweet.*

*Still a smooth talker, smooth fibber, too.
LOL*

> *Are you saying you don't dream about me?
> I'm crushed.*

*Every night, handsome, every night.
Goodnight.*

Chapter 12

essa awoke the next morning, groggy after a restless night. It was 6:00 am and the sun wasn't up yet, but the pink streaks in the sky promised an appearance. She called room service for some coffee and pastries. She glanced out her window, watching the few people scattered out on the sand and thought about taking a walk before it got crowded. With a deep yawn that caught her off-guard, she changed her mind. Turning on the local news, she snuggled into her blanket. A light knock on the door announced the arrival of room service with her breakfast. As the attendant wheeled the cart into her room, the scent of coffee washed over her. Coffee had long been one of her favorite smells. That and roses. She could sniff roses all day. They always reminded her of the ones Dylan gave her, her first flowers from a boy. Tessa tipped the attendant and poured herself a cup of caffeinated heaven. After doping it with sugar and creamer, she walked back out onto her balcony to watch the sun come up.

Looking to her right, she saw the first rays of the sun starting to shine through the ebbing darkness. Setting her coffee down, she picked up her phone to take a picture. Distracted by the message notification, she opened it.

Good morning sunshine!

Dylan sent it an hour ago. Focusing on her photo op, Tessa opened her camera app, aimed it toward the sunrise, and captured the moment. Attaching it to her reply, she responded.

Good morning yourself! You're up bright and early.

It's an hour earlier here remember?

True. I actually slept in. It was nice for a change.

I'm sure it was. Not that you need that much beauty rest. You're still as pretty as ever. That sky is beautiful, by the way.

That is my current view.

Breathtaking. Just like you.

I'm sure you are still as handsome as I remember.

Probably not, but let's not go there.

LOL. Okay, if you insist.

I do. So, you have a massage today. Do you have anything exciting planned?

Have you ever had a massage? They are so relaxing. And to me being pampered IS exciting.

Good to know. I'm happy to excite you anytime. Whenever you need a massage, let me know!

You give massages?

Not yet, but I can learn.

You are a mess. I usually only get them when traveling. By the time I get home, I 'm ready to be back to normal.

I can't believe we live so close to each other and didn't know it.

I know! Crazy, isn't it?

Yep. How did you sleep?

Not well. But I usually don't the first night or two in a strange bed.

I know the feeling.

I guess a lot of people are that way.

Probably.

How did you sleep?

Not too good. I never do.

*I remember that. You work too hard, always
have.*

Nah, I just do what needs to be done.

Still, you have to take care of yourself.

*I'm fine. I'm tough. I don't do much
construction on my projects anymore, but my
son is a builder. I push a lot of my customers
his way, and in return he lets me work with
my hands on occasion. Sometimes I like to
get in and get my hands dirty.*

*All right, tough guy. You're not getting any
younger, ya know?*

*None of us are. Trust me, I know. I feel it in
my bones.*

*You and me both. Being on the water doesn't
help much.*

She snapped a quick picture of the ocean outside her window and
sent it to accentuate the point.

Is that a woman lying naked on the beach?

Tessa scanned the beach. Sure enough, there was a woman lying
naked under the morning sun. She laughed out loud.

*I guess it is. Maybe I should look before I
snap a picture. I didn't know this was a
nude beach. There are lots of families in this
hotel.*

*Nude beach, huh? What hotel are you at? I
will book the first flight out!*

61

Ha-ha. NO YOU WON'T!

> *Now, you better not be going naked out on that beach. The police will be called due to all the men fighting over you.*

LOL You are so funny. Have you already hit the bottle this morning?

> *No ma'am. Just speaking from the heart.*

With all that charm, why has someone not snatched you up yet?

> *Because nobody can fill your shoes.*

Awe, you're makin' me blush. Except, you're so full of crap your eyes should be brown.

> *That's a lot of sass for so early in the morning, little lady.*

You know I come by it naturally. Mama taught me well. I get told that I look like her now, too.

> *Yes, you do. Mom had some pictures from when we all lived next door to each other. You're the spitting image of her from back then. I really noticed it the last time I saw you 20 years ago when I saw you together. Remember that? I think our moms visited the whole time.*

They did. Mama gushed all the way over there about living next door to you guys. So many stories. Apparently, you didn't want any "icky girls" in your room, so I had to hang out with the adults back then. Thanks for that, by the way!

> *Trust me. If I knew then what I know now, I would have trapped you in my room.*

*As I recall, you did a few times when we were
dating. I'm pretty sure it was that amazing
smile of yours that did it.*

Now who's making who blush?

*What? I made you blush? I better mark the
time and date!*

*Very funny. I'm going to get grab a shower.
Got a busy day today. Meeting a new client
and hopefully finishing up a drawing so I can
get paid. Broke gets old.*

*Broke huh? Yet here you are, offering to spoil
me...*

*I don't need to eat that bad. I'd do anything
for you.*

Go get your shower. We'll talk later, silly.

If you insist. Enjoy your massage.

Will do, Have a good day.

Tessa stretched. She'd slept a little better last night. After pouring
a fresh cup of coffee, she picked up a cherry turnover and took a bite.
She closed her eyes as she chewed. It was so good. Twenty minutes
and two pastries later, she headed to the shower. Emerging from the
hot water, she felt ready to take on the day. With a little time before
she needed to head to her appointment, she switched the tv to a
country music video channel. The song playing quickly caught her
attention. The lyrics told the story of high school sweethearts
reconnecting. The coincidence felt fated. She took out her phone,
texting Dylan to listen. He responded within a few minutes.

*Yep, one of my favorite songs. It reminds me
of you, actually.*

*Funny you should say that. It made me
think of you.*

*Nope, I found it first. You have to find your
own.*

You're just a meanie. :P

Deal with it! :P

Ok, Mr. Meanie! I will. I'm out of here and headed to my massage. I might even get my nails done today.

Good, I hope you do. Let me know if you start running low on money.

You just told me you were broke! I have a credit card if I start running out. You go have a good day. We'll chat tonight.

Will do. You have a good day too.

Chapter 13

Tessa had an exciting morning. She had barely started on her coffee when the police showed up and arrested the nude sunbather outside her window. Guess it wasn't a nude beach after all. She couldn't wait to tell Dylan. He'd be crushed.

Shortly after the police lights faded from view, Tessa headed to her scheduled massage. This wasn't her first time. She'd frequented one particular spa on vacation a few times before, so she figured she knew what to expect. She figured wrong. The paperwork process in the waiting room felt familiar enough. She filled out a form requesting a list of health issues, current medications, that sort of thing. After she handed back the clipboard, she was ushered into a dark room where a massage table waited. Following instructions, Tessa removed all her clothes, neatly folding them and placing them on a nearby chair. She situated herself on the table so that her face fit as comfortably as possible into the cutout and covered herself with the sheet. Just as she started to relax, the door creaked open. Soothing music poured softly from a small portable speaker in the corner of the room. She didn't raise her head to look at the massage therapist when she heard the rustle of footsteps approaching, but she did notice the size of the feet as they came into view. Then he spoke.

"Good morning. My name is Stephen, and I'll be your masseuse today." After a weighted pause, he continued, "Any problem areas you would like me to focus on?"

Tessa thought for a minute. She had never been asked that before. "No, not really. I'm just here for a basic relaxation massage to help me unwind and enjoy my vacation."

"I promise you will be very relaxed when you leave."

"Uh, ok," she stuttered. She'd never had a male masseuse before. She raised her head to get a peek at Stephen and almost passed out. He was sexy and ripped. "Just the basics would be fine. I don't need anything fancy." Then she quickly poked her face back into the hole in the table. She had no doubt she was blushing from head to toe.

Stephen stepped back, pausing to ask, "Just the basic massage? Are you sure you don't want to go with the facial too? It's very relaxing and the perfect way to complement your vacation. When it's time to roll over, I'll place a warm towel over your face to help open the pores. Then I'll apply a cleanser with aromatherapy properties, followed by a deep moisturizer. It's the ultimate in relaxation."

Convinced, Tessa gave the approval. "Ok. Give me the works. What the hell, I'm on vacation, right?"

"Now, you have the right idea. If, for any reason, you feel uncomfortable at any time, please speak up. We want our customers to leave feeling relaxed, not distressed."

"Okie, dokie…" Tessa replied nervously. Her head was spinning, wondering what she had just agreed to. Telling herself to calm down, she shrugged under the sheet. It'll be fine.

Stephen began the massage, working her shoulders, arms, and torso. Walking to the end of the table, he raised her right foot and started working the arch. She felt the tension draining out of her body, and it felt amazing. As her muscles eased, her mind wandered back to Dylan. In their messages she was finding the same sweet guy she remembered. Protective, generous. He had a way of making her feel like the only girl on the planet.

Stephen put her foot down, sliding her leg to the right. Then he started on her calf and thigh. She became very aware of how far his hands traveled, but oh, they worked magic on her muscles. Moving back to the bottom of the table, Stephen turned his attention to left foot.

As he worked his way up to her left calf and thigh, she drifted back to thoughts of Dylan. She contemplated what the future might hold for them now that they were talking again. Then her thoughts turned to what it would be like when they saw each other next week. It's not like they hadn't seen each other in the forty plus years since they broke up. But even with those occasional encounters, it had been a couple of decades. It wouldn't be a complete shock that they have both gotten older, but she didn't know what to expect. Life had a way of doing that. She decided that talking to him first, getting reacquainted over chat, would only help. At least he had the benefit of looking at her pictures on social media. She hadn't a clue what he looked like now. Not that she was worried. Her attraction ran deeper than that. *Wait, did I just admit I'm attracted to Dylan?* She twirled the word around in her mind, considering. *Hmmmm… Yeah, guess that's the right word for it, all right.* She had never stopped loving him anyway, she finally admitted to herself—even during the best moments of her marriage.

Stephen interrupted her epiphany, instructing her to turn over. As she complied, she noticed he had turned his back, giving her privacy to transition while getting something off the shelf. He returned with a warm washcloth, placing it over her face. Urging her just to relax, he suggested she find her inner happy place. Tessa closed her eyes and pictured herself back on the beach, sipping a Pineapple Upside-Down Paradise. Her arms, then hands, melted under Stephen's touch. With her upper limbs thoroughly liquified, Stephen moved back to her thighs. Pushing the sheet up to the bend of her left thigh, he started massaging from the inside, working his way out. As she became hyper-aware of her reaction to such an intimate touch, she quivered.

"Too much pressure?" he asked.

"No, not at all," she said.

"Ok. Remember what I said. If you start to feel uncomfortable, just speak up."

Tessa nodded her head, but kept her eyes closed. He continued the massage, working her whole thigh, then moving to the other side. Using more oil, he rubbed it into her lower legs and the sides of both calves. Tessa puddled, scarcely noticing as Stephen removed the washcloth from her face and applied a soft exfoliating cleanser to her face. He switched on the small round brush with feather-soft bristles.

After washing the scrub away, he applied a toner, then smoothed a fragrant moisturizer into her skin with the tips of his fingers.

Instructing her to flip over again, he explained, "I always save the back for last. You might fall asleep, and that's perfectly ok." Starting at her waist, he eased the muscles in her back and shoulders, allowing all the muscles in her body to relax completely.

Stephen's soft voice found her, telling her to take her time getting dressed then he would meet her out front when she was ready. After laying there for a long moment, she slowly got dressed and somehow made it to the front lobby. Stephen was there waiting for her as promised. As Tessa paid for the massage, adding a generous tip. Stephen stepped around the counter and gave her a hug. "Come see me again before your vacation is over. I have never had a client relax quite like you did."

Tessa was sure she was blushing as she stepped out into the bright sunlight. Her stomach informed her it was almost lunchtime. Her early breakfast seemed to have also melted away during her sensational massage. She decided a salad at the hotel restaurant sounded good, then she'd find a salon and indulge in a mani-pedi. Ordering a sweet tea with her small chef salad, Tessa pulled her phone out to check her messages. Sure enough, a message was waiting.

> *Don't go looking for any hot surfer dudes while you are there! And enjoy the massage… but not too much. ;)*

I'm not interested in any hot surfer dudes, and my massage was AMAZING. Stephen is very good at what he does.

> *Then I guess I'm going to have to look up how to give an amazing massage so I can try to be better than Stephen.*

Tessa was still giggling as her salad and tea arrived.

My lunch just arrived. We will discuss what you should and shouldn't be looking up later. Talk soon. Enjoy the rest of your day.

Tessa dug into her salad, enjoying another trip down memory lane.

June 1979

The sun had gone down, but the heat lingered. It was almost curfew, and Tessa and Dylan walked out to his car hand-in-hand. Dylan suddenly swung her around, leering at her backside. "Before I take you home, I'm gonna need a handful of that butt."

Tessa rolled her eyes and laughed.

"Why are you laughing? I'm serious!" He feigned shock at her dismissive reaction. "You know I love your butt, and since I don't get to see you for an entire week, I need to get a handful of it so I don't forget what it feels like."

His dad had entered his car in a car show in Arizona. Dylan and his brothers were all going with him, and they were leaving first thing in the morning. "Thanks for reminding me," she complained, giving him her best sad face.

He stopped, pulling her against him. She leaned her head into his chest, trying not to cry. She knew she was being silly, but she couldn't stop her emotions from showing. He tipped her head up by the chin and said softly, "Hey now, none of that. This week is going to fly by. You just wait and see."

"I'm sure it will for you, but to me it will seem like forever." She stuck her lower lip out even further.

"You will be fine."

"Probably. But don't be looking at any hot girls while you're there." She countered, shaking her finger at him

"I only know of one hot girl, and she is right here in my arms." As he said the words, Dylan impulsively stuffed both hands down the back of her jeans and grabbed her butt. He hissed, "Damn, girl, your butt is sweet!"

Tessa blushed. Looking down, she teased, "I can feel your excitement. I might need to cop a feel of my own before your leave." And she did.

Just as things were really heating up, Donnie stuck his head out the door and warned, "You better get her home and get your butt back here. We have a lot to do!" Dylan reluctantly removed his hands, then opened the passenger door for her. He turned, walked around to the driver's side, then stopped and just stood there.

Puzzled, she asked, "Hey, get in. What are you waiting for?"

"I'm waiting for things to settle down so I can sit without breaking anything." Tessa bit her lip and looked away, struggling not to laugh.

Outside her house, Dylan took her face in his hands and looked her straight in the eyes. "You better stay home while I'm gone. I don't think I can fight off more than… say, a thousand guys at a time to keep your from being taken from me."

Tessa shook her head and giggled. "There you go, talking crazy again. I'm not interested in anyone but you."

Chapter 14

Tessa was still relaxed from her day of pampering. She had found a cute little salon just off the beach. The lady who did her nails had to be at least a hundred years old. But she had shared some delightful stories and did an amazing job on her nails. Tessa decided to go bold and selected the "flavor of the month," a perfect Floridian hot pink. Her spirits were high as she sauntered back to the hotel. Oh, how she loved it here.

Rounding the corner of the shopping center, Tessa spotted a vendor selling beautiful handmade sandals. She opted for some flats with bold colors made from silky material. They felt so light and comfortable on her feet and perfectly framed her pedicure. The vendor appeared young and sweet. She spoke in broken English, but she knew enough to have a successful sale. Tessa noticed a young child contentedly watching her from a play pen behind the register. She pointed, asking "yours?"

The young lady beamed and smiled, nodding her head. "She is so precious," Tessa cooed, handing her $40 for sandals marked $30 and telling her to keep the change. The young mother gushed with gratitude and Tessa left feeling like a million bucks.

When she got back to her room, Tessa took a picture of her freshly painted toes and new sandals and sent it to Dylan.

I splurged on me! I haven't done that in a very long time.

Nice. Those shoes are very pretty.

*I thought so. The young lady selling them
wasn't from around here. Her baby was
adorable. I feel good supporting a new mama
that probably needs the money more than I
do.*

You are a good woman, Tessa.

Boy, did I screw up.

Where did that come from? Are you okay?

Yeah, I was just thinking…

Waiting….

*Ok, well… today I was thinking about that
Fourth of July, when we were in your room,
and Nelson almost caught us. Remember?*

*Yes, I remember it well. I almost lost my
virginity that day.*

*Yes, you did. I would like to think I would
have stopped it, but at that point and time, I
don't think I was that noble.*

*Yes, you were. You knew that it was
important to me to save myself for marriage.*

*I don't know. I can't say for certain that I
would have. You had me pretty worked up.
Hell, just thinking about it today had me
worked up all over again.*

I can relate. Especially these last few days.

*Wait until you see me now. That'll fix that
problem.*

*Don't bet on it. You still have a special place
in my heart, Dylan Wilson.*

And you mine.

So, you've been thinking about that Fourth of July, huh? That was our second Independence Day.

Yep. Then I started thinking about how we broke up the following month. I know it was me who broke it off, but I don't know why.

Does it really matter anymore? I mean, we both moved on. We both still think about each other. We don't hate each other. A lot of people can't say that. I get it. It bothered me, too, for a while after it happened. To say I was heartbroken would be an understatement. Then I dated a few losers who were not even half the gentleman you were. I even had to fight one of them off.

Tell me his name, and I will hunt him down and make him regret it.

LOL, I think it's a little late for that. He probably forgot me and moved on to the next victim. Besides, I don't even remember him, really. You are the only one who stands out in my memory.

Wow, you must have dated some real losers.

Stop. You weren't a loser then, and you're not one now.

You don't know that.

I do know that. I know what kind of man you are. So, tell me, how was your day?

It was good. Not as good as yours was, apparently. Maybe tomorrow I should get MY toes done? What color do you think?

Definitely peach. Peach is safe with just about anything. LOL

73

*Um, NO! Something more manly. I was
thinking like... hunter green.*

*Hmmm. I don't know. That would clash
with your eyes... Maybe something lighter.
Seafoam? Or sage maybe?*

*I have no idea what the hell you just said.
Think I'll just stick with natural.*

Ha ha, that's probably a good idea.

*My feet are ugly. I don't let anyone see them
anyway. Except when my sock has a hole in
the toe when I go get new boots. Then all bets
are off.*

*You are so funny. I'm sure you don't have
holes in your socks. You were always picky
about keeping your feet dry if I remember
right.*

You seriously remember that?

*You would be surprised what I remember.
The lake on Valentine's Day. And the way
you complained all the way back because your
feet got wet while changing the flat tire when
we were headed back to town.*

*Wow, I'm impressed. You have a good
memory. I remember you forcing me to keep
watch while you... took care of business.
You drove me crazy that day.*

*Oh, I remember that too. And how I received
my very first bouquet of flowers that day.
Roses have been my favorite ever since.*

*That's what you remember? That and the
flat tire?*

*Well, I also remember getting your windows
all steamed up.*

I kind of remember that.

Kind of?

> *Yeah, as in I kind of thought about it a lot—several times today alone. And might I add, indulging those kinds of memories while I'm working is not the best idea.*

How is it I always end up blushing when I talk to you?

> *Well, I don't know. Maybe you have been hanging out with the wrong kind of people if you don't blush at least once a day. I remember how big your eyes get when you blush. Have I told you today how pretty your eyes are?*

I'm not sure. I lose track, lol.

> *Well, here's something else I remember. Those eyes are beautiful, and they sparkle when you laugh. Hopefully, we can go get that pizza soon and I can check to see if it still stands true.*

I'm really looking forward to it. You know what would be nice? You could send me a picture so I can see what you look like now.

> *Hang on, I think I have one.*

Tessa sat patiently, waiting for the picture.

> *Found one. Hang on, I will send it your way.*

The picture came through, sending Tessa into a fit of laughter. It was a picture of a picture of him, taken back when they were dating. Shaking her head, she saved it to her photos.

OH WOW!!! You haven't changed a bit!!

> *LOL. That was taken the day after I met you. Cal had gotten a new roll of film for his*

75

camera and snuck up on me. That's why I look like that.

I love it.

I saw a picture of you with your kids. I remember Shelly telling me you had twins. I can see they look a lot like you. And your son is tall. That must have been fun for you, looking up to him.

Twins were actually easier than just one. They kept each other entertained. And yes, he is tall just like his daddy was. Over 6 feet. He's very protective of me but loves to call me a troll since I am little over a foot shorter than he is.

They are pretty, but not near as pretty as their mother.

Stop, you are making me blush again. They are amazing. All my kids. My girls were my rock when my Tom passed away. I would have been lost without all three of them.

Mine are pretty special too. I can't believe I was a part of creating such pretty kids.

Oh, I can believe it. You were mighty fine looking. I bet you still are. Do you have a picture of them?

I do have a picture of them. Give me just a second.

Moments later, another picture appeared. This one of Dylan with two of his kids. Dang, he really did still look good. His son looked just like him, too. His daughter was very pretty, and that look on her face said "Daddy's Girl" all the way. She must have inherited that Wilson protective streak. Intent on examining the photo, Tessa didn't respond right away.

*Is it that bad? Are you going to stop
speaking to me now? I just figured I would
kill two birds with one stone. That one was
taken before I remarried and had two more. I
have a picture of them. Gimme a minute, I'll
send it.*

*No, definitely not bad. Not at all. I'm just
in shock. Your son looks like your twin.
And you look as handsome as I remember.*

Another picture appeared in the message. It was Dylan alongside
two blond haired boys, all three cute as could be.

*That one was taken a few years ago. Not
long after my second wife passed. We were at
Cal's for Christmas."*

You haven't changed much at all.

You haven't either. We both just got older.

I'm feeling it, too.

*Yeah, I know what you mean. I'm going to
get off of here for a bit. I have an estimate to
write up, and I need go get some dinner.
Talk later?*

*I should probably get something to eat myself.
I walked that salad off a while ago. I'm
going to head down to the beach, maybe grab
a taco and a beer.*

*Don't drink too much, now, and let some hot
surfer dude sweep you off your feet. Looking
at you, he would think you were in your early
20's.*

Go do your estimate and stop with the BS.

*It's not BS. You are still as pretty as I
remember.*

And you still know the way to my heart.

> *Behave yourself but have fun.*

I can't do both.

> *I'm sure you'll find a way.*

If you insist.

> *I do. Later, Tessa.*

Chapter 15

Tessa savored her taco and the sounds of the waves whispering to the shore. She'd opted for her signature drink over the beer, and she watched as beads of moisture ran slowly down the hurricane shaped glass. A breeze gently caressed her, lifting her hair off her face as she allowed her mind to replay her last text conversation with Dylan. Suddenly she remembered the story she had to tell him. Smiling broadly, she reached for her phone. She knew he had estimates to work on, but this was too good not to share.

> *So, I'm sitting here on the beach having my second drink. I'm definitely going to have to learn how to make these before I leave, btw. I just realized something I forgot to tell you earlier. That nude sunbather was arrested this morning. Rumor has it she left a party pretty sloshed, went skinny dipping, then passed out on the beach sometime during the night. I'm not sure if they ever found her clothes or not.*

> *Are you serious?*

> *Yep. I guess the party got a little out of control. It must have been at another hotel though, because I didn't hear any wild parties last night.*

> *Just don't go joining any wild parties. I would hate to fly up there and beat the snot*

out of some young college kid. But I will if I have to.

You're just looking for an excuse to fly to Florida, aren't you? And why do you keep worrying about me finding someone young? I couldn't handle any of the young studs down here.

I wasn't really worried about it before but now that you're calling them studs, maybe I should fly in.

LOL. I give up. You do what you feel you need to do. Who am I to tell you what you can do?

I'm really tempted.

Well, what's stopping you then?

Oh, I have a special project I'm working on. I hope to unveil it next week.

Intriguing. But you know I was just kidding, right? I told you I'm busy the rest of the week anyway, you goober.

Yep, I remember.

Maybe someday you and I can come back together.

Anything is possible. How is the vaca going?

I'm great! It doesn't get much better than sitting on the beach with a drink in your hand.

Are you getting tipsy again?

Not yet, but the night is young.

Be careful.

I'm good. I know my limits.

Good to know. I'm about to head to the
house. I will hit you up when I get everything
unloaded and I'm settled.

Sounds good to me. My follow-up taco was
just delivered anyway. With my third drink.

I'm glad you are eating something to absorb
the alcohol.

Whatever, I haven't had that much. Go
home, we will talk soon.

Yes ma'am. Behave.

Always. Drive safe.

Tessa took a bite of her taco, pressing the photo app to look through some of the vacation pictures she had taken so far. Scrolling, she was surprised she had so many. She considered having some printed to hang in her house. Swiping to the final shot, she chuckled. Not the one with the drunken nude sunbather sprawled out on the beach, obviously. Maybe she should take some of the sunrise in the morning.

Glancing up, she realized she was missing the sunset. She paid her bill and hurried down to the beach. She remembered spying a pier on the way back from the nail salon and headed that way. A couple loitered underneath, clearly in their own little world. The young man was holding both of her hands, speaking softly but intently to the pretty young woman standing across from him. Suddenly, he dropped down on one knee. Tessa heard the woman squeal with delight. Tessa paused, waiting so they could have their moment without interference. Arm in arm, the couple turned the opposite direction and Tessa continued on her way. As she reached the pier, she caught her breath at the brilliant colors surrounding the retreating sun. Wanting to capture it, she framed the scene perfectly to capture the colors reflecting on the water, the diamond glints of the sand, and the sun taking its final bow for the evening.

As she turned to walk back to her hotel, new sandals dangling from her fingers, Tessa saw that the beach was clearing out. Enjoying the warm air on her face and the feel of the sand between her toes, she took her time. Couples walked hand-in-hand on the beach. Squeals and laughter erupted as one couple dashed inland, narrowly escaping being soaked by the waves crashing up on shore. She smiled wistfully. She missed being a part of a couple. Tessa caught herself fantasizing about sharing this view with Dylan on day. Don't get ahead of yourself, Tessa.

Tessa returned to her room and showered. Worn out, she slipped on shorts and a tank top, then climbed under the covers. She stretched, plugged up her phone, and reached for the tv remote. While scrolling through the channels looking for something to watch, she heard her phone chime. Her niece wanted to confirm their shopping trip. Tessa responded, then turned her attention back to the tv.

Her phone chimed again. This time, she found a message from Dylan.

Hey there pretty lady, you still up?

I am. I just climbed in the bed. What are you doing still up?

I'm a little wound up. Excited and worried.

?

Excited to see you again. Worried you will run screaming when you see me.

I don't see that happening.

If you say so…, but I have a plan just in case. We meet before we go for pizza. Say a park somewhere or something like that. That way if you're disappointed, we can skip the awkwardness of the date and just keep in touch?

Not necessary. You're just trying to get out of taking me to our old pizza place.

Not even! I'm looking forward to seeing you. When do you get back?

*Should be back Friday afternoon. I think
I'm scheduled to arrive around 2 or 3. I do
have a 3 hr layover on my way back. Not
looking forward to that.*

> *If something changes and you need a ride, just
> let me know.*

Awe, well aren't you the sweetest?

> *Nope, just can't wait to see if those pretty
> blue eyes still make me weak in the knees.*

Stop, you're making me blush.

> *Dang it, I'm missing seeing you blush?*

Seriously, stop.

> *If you insist. I mean every word of it, though.
> And I can't wait to see you again.*

Soon, I promise.

> *I'm gonna hold you to that.*

*Ha-ha. Holding me might be your best bet. I
might get nervous and run.*

> *Then I will chase you until you tire out.*

*Well, considering how out of shape I am, that
shouldn't take very long. LOL*

> *I see you still have that quick humor. But it's
> late and I have to get up early. Goodnight,
> pretty lady.*

Sweet dreams, handsome. :)

Chapter 16

Tessa woke the next morning in a good mood. It was the first time she felt this well rested since Tom passed away. She refused to question it. Getting dressed, Tessa headed down to the restaurant looking forward to coffee and Eggs Benedict. Sliding into a chair at what was becoming her regular table, Tessa pulled out her phone.

Morning.

Good morning to you.

How did you sleep? I slept like a baby.
Feeling great this morning.

Not too good here. I woke up several times.

I'm sorry to hear that. That sucks.

I'll be alright.

Well, I guess that's a good attitude to have anyway.

Doesn't do any good to complain, nobody listens. And I have enough going on today I shouldn't fall asleep.

If you say so. I'm shopping with my niece today. Then I think I'm having dinner with her and my nephew."

*That should be fun. You need to be around
other people. I worry about you being there
alone.*

*That's sweet, but you don't need to worry
about me.*

*I will worry about you until you are safe at
home. We have a date coming up. I don't
want to miss it.*

*LOL. You crack me up. But you don't gotta
worry about that. I wouldn't miss it for the
world.*

*Good. I think I'm going to lay back down
for a little bit. Talk later?*

No problem. Get some rest.

Tessa finished her breakfast and took her coffee outside to watch the beach wake up. It was so peaceful. She still had a few hours before her shopping excursion, giving her the perfect opportunity to get some pictures of the mostly empty beach at dawn. She captured a beautiful shot from the pier of the sun emerging above the ocean. Fishermen began to line up, dropping their lines into the water. The smell of bait assaulted her senses, prompting her to move further down the beach. As she trailed along the water's edge, looking for shells and taking pictures, thoughts of Dylan surged again. She sighed, content. A seagull overhead called, pulling her from her reverie. She glanced at her watch and realized she only had an hour before Liz came to pick her up. Making her way back towards the hotel, she soon realized how far she had wandered. Still clutching a few shells in her hand, she finally made her way up to her room, changed shoes, and pulled her hair up.

Twenty minutes later, Liz arrived, thrilled to see her aunt. They hadn't seen each other in several years. Since Tom died, Tessa had been back to his hometown in Florida at least once a year, but the timing had never worked out. Tessa had remained in touch with his family because, well they were her family, too. Since Jamie and her parents passed away, and Nelson was busy with his own family and life, she felt blessed to remain so close to her in-laws.

Liz wanted to take Tessa into Destin, a nice town with a big shopping center where she would be able to get just about anything she could want. After browsing through several stores, Liz asked Tessa if she was hungry. "I could eat," she replied quickly.

"What are you in the mood for?" Liz asked. "There's a nice food court not too far from the store I told you about. Where you wanted to find a gift for Nelson?"

"Sounds perfect. Let's head that way. We could eat, hit that shop, then maybe look at a few other places? I want a few sun dresses to take home."

At the food court, Tessa chose a slice of pizza and sweet tea. Liz opted for a seafood sandwich and a Coke. As they ate, Tessa and Liz visited, catching up on family and sharing girl-talk. They discussed how life as an Air Force wife was treating Liz and what it was like for her living in Pensacola. The day flew by, and before she knew it, Liz and her husband were dropping Tessa off at her hotel after dinner. Yawning, Tessa was thinking she might squeeze in a quick nap and then devote her evening to some quality beach time. Tomorrow was her last full day in Florida, and there were so many ways to fill it. She wanted to do some sightseeing before she left. Maybe work on her tan or go out on a boat. She smiled, shrugging. She knew, realistically, she was probably going to sit in a beach chair, drinking and reading all day. She thought about Dylan. Of course, Dylan had scarcely left her thoughts all day. She'd almost mentioned him to Liz, but then thought better of it. If she didn't want the whole family to know about him, it was best to keep this under wraps for now.

Lying on the bed, she felt her phone vibrate in her purse next to her. Grabbing the strap, Tessa pulled her purse toward her, then fished out the phone and checked her messages. She had a message from Dylan. Several actually, from throughout the day.

Having fun yet?

Hello?

Okay, now I'm getting worried.

Tessa, I'm choosing to assume you are out having fun with your niece and your phone is

just dead or buried in the bottom of your
purse. I just finished lunch, and I'm headed
back to the job. Enjoy the rest of your day.
Chat later.

Hey lady! I'm home early. I missed chatting
with you today. Hope you are having a good
time.

Tessa felt a twinge of guilt reading his messages. She tapped out a response.

Hey! Sorry my phone was in the bottom of
my purse, LOL. I had a great time with Liz
and did a lot of shopping, of course. Mainly
got stuff for the kids, but I picked up a few
things for myself, too. Dinner with them was
awesome. I had a really good steak. I'm
thinking tomorrow I'm going to catch up on
my reading while sunbathing. With glasses of
Pineapple Upside Down close by, LOL.

So, you had a good day? Great to hear.

I did. I'm a little worn out, but in a good
way. I think I am finally adjusted to the time
change. It's so pretty here, but I am ready to
get home to my bed and my house, too. Wish
I could bring housekeeping back with me,
though. Getting a little spoiled with my room
being cleaned by someone else every day.

I can make arrangements to have that done,
if you like?

Stop, you are too much. I'm not that lazy but
it has been nice.

Ok, but all you have to do is ask, your wish
is my command.

Tessa wasn't sure how to respond. Tom had tried to spoil her, too, but it always made her uncomfortable. She appreciated it, understood that it came from love. She just didn't know how to accept it. She never truly felt deserving.

Such a sweetheart. I see some things never change.

I'm just a simple man. I believe women should be spoiled and protected and I have plenty of money and nobody to spend it on.

Thanks, Dylan, but I'm fine, really. But I promise if I need anything, I will let you know.

I'll hold you to that. Listen, I'm meeting my son and daughter-in-law for dinner. It's my granddaughter's 3rd birthday, and we're taking her to her favorite fast-food restaurant so she can play in the kiddie area. Saturday's the party, but I like my time with her without a lot of curtain climbers around. I'll go to the party, but this will be our time.

Awe, I see you like to spoil her, too! Such a good grandpa. You go enjoy your time with her. I think I'm going to relax, call the kids and check in. Message me when you get back. We can do a video call if you want, and I can show you what I got today. I might need to pick up another suitcase to get it all home. LOL

Funny. I will let you know when I make it home. I'm going to hop in the shower.

Need me to wash your back?

Stop teasing.

Tessa put her phone down and started going through her purchases. She had done well. Her haul included several sundresses, two pairs of shoes, a new purse, sunglasses, and a few souvenirs for herself. She had also picked up some fun shirts for the family declaring that she'd gone to Florida and all they got "was this lousy t-shirt." Not original, but she couldn't resist. With her gifts safely packed away, Tessa put on her swimsuit and new sunglasses, grabbed her book, and headed for the pool. Relieved to find it vacant, Tessa found an empty chair facing the beach, settled in, and opened her book. She tried to focus on the time-travel romance, but she was having trouble getting into it. She liked the characters, but the story line was difficult to follow. Determined, she restarted the page.

Sam, the waiter she'd met that first night, approached her. With a mischievous smile, she asked him if he remembered her and quizzed him, asking if he knew which cocktail he'd introduced her to. He assured her that he did remember, then with a wink, he disappeared to fetch her one. She was finally lost in her book when he returned with the Pineapple Upside Down Paradise and a small plate of nachos. Puzzled, Tessa protested, "I didn't order these."

"You really seemed to enjoy them the other night, so I took liberty and brought you some, on the house."

Tessa laughed. "I was a bit tipsy the other night, but I do remember how good they were. Thank you. But I insist on paying."

Sam scratched his head. "Well ma'am, I can't really charge you for them since, in reality, you didn't order them. Besides, we like to take care of our favorite clients. We're hoping that when you come back, you'll stay with us again."

"That's very sweet. And it worked. I will definitely be back."

Book discarded, and half of the nachos gone, Tessa was starting on her second drink when she checked her phone. No messages, no missed calls. She gazed off into the ocean, mesmerized. The sound of her ringing phone shook her out of her trance. She jumped, then saw the video call request from Dylan. She smoothed her hair, worried about how she looked. Accepting the call request, she flipped the camera around to face the beach.

"Well, hello stranger." she drawled.

Dylan responded with a laugh. "What the hell are you doing? Turn the phone around. I want to see you not the beach. I mean, it is pretty. But I have no doubt you look much prettier."

Tessa stalled. "I will. Just give me a second to make sure I look ok and nothing is hanging out."

She could practically hear the cheesy grin as he said, "Turn the phone around, and I'll let you know if anything is hanging out."

"You crack me up. Hang on one second."

She saw Sam walking by and snapped her fingers, whispering, "Hey! Hey!" As he turned to look at her, she called him over with a finger. Holding her finger to her lips, she pointed to her phone.

He gave her a puzzled look, whispering "You ok?"

"Yes, I'm fine… but how do I look? "

Confused, he responded, "You look great, why? Do you not feel well?"

"No, no. I feel fine. My old boyfriend is on the phone, wanting to video chat. We dated forty years ago, and it's been half that since we've seen each other. I don't want to scare him off," Tessa explained in a low voice.

Dylan's amused voice cut in. "Uh, Tessa, sweetie, I can hear you. I'm sure you look great. Now turn the phone around, please." Tessa giggled as Sam stepped between her phone and Dylan's ocean view. "You are right, sir. She is stunning, and apparently very fond of you, judging by that blush."

Tessa wanted to tunnel into the sand. "Well, thanks for making me want to cringe. I thought you were on my side?"

"Sorry ma'am, I cannot tell a lie." Sam quipped with a wink.

Tessa rolled her eyes and flipped the camera back around, looking at Dylan like a child caught with her hand in the candy dish. "Don't pay any attention to him. He's a kid and doesn't know what he's talking about."

"Oh, really?" Dylan continued with a smirk, "Looks to me like you are still blushing."

"Wipe that grin off your face, mister," Tessa chided, trying not to crack a smile. "And hello, you haven't changed one bit. Still handsome as ever."

"Tessa, we have known each other for a long time. Don't start lying now."

"Oh, I think you know me better than that. I don't lie, and I am entitled to voice my opinion. You are still handsome, and I'm not going to argue with you about that."

"Well, you look amazing. The beach was a pretty great view, but you… you take my breath away."

"Well, thank you," she choked out, blush deepening, "that's very sweet. How was your day?"

"Typical. Except my mind kept wandering to what you might be doing. Seeing you now, I would guess the warm air and sunshine agree with you. But that doesn't mean you can stay. I'm looking forward to our pizza date."

"Me, too. And seeing you now, I am even more excited."

"Is that right? Why is that?" he prodded.

"Well, honestly I'm not sure how to answer that. Just the anticipation. And now that we've seen each other, we both kind of know what to expect." Tessa trailed off, wondering if she was making sense.

Dylan nodded. "True. However, I didn't expect for you to look better than you did last time I saw you. You get more and more beautiful every time I see you."

"Have you been drinking?" she asked, one eyebrow raised.

Dylan laughed. "No, I haven't been drinking. Of course, it wasn't a complete surprise. I'll admit I have been studying your pictures. I can't believe how well you have aged." Dylan paused, then continued, self-consciously, "I haven't been as lucky."

Tessa shook her head. "I wouldn't say that. Dylan, you look great! We've both aged forty years since we dated. And that takes a toll. You, however, have just become more handsome. Distinguished looks good on you. Now let's change the subject."

"Okay…" Dylan turned the conversation to her arrival back home. "Are you sure you don't want me to pick you up at the airport? I can bring someone with me to drive your car back."

"I'm sure. Besides, I will want a shower and to unpack and get my laundry going when I get home."

Dylan sighed, defeated. "Well, alright then, but don't you go getting all busy and forget we have a date!"

Tessa rolled her eyes. "Like I could forget that! You just let me know when and what time to meet, and I'll be there."

"What?" Dylan feigned shock horror. "No, this is a date. I will be picking you up like a proper gentleman. I was teasing about meeting at a park."

"You always were a gentleman," she conceded.

"I'm sure there are a few people who would disagree with that, but you always were special and always will be."

"They obviously don't know you as well as I do. And you are special to me as well. I have thought about you so much over the years. Always hoping you were happy. You deserve to be spoiled, too," Tessa said.

"I wouldn't go that far," he scoffed. "Spoiled is for women and children, not grown men."

Tessa rolled her eyes. "Says who? Men can be spoiled too."

"If you say so."

"Spoken like a true man," Tessa chuckled. "Back to our date. What do you have planned? I know we are going to our old pizza place. Is it still casual?"

Dylan scratched the side of his chin as he thought it over. "I'm not sure. I haven't been there in years. I doubt it's formal dress. Just wear something comfortable."

"Okay, that's what I will do," she said.

Dylan needed to take care of a few things in the shop before he went to bed, and Tessa wanted to finish her nachos and possibly get a few more pictures in. They said goodnight and promised to chat again soon. Tessa ordered another drink to take to her room. She smiled as she swiped through the stealthy screenshots she'd snagged while talking to Dylan. He had changed; everyone does over the years, but he still looked good. His hair had turned gray, but he still had a head full of it. He had wrinkles now, but so did she. Life has a way of marking the passage of time. But he still had that amazing smile. She couldn't wait to see him in person soon. Tessa had soured on dating, but her heart was softening–for Dylan.

Chapter 11

Tessa's final day of vacation went fast. She managed to take in a few sights, even took a short trip over the water on a fishing boat. She had been fishing as a girl and accompanied Tom a few times when they were first married, but she really wasn't interested in fishing. What did excite her were the amazing photographs she took of the fisherman reeling in "the big ones" that would become legends at the local pub. Most endearing were the shots she'd taken of Jeffery, an eight-year-old whose excitement at his outing with dad could barely be contained on film. Tessa got his dad's e-mail address and promised to forward the pictures to him when she got back to the hotel.

Tessa disembarked, then took one last walk along the beach while enjoying a quick burger before heading up to her room to shower and start packing. She'd just stepped out of the shower when she heard her phone ringing in the other room. Wrapping the towel around her, Tessa ran toward the sound. The phone stilled as her fingers made contact. Damn, she missed it. A video call from Dylan, she chuckled to herself. Well, she wouldn't have answered it for a million dollars anyway. She decided to send a quick text.

Hey, Sorry I just missed your call. I was just getting out of the shower. Give me about 10 minutes and I will call you back?

                Just out of the shower huh? Does that mean you are not dressed?

That's exactly what that means. I will call you back.

She set the phone down and started back to the bathroom to grab her clothes. The phone rang again. This time she answered.

"Seriously, Dylan?" she huffed.

"What?" he feigned innocence. "I just want to make sure you are OK."

"Funny. 10 minutes." Tessa said evenly.

"You can't blame a guy for trying." Dylan responded, clearly amused.

"No, but it will be a cold day in hell before you see me right out of the shower," she flung back.

"Don't bet on that." Dylan's voice held plenty of the cockiness she remembered from their youth.

This time, she heard a trace of amusement in her own answer. "10 minutes, Dylan."

"Okay, Okay. You win. 10 minutes."

"Bye!" And she hung up the phone, shaking her head, and smiling from ear to ear.

On the clock, Tessa went back into the bathroom to get dressed. She'd miss the beach, but she was looking forward to getting back. Mostly, she was looking forward to her date. As she styled her hair and put on a trace of makeup in the mirror, she thought back to that first evening when Dylan asked her mom for permission to take her out. The shock and excitement when her mom actually said yes, still made her smile. Nine minutes after hanging up the phone, she stepped out on her balcony to make the video call. Before she could hit the call button, her phone rang again. She knew who it would be before checking. Smiling, she hit the accept call button. He appeared on her screen, sitting outside.

Skipping hello, Tessa began, "I was just fixing to call you!"

Dylan looked skeptical. "You sure about that? I'm starting to think you are avoiding me," he answered, begrudgingly.

"Not on your life," she protested, vehemently shaking her head. "I had just got out of the shower and was naked. If I'd answered when you called before, you would have changed your mind about our date. And I'm really looking forward to that pizza."

Dylan gave her a leering look. "I don't think so. But you could have at least allowed me to make that decision."

Tessa laughed nervously, "You are sooo funny."

"Well, you answered this time, and once again you look amazing," he said, accentuating the last three words with dramatic pauses.

"You are going to make me blush again," she responded, batting her eyes.

"I'm just a simple man who tells it like it is." He watched her, clearly enjoying the deepening of her complexion.

She squirmed, not sure how to respond to his steady stream of complements. "I'm not going to argue with you. Besides, simple is nice. With you I know what to expect, and I don't have to deal with any man drama." She emphasized the last two words.

"Man drama? Is that a thing?" Dylan asked with a puzzled look on his face.

"You would be surprised," she said evenly.

"Probably not," he admitted with a shake of his head. "Things are definitely not the same as they were when we were dating."

"Not even close," Tessa agreed. "I have a friend who is trying to set me up with some guy she works with. Apparently, he's part of some role-playing group. Something about knights and kingdoms. I told her not only am I not interested, but that he might want to keep some of these hobbies under wraps if he ever wanted to date again." She failed to stifle her laugh.

Dylan snorted. "Well, you are off the dating market anyway." His stern glance meant business.

"Is that right? And who gave you the right to decide that?" she asked, playfully.

"Oh, it's right. It's been decided." Dylan crossed his arms and raised an eyebrow at her. "We have a date in a few days, remember? That means you are definitely off the market," he insisted.

"Truth be told, I've never really been on the market anyway. My heart was stolen a long time ago," she shot back, blushing.

Dylan nodded, flashing his signature cocky grin. "Mmmm… good answer. Now remind me, when do you get back?"

"Dylan, I've told you twice now." She went through it again. "Tomorrow afternoon. I plan on getting to the airport around 8 in the morning. I'll get checked in and relax for a few, then get on the plane."

"Damn, I have an appointment at 2 tomorrow." Dylan's eyes twinkled with mischief. "Otherwise, I would meet you there."

Tessa rolled her eyes. "I told you, my car is there. And I have a lot to do when I get home. Besides, you need to take care of your business. We will see each other soon." The man was maddening. He was acting like a child waiting to go to Disneyland.

Confirming her thoughts, he muttered, "Not soon enough." He leaned in closer to his camera, looking her straight in the eyes, "Really, Tessa. I can't tell you how much talking to you this past week has lifted my spirits. The guys are already teasing me about having someone new, and I haven't even said anything to anyone yet."

"Wow, you must usually be a grouch," she teased. Returning his gaze, she admitted, "If it makes you feel any better, I've had a bounce in my step all week. Even Liz noticed it and she doesn't see me that often." She paused, as the simply looked at each other in the stillness. "You know, I still can't believe I looked you up. It's so unlike me. But for some reason, I haven't been able to stop thinking about you."

"I guess I have been grumpy," he conceded with a small shrug. "Never really thought of it that way. I'm always just focused on the task at hand. But my son mentioned my change in demeanor, so I guess you've done something to me." He pointed at her, a silly grin on his face.

Tessa chuckled lightly. "You've always been focused. But that's why you have a successful business," she said. Unable to resist the urge, she baited him, "Of course, you're a little bullheaded and stubborn, too, if I remember right."

Dylan shrugged. "That is one thing that hasn't changed. Well, and I'm still hot, of course," he teased, laughing out loud.

"You crack me up. But I have to agree, you are still hot." She smiled, looking at him, then turned the camera to face the beach. "Look at that beautiful sunset."

"Wow, that is pretty, but not near as pretty as you. Maybe someday we can go and enjoy it together."

Tessa turned the phone back around so he could see her. "See, that's what I'm talking about. You melt my heart when you say stuff like that."

He waved his hand, dismissively, "Nah, you're just easy to impress."

"Not really, I just haven't had anyone say sweet things to me in a while." Tessa shrugged, then wrapped her arms across her chest.

"So, what, are all the men around you blind?" he scoffed.

Tessa looked out toward the ocean again, thinking about how to answer. "I'm not really around men, hence the reason my friends keep trying to set me up."

Dylan sat quietly for a moment, just looking at her. "Why haven't you let them set you up before now?"

Tessa looked down, fiddling with her hands. "Well, I haven't really given dating much thought. Besides, I'm waiting for Mr. Right," she joked.

Dylan leaned back in his chair. "So..." he drawled, "I should think about changing my name?"

"Wow, you really are on your game tonight," she said, trying her best not to laugh.

Dylan grinned, clearly proud of himself. "Why do you say that?"

"It's almost as if all the right words just spill out of your mouth."

He shrugged, "I told you. I call it as I see it. Now, what's on your agenda for tonight?"

"Just packing up and getting ready for the trip home tomorrow." She sounded fatigued just thinking about it.

"I'm sure you are ready to get back home," he said, reassuringly.

"I am," Tessa groaned. "Don't get me wrong, it's beautiful here. But there truly is no place like home."

Dylan nodded. "I know what you mean. When we do a job out of town, I'm always eager to get back home and to my routine. Speaking of, it's getting late here. I need to hit the sack. We are starting a new job tomorrow. It's actually a rework of a project the previous contractors messed up, and those are more work than the projects we start from scratch." He rubbed his face with both hands.

"Alright, I need to get busy packing anyway." Continuing, she perked up, "and maybe catch up on my reading!"

"Have a good night. I'll text you in the morning," he smiled, but his fatigue showed around the eyes.

"Or you can call me," Tessa hinted.

Dylan's smile widened, reaching his tired eyes this time. "I figured you'd be busy in the morning."

"Never too busy for you," Tessa flirted, batting her eyes.

Laughing, he scolded playfully, "Okay, baby girl, stop with the sweet talk or we will never get off of the phone."

Tessa knew they both needed their rest, but she wasn't quite ready to hang up. "Don't you like talking to me?" she prodded, relentlessly.

"Whatever," he countered dismissively.

Tessa gasped in feigned shock. "I can't believe you'd talk to me like that!"

Confused, Dylan questioned her. "Like what?"

"Whatever. It's basically saying, 'f you.' That hurts my feelings, Dylan." She faked a sniff.

Dylan shook his head and laughed. "Goodnight, Tessa."

"Fine. Goodnight," she relented. Then she hung up the phone with a smile.

Tessa went back inside to start packing. About ten minutes later, she heard a knock on the door. She opened it to reveal a young lady delivering a package. Confused, Tessa stood there a moment before the lady went on, "The guy said to make sure you had this before you went to bed. He was insistent that you get it tonight."

Thinking the lady might have the wrong room, she asked, "Are you sure that's for me? My name is Tessa Bentley."

"Oh!" Now the delivery girl looked confused. "Maybe I do have the wrong room. This is for a Tessa Peterson."

Tessa smiled broadly, suddenly sure who had called in the order. "No, that's my maiden name. I know who it's from."

Directing the girl to place the package on the table, Tessa fished $5 out of her purse for a tip. Protesting that the caller had already provided her with a generous tip, she refused it. Tessa tucked the money back into her purse, accepted the package, and thanked her. Wishing her a goodnight, Tessa closed the door behind her, then returned to the package. Taking it to the bed, she sat down and opened the envelope. Inside was a card with a note that read, "I can't wait to see you again. Have a safe trip home, but hurry back. Love, D"

Touched, Tessa opened the box to find a charm bracelet with several charms inside. She inspected each charm: a dolphin, a seashell, a slice of pizza, a muscle car, and a small ring complete with a tiny diamond. Tessa blinked back tears. She was amazed at how artfully thought out each charm was, blending past, present, and future. Aching to call him, she remembered he was headed to bed, so she sent a text instead.

You just blew me away…

I have no idea what you are talking about.

Oh yeah? We will see about that.

Goodnight, handsome.

Goodnight, baby girl.

Knowing he needed to rest, she moved outside to the balcony for one last picture of the ocean, moonlight dancing across the water. She stood, watching, feeling very young again.

Chapter 18

Tessa awoke the next morning feeling conflicted. On one hand, she was so ready to be home. On the other, she was dreading the flight and oh, how she would miss the beach–the sounds, the warmth, the beauty. Hopefully, she could finish the last few chapters of her book.

As she lay in bed thinking about what she needed to get done, Dylan flooded her thoughts. She looked at her bracelet and smiled. How could a man she hadn't seen or talked to in twenty years be so darn sweet? She'd been surprised when Dylan told her about running into her mom occasionally. She thought it was strange she never said anything. Why, Mama? Why not mention it? Her mind raced, but she would never have the chance to ask. She sighed, missing her mom even more in that moment. She had always thought that her mom liked Dylan. Afterall, she had relaxed her dating rules for him and been such good friends with his mom. In fact, when Dylan's dad passed away some twenty years ago, they'd attended the funeral together. Her mom and Dylan's had spent most of the day together. After the graveside services, Tessa's mom admitted that they had discussed Dylan and Tessa's relationship briefly, and the mutual feeling that their kids still loved each other. But then, despite Tessa's prodding, her mom had nothing more to say.

Tessa shrugged off the speculation about her mom's feelings regarding Dylan, got out of bed, and went into the bathroom. After brushing her teeth and running a brush through her hair, she decided to skip her shower and take one when she got home that evening. She quickly dressed, then went down to the restaurant for breakfast. The

101

waitress seated her and handed her a menu, but Tessa barely glanced at it. She ordered a cup of coffee and the #2, fishing her phone out of her purse. She had to text Dylan.

Good morning, handsome. Did you sleep ok?

I actually did, you?

I slept alright. Woke up a little stiff, but you know how that goes. Getting old sucks.

You are not old. You still look the same as you did the last time I saw you.

I was just thinking about that day last night.

It wasn't the best day of my life. Having you there helped, though.

I always told you I would be there for you. Twenty years apart wasn't going to change that. I just wish it had been under better circumstances.

That makes two of us… Have you packed yet?

No, I'm having coffee and just ordered breakfast. When I'm done here, I'm going to get some more pictures of the beach. I still have a few hours, and I got a lot of packing done last night.

You better not miss that plane. We have a date in a few days. I would hate to have to drive to Florida to pick you up. But I will if I need to!

LOL, you are too much. I won't miss my plane. I have already requested a ride to the airport. They are meeting me in the lobby at 7:40. Just cool your jets, Mister!

You might want to put a lid on the sass. ;)

You're forgetting who you're talking to.

Ha

*You get back to work. My breakfast just
arrived. Be careful and we will talk later.*

> *Yes ma'am. Let me know when you make it
> to the airport. I want to make sure you don't
> miss your flight.*

Sure, if it will make you feel better.

> *It will. Later.*

Later, gator

Tessa ate her two eggs with toast and hash browns. She didn't normally eat a big breakfast, but for some reason, it just sounded good. She eyed the sliver of toast and bite of hash browns left on the plate. She couldn't believe she ate so much. After finishing her second cup of coffee, she went to the register to pay her bill. The cashier noticed her bracelet and commented on how pretty it was, asking if the charms represented different things. Tessa smiled and explained, "Oh, yes! The muscle car and ring are both for my first boyfriend. Forty years ago. He actually sent it to me last night. Way back in the 70's we dated for a little over a year and a half. I wasn't old enough to drive yet, but he had a nice car. And he gave me a promise ring our first Christmas, right before my 16th birthday. I remember it like it was yesterday. The dolphin and the seashell are for me to remember this past week here at the beach. The pizza slice is looking forward to a pizza date we have this Sunday night, at the same restaurant we used to go to when we dated."

The cashier gushed at how romantic it all was, acting as if she was more excited about the date than Tessa was. But she knew that was impossible. Tessa was nervous as hell, but she couldn't wait. Finally escaping the restaurant, Tessa made it up to her room and finished packing. She still had almost an hour before she had to meet the driver in the lobby. Glancing around the room, she reminded herself to pack extra shoes in her carry on. No way would it be warm enough to wear flip flops once the plane landed back home. She tucked her favorite pair into the bag and hurried out the door, towing all her things.

Exiting the elevator, Tessa asked if she could leave her luggage in the lobby while she took one last stroll on beach. She wanted to get some pictures of all the cute little shops close by—except maybe not the massage parlor. She wasn't sure she should wander that far from the hotel, but more importantly, she still blushed every time she thought about that massage. No matter how much that may have factored into how relaxing the last five days were.

After capturing several good snapshots of the shops, palm trees, and her beautiful beach, she headed back toward the hotel. Along the way, she stopped by the bar on the beach just as Sam, her favorite server, arrived. Tessa asked a fellow beach wanderer to take a few pictures of them together. She took several cute photos, including one of Sam leaning Tessa back as if going in for a kiss. Tessa was most excited when he gave her the recipe for her Pineapple Upside Down Paradise. She knew she would miss him. Sure, he was a great waiter. He made sure her glass was never empty when she visited the beach or pool. But he also felt like a friend. She had to remember to stop and tell the manager what an asset Sam was. Stuffing a twenty-dollar bill into his hand, her final tip, she said goodbye and headed off to find the manager.

Her ride pulled up just as she returned to the hotel. She climbed into the back seat as her bags were loaded into the trunk. The driver kept talking to someone on his phone, an earpiece stuffed in one ear, which was fine with her because she wasn't in the mood to chat right now anyway. After arriving at the airport, the driver unloaded her luggage, still talking to someone about a party this upcoming weekend. She tipped him the minimum and rolled her luggage through the sliding glass doors. Looking around, she was glad she arrived early. The airport was packed. An hour passed in line, then finally she got her luggage checked and made her way to the terminal. She entered one of the gift shops, hoping to snag some snacks for the flight home. Grabbing an iced caramel mocha at the coffee shop next door, she sat down and pulled out her phone, sending Dylan the promised text.

*I made it safely to the airport. Luggage is
checked and I'm waiting for my plane to come
in. How is your morning so far?*

Fifteen minutes dragged by before she heard the answering ding.

> *Busy as always. I was starting to worry.*
> *Were you late getting there?*

No, there was just a long line at check in.

> *I see. How long before you take off?*

I still have about 45 minutes. I got some
snacks for the flight back and I brought a
book to read. But I am almost finished with
this one already. I had planned to finish it
earlier and start a new one on this flight, but
someone kept me distracted.

> *Hmmm. Is that a complaint?*

Not even! If anything, you made my vacation
better. Oh, gotta go. They're calling for
boarding.

> *Fly safe!*

The flight was smooth, and Tessa was able to finish her book. As they taxied to their terminal, she took her phone out and turned off airplane mode. Immediately, her phone dinged. She opened the message from Dylan, sent ten minutes ago.

> *Let me know when you land. I'm getting*
> *ready to meet a new client so it might be a*
> *while before I can respond. But knowing you*
> *are safe on the ground will make my meeting*
> *go smoother.*

Just landed. Should be unloading soon.

> *Good to know. Drive safe and we will talk*
> *tonight. Welcome home.*

Tessa smiled and slipped her phone back into her purse. Knowing the air would be too cool to wear her flip flops now, she started changing into her tennis shoes. She stuck her lower lip out in protest. Noticing the tan line her beloved flip flops left, she couldn't help but smile. It was a nice reminder of a good vacation!

As she waited for her suitcase to show up on the conveyer belt, she remembered how just less than a week ago she was a nervous wreck because Dylan had responded to her message. Now, looking back, she knew that was why her week was so awesome. Well… that, and the sand, and the shopping, and the drinks… She smiled. She was glad to be back home but was already missing the beach.

After retrieving her luggage, Tessa made her way to her car. Waiting for the car to warm up, she scrolled through their last few texts and smiled. Traffic moved smoothly, and Tessa was home in no time. Feeling relieved to be home, she pulled in the garage as another message from Dylan came through.

You home yet? Can I call you later?

Yes. and yes. But not video. After traveling all day, I look like hell.

I bet you don't. But I won't argue with you. I've gotta get some work done. Talk soon.

Tessa hauled her luggage out of the car, plopped it onto her bed, and started unpacking. She couldn't believe she had bought so much stuff. A little at a time adds up. She sorted the laundry and started a load. Putting away her bath soaps, shampoos, and lotions, she thought about the fancy shop where she'd found the best smelling body care products. There were so many, but some were gifts for her daughters and daughter-in-law. Smelling each one, she realized she still needed to decide who was getting what. It would have been so much easier if she'd bought multiples of one thing. She shrugged and decided to let them fight it out when they came over for dinner. Snagging her favorites from the pile, she dumped the rest back in the bag and set it aside for tomorrow.

Treasures unpacked and suitcases stowed in the top of the closet, Tessa hit the shower. As the warm water ran over her body, she thought about Dylan. Hell, when didn't she think about him? He was constantly on her mind, even more now that they were talking again. The past week was magical, almost as if they had never broken up, never married other people or led other lives. She was just finishing getting dressed when her phone rang. It was him.

"Hey, what's up?" she answered, trying to keep the fatigue from her voice.

"Nothing just got home. What's up with you?" he asked.

"Not a lot now. Got home, unpacked, and took a shower. I have laundry going and I'm about to indulge in a cup of coffee. It's always so much better at home." She poured a cup and leaned over, taking in the heady scent.

"You got that right. I'm glad you're back. There's something… comforting knowing you are in the same state." His voice deepened, sounding warmer as he found the word he wanted to say.

Tessa couldn't help but think about how comforting she found the sound of his voice. "Awe, that's sweet. How was your day?"

"Not too bad. I always feel awkward when meeting with new clients, though. They're not always easy to read. How was your flight?"

She smiled at the thought of charming Dylan worrying about connecting with clients. "I can't complain, no screaming kids on the flight back. It was nice and quiet. Had a lot of time to think, to remember how much fun we had when we dated before."

"Sounds like good memories," Dylan suggested, hopefully.

Tessa nodded subconsciously. "Definitely good memories. I keep thinking about Laura, too, and how she would freak if she knew we were going on a date again. I would give just about anything to have her here." She cleared her throat, dispelling the wistfulness she heard there. "Oh, and remembering our letters! She always signed, 'Laura loves Clayton' and 'Tessa loves Dylan.' We talked about the two of you all the time. She was always angling to hear more about how things were with us." The memory tugged at her heart and smile.

Dylan added, self-consciously, "I'm sure that changed after we broke up."

Tessa wasn't sure what to say. Her best friend had been understandably livid when he'd shattered her heart. She waited a beat, then decided to be honest. "Well, yeah, a little. You did hurt her "bestie."

Both sat in the quiet a moment before Dylan pierced it with his soft, low voice. "I'm sorry I hurt you, Tessa. I wish I could remember what I was thinking, why we broke up."

She was quick to reassure him, wanting to leave the past behind and embrace the excitement of the near future. "It doesn't really matter anymore. But just know, all these years you were never unloved."

Dylan cleared his throat then, too, and followed her lead. "So, my son, Tommy is starting the next job tomorrow. It's local. Not too far from your old house."

"Really? Lots of memories in that driveway..." Tessa trailed off with a smile.

"Yes, there are. All good, I might add." Dylan sounded happily nostalgic. "I really can't wait to see you again."

"I'm looking forward to it as well," she agreed.

He was quiet for a while, and Tessa wondered again what was going through his head. "Well, I guess I should let you go so you can finish unwinding and be ready for our date."

Tessa laughed "Oh, I've been ready."

Dylan protested, chuckling, "It's been a long time, Tessa," mischievously adding, "What if I grew another head you don't know about?"

"Well, if you did, I somehow didn't notice when we had our video chats," she pointed out. "But that would be interesting for sure."

Dylan yawned. "Goodnight, talk to you in the morning, ok?"

"Yep, goodnight, and sweet dreams," she responded sweetly.

"I might have already had a few of those this week," he added, suggestively.

"Me, too, Dylan. Now get some rest."

Tessa hung up the phone with a smile on her face. She put away the clothes in the dryer, then transferred the load from the washer. With a fresh cup of coffee, she sat down to read through their messages from the past week. It was obvious that he was a family man, and his kids were his world. This didn't surprise her because his father was the same way. Her marriage hadn't been perfect, but in the end, she was madly in love with Tom and wouldn't change the past for anything. That didn't stop her from wondering what being married to Dylan would've been like. Would they have made it? A vow meant something to her, but she acknowledged their differences. Dylan could be a bit controlling and old fashioned in terms of expectations and roles in a relationship. That, too, was a trait he inherited from his father. Their lives were structured, no-nonsense, and adhered to specific expectations. Tessa tended to fly by the seat of her pants. She knew what her responsibilities were, and they were always taken care of, but she liked doing things her own way. Her attitude didn't cater to following a man's rules. She doubted that would change. Hanging up the last of her vacation clothes, Tessa climbed into her bed. Within minutes she was fast asleep.

Chapter 19

Tessa woke up feeling like a million bucks. She stretched, long and luxurious, before getting out of bed. It was so good to be home. She settled quickly into her morning routine, from coffee pot to couch, soon curled up watching the local news. Her phone chimed, interrupting the familiar chatter. Expecting a message from Dylan, she opened her chat app, finding a message from her daughter, Sandra, instead.

> *Hey mom! Welcome home. Are we still getting together for dinner?*

Of course, I'm looking forward to it.

> *Me, too! I confirmed with everyone last night after you said you were back. We missed you.*

I am so lucky to have such wonderful kids. I'm excited to see you all.

> *Awesome! I'll bring the chicken.*

Thanks, sweetheart. I really don't want to cook. I'm not reacclimated to this time zone yet. Oh, I have a lot of pictures to show you all, and a few presents...

> *Mom! I told you to not worry about us. But I'm excited to hear about your adventures and how Liz and her family are doing. See you around 6.*

Tessa smiled, looking forward to time with her kids, then poured another cup of coffee. She inhaled the scent before taking a sip. Mmmm, just the way she liked it. Not too strong. Taking another sip, she pulled up her chat app and noticed Dylan was online.

Good morning, handsome.

> *I think you have the wrong number.*

Ha. You think you're cute, don't you?

> *Cute, maybe. Handsome is pushing it.*

I don't know. Handsome fit pretty well from what I saw.

> *Hmmmm… and how long has it been since you had your eyes checked?*

LOL, last month, smarty pants. My eyes are fine, thank you very much.

> *Your eyes are beautiful.*

:) Ok, enough mushy stuff. How did you sleep?

> *Great, knowing you made it home safe. You?*

Like a baby.

> *Oh? You woke up every few hours to be fed and burped?*

NO, goober. I slept like a rock. Is that better?

There truly is no place like home.

> *Ok Dorothy, settle down.*

You are quite the comedian this morning.

> *I'm just in a good mood. I have a hot date tomorrow night. ;)*

Really? Anyone I know?

                    Maybe… little hottie that hung out in my
                    room quite a bit. Sound familiar?

Hmmm… I thought I was the only one who
hung out in your room. Is there something
you have been hiding from me all these years?

                    This little hottie used to have the initials TP.
                    Looked a lot like you. Go look in the
                    mirror; I'll bet you remember.

You are making me blush again.

                    Good, I still got it!

You are too much. Busy day today?

                    Eh, not really. I'm going to go look at a piece
                    of land and visit with the clients about what
                    they have in mind for their house. Then, I'm
                    going to my daughter's place to see the
                    grandbabies.

Nice. My kids are coming over later this
evening for dinner. I got them all gifts in
Florida. We usually try to get together once a
week and catch up. I'm excited to see them.

                    I'm sure they are ready to see you, too. I
                    know I am. I'm sure today is going to drag
                    and tomorrow, time will slow to a crawl.

I'm looking forward to tomorrow, too. I just
hope I don't scare you off.

                    Scare me off?

Come on. It's been 20 years.

                    You're still Tessa. There's no scaring me off
                    from that pretty, blue-eyed sweet girl who stole
                    my heart 40 years ago. I was a fool to let you
                    go.

I was the fool for not fighting to keep you.

We were both fools.

Right.

*We can't undo the past. But we can move
forward and see where this thing goes.*

*I want that, too, Dylan. But I'm still a bit
nervous. Trust me. I have changed.*

*Wait. changed how? Did you sprout a third
arm or leg? I'm not sure I could be seen with
someone who had an extra appendage.*

*Silly. It's just… I've grown. I didn't have a
clue what I was doing or where I was going
back then.*

*I had certainly had no issues with what you
were doing…*

You really need to stop making me blush.

I bet you look cute blushing.

Dylan, stop.

Alright, fun killer. ;)

*I need to shower and get ready for my
appointment, anyway. Enjoy your day*

You, too!

*Starting the day chatting with you makes it
good. Talk later.*

Tessa headed to the corner drug store to print off some of her
favorite vacation pictures to share with the kids. As she pulled into her
parking spot, a familiar song came on the radio. This one was from the
early days of her marriage. She sat in the car, motor running, allowing
memories to come crashing back. Her husband was a good man. He
worked hard and provided for her and her children. Still, the early years
were shaky. Friday nights were lost, then some Saturdays, too. Tom
often stumbled in drunk, but never violent. He never once hit her or
verbally abused her. But one night still haunted her. At 2:00 am she'd

received a call from a woman saying that he had left his wallet at the hotel. Not knowing what to say, Tessa hadn't said much at all. Ten minutes later, Tom came home. She never questioned him about it. She had loaded up the kids the next morning and taken them to visit Mama, then for a drive. But she never told anyone about that call.

Tessa's mind jumped to another night, about a year after they were married. That night she told Tom that she was pregnant with their first child. He was so excited, an unplanned surprise.

Fast-forwarding to her first delivery, Tessa remembered a normal pregnancy, ending six weeks early. After twenty-four hours of failed attempts at stopping labor, their beautiful baby girl emerged. Exhausted but happy, Tessa glanced at the doctor, becoming concerned. With a "what the hell" look on his face, he shocked both parents with the announcement that another baby was coming. Soon, their second baby girl was born. They weren't prepared for two babies, or the stay in the NICU, but they were blissfully happy that both girls were happy and soon gained weight and came home.

Tessa was born to be a mom. And within a few years, she gave birth to her youngest, a little boy with a head full of hair. She sometimes thought the twins were easier than her son. He demanded more attention and always seemed to be hungry. But their lives were perfect: nice house, reliable car, and pretty much anything a girl could want. She was able to stay home with the kids. And her husband spoiled her... but that thought brought Dylan to mind again. She loved her husband, but Dylan was her first love. This felt different. She missed her husband, couldn't count the time she had cried because her children would never know their father, and for what she had lost.

The DJ interrupted the music and Tessa's thoughts. She switched off the ignition and headed into the store to retrieve her photos. She'd printed a million of them. Well... not really, but she had amazing beach shots, some selfies with Liz, and picturesque store fronts. Looking at the moments she'd captured, she could almost feel the sun on her shoulders and the sand under her feet. And she detected the faint taste of Pineapple Upside Down Paradise. She couldn't wait to arrange them in the album she'd bought in Florida. Looking at her watch, she realized she needed to get home before the kids arrived. She grabbed some gift bags for their souvenirs, paid for her purchases, and drove home.

Tessa put the gifts in the new bags, then sat at the table, photos spread across the surface, putting them in the album. The girls were the first to arrive. They came bearing food from her favorite chicken place and were thrilled to see her. Her son wasn't far behind. Soon, they gathered around the table, eating and chatting animatedly. The kids asked questions about her trip, and they all agreed to head there together soon for a family vacation. All three women opened their gifts, fawning over the scented goodies.

The four women cleaned the kitchen while Justin and his brothers-in-law caught the end of the football game they all wanted to see. The women laughed at the startling cheers that came from the living room as their team won.

The family spent the rest of the evening combing through her vacation photos and enjoying their time together until the sun went down and Tessa's brood all headed home. In the roaring quiet their exit left behind, Tessa straightened things up, readied her coffee pot for the next morning, then messaged Dylan.

Hey stranger.

Hey, yourself. Are the kids still there?

No, they left a while ago. It was so good visiting with them. We talked about going back to Florida for a family vacation and looked through all my pictures. And they brought food, so I didn't complain, LOL

Nice. Did you tell them you are talking to your first ever boyfriend again?

It didn't come up. Sorry.

No worries, I was kidding.

It's hard to tell when messaging. Anyway, how was your day?

Good. Got a lot accomplished and didn't cut off any body parts.

115

Ha Ha, that's always a plus.

> *Yes, ma'am. Are you still sure about tomorrow's date?*

Trying to back out?

> *Hell NO! I'm so excited about it I probably won't sleep tonight.*

I probably won't either.

> *Pick you up around 6:30ish?*

Works for me. I'm not going to lie, I'm a little nervous.

> *What are you nervous about? It's not like we're strangers.*

I know but still. We've both changed. It's been a long time since we met. I will never forget the butterflies I had in my stomach every time you looked my way.

> *You did blush a lot that night.*

You know you really set me off when you took that letter out of my pocket and took off running.

> *LOL Good times! I couldn't run that fast now if my life depended on it.*

Same. Still, you were still adorable.

> *Were, huh? Never mind. We can revisit this after our date tomorrow night.*

There's that word again. So, we are considering this a date?

> *I would like to think of it as the first—again. Of many.*

Getting a little ahead of yourself, aren't you?

> *No, ma'am. Just keeping my fingers crossed.*

I have no doubt we will have a lot of fun. As far as I'm concerned, we have some great memories to reminisce about.

We do. And I'm looking forward to seeing those pretty blue eyes again.

Still a charmer, I see.

Well, there's something I have never been accused of.

Eh, maybe it's just me. I have that effect on people.

LOL. Ok, now who's the comedian?

Just saying…

Good night, Tessa. Go to sleep. Not that you need any beauty rest. You're still the adorable girl I fell for 40 years ago.

Adorable, huh? That's something I have never been accused of.

You can't say that anymore.

I guess you are right, there.

I'm what now?

Right, Dylan. I said you are right. But don't get use to that. I don't expect to say it often.

HA HA. Say goodnight, Tessa

Goodnight, handsome. Sweet dreams.

After turning off all the lights, she crawled into bed and fell right to sleep, dreaming about Dylan. They were at their pizza place, celebrating her sixteenth birthday. Dylan had surprised her with roses and dinner. The place was packed for New Year's Eve, and they had to practically yell at each other over the noise. Words were lost, but she did remember flirtations winks, suggestive smiles, and an amazing night in his room, not to mention her first New Year's kiss at midnight.

Chapter 20

Tessa opened her eyes, refreshed and excited for her big date. Lured to the kitchen by the sweet smell of fresh coffee, she poured herself a cup and sat at the table, scrolling through her social media wall. Surveying the posts she'd missed, she realized she hadn't really been on in a while, other than messaging Dylan. It felt crazy that she'd survived a whole week without social media, and she'd barely noticed. Her phone chimed. She had a message from Dylan.

Good morning beautiful. You ready for your hot date tonight?

Hot date huh? Is that what they still call it? LOL, I remember telling Laura about our first hot date all those years ago. She couldn't believe Mama let me go out before I was 16.

I'll be honest. I don't remember our first date all that well. I do remember the look on your face when your mom said I could take you out. I wasn't sure at the time how to read it. Couldn't tell if it was a "Crap, now I have to go out with him" or an "OMG, she said yes!" look.

I was totally in shock when she said yes, but trust me when I say I was excited. That time spent with you are some of my favorite memories.

*Mine, too. I'm hitting the shower. I need to
ready your chariot for the evening. And take
care of a few other things.*

*Alright then. I have a few things to tend to
myself.*

See you soon. Text me your address please.

Will do. Until then, have a good day.

*Oh, I'm sure I will. What do you want to
bet it goes slooooooow? 6:30 can't get here
quick enough.*

LOL, can't wait.

Tessa scrolled for a bit longer, catching up on her social media, then headed out to her hair appointment. Just a wash, trim, and style. She then drove the short distance to the nail salon for a color change. She chose a pretty pastel pink, then sat back to enjoy the pampering. She began to reminisce about their original first date, how nervous she was, how handsome he looked, and how she'd shared it all with Laura. How she wished she could tell her all about this.

Tessa jolted back as the manicurist said, "All done." Tessa looked down at her hands and smiled, pleased with the results. She decided she'd treat herself luxuries more often. Sliding into the driver's seat, Tessa checked the clock on the dash. It was just after noon, and she was craving a chicken sandwich and some sweet tea. Tessa ate her sandwich in the car, then ran a few more errands and checked the clock again. Dylan was right, time was crawling today.

Tessa headed home. As she pulled into the garage and hit the button to close the door, her phone dinged with a message from Dylan.

*Today is creeping by so slow. I knew it
would. I 've gotten a lot done already, though.
I don't want anything on my mind,
distracting me from my hot date tonight.*

*LOL I must admit, it does seem like time
has slowed down. I just got home from
running a few errands.*

The chariot is shining like a new penny.

*You didn't have to do all that. I'm excited
about seeing you, not your vehicle.*

*Eh, it gets cleaned every weekend. I'm a bit
of a clean freak.*

*Really, you, too? Well, I wouldn't go so far
as to say I'm a freak, but I do like things to
be clean and orderly. It just makes the day go
better. My car on the on the other hand can
get a little out of control. Sometimes it looks
like I live in it. Good thing we are not taking
it tonight.*

*To be fair, I work out of my truck, so it's
kind of a necessity to clean it every weekend
or it might get messy, too.*

You still sure about going out tonight?

*Sure am! Baby girl, I 've been looking
forward to this since the first time we
discussed it. I'm like a kid on Christmas
morning.*

Tessa sat, quiet and still. He'd always called her baby girl when they were dating. Even when she showed up at his father's funeral, when he embraced her for a hug, he'd whispered, "It means so much to me that you are here, baby girl." She'd melted when he called her that years ago and she was melting now.

Tessa, You there?

*Yeah, sorry. I got lost in my thoughts for a
second.*

Did I say something wrong?

No, not at all. Just the opposite.

?

120

Nothing bad. Just, you always called me
baby girl when we were dating. It took me
back.

So, that's a good thing, right?

Yep, that's a good thing. Hey, I'm sitting in
my car in the garage. Give me a few minutes
to get in the house.

Take your time. I have another errand to
run, anyway, so I'll hit you up later. 4 more
hours!!! It can't come soon enough. I got your
address and mapped it. I'm 22 minutes
away.

Good to know. 22 huh? Not 20, not 25, 22
miles?

I could make it in 10 or 15 if need be.

Nah, let's keep it safe at 22.

Alright. I will see you soon. I can't wait.

Me either. Later.

Tessa gathered her few bags and went into the house, locking the garage door behind her. She had started making that a habit since the house across the street had been broken into in broad daylight a few years ago. You could never be too careful. Before she knew it, it was 5:45, and she was ready and pacing the floor. She had checked her appearance in the mirror at least a dozen times and tried on four different outfits before settling on deep blue fitted jeans with a nice crease down the middle, a red blouse, and black ankle boots with a small ½ inch heel. Red was a good color on Tessa, her complexion glowed. She had already applied eyeliner with a light coat of mascara. She knew blush wouldn't be needed considering she was a nervous wreck. Glancing at the clock again, she fidgeted and returned her attention to the mirror. Should she change into slacks? Weighing her options, she decided against it. Jeans were comfortable and casual, besides slacks would require a different pair of shoes. She paced the floor, and she waited. And she waited for what seemed like forever.

When the doorbell rang, Tessa almost jumped out of her skin. She turned off the tv and headed to the door. Stalling, she stretched up on her toes and looked through the peep hole. Seeing him there, her breath caught. She stepped back and took a deep breath. Dylan rang the doorbell again as she opened the door. "Lay off the doorbell. Patience is a virtue," she teased.

As she stepped aside and held open the door, he entered with a broad smile on his face. With a quick kiss on the cheek, and he asked, "You ready? I have a pit stop lined up before we head to the pizza place."

She cocked her head inquisitively. "Pit stop? Dare I ask?"

Dylan chuckled. "Don't worry, you'll like it. I promise to be a gentleman."

Tessa looked at him a moment, slightly disappointed at the promise. Ignoring the knowing smile Dylan wore, she grabbed her purse and keys as he held the door open for her to exit. She turned and locked the deadbolt, then put the keys in her compact purse and waited to see what he would do next.

Chapter 21

Dylan walked beside her, guiding her with his hand on the small of her back, then opened the passenger door to his truck. The step automatically extended for her to step up. As she waited for Dylan to walk around to the driver's side, she thought how much this felt like old times. "Buckle up," he said as he climbed in. He looked over at her and she saw a red tinge creep across his face.

"Why do I need to buckle up? Your driving hasn't improved over the years? That's scary!" She grinned at him.

Shooting her the dad-look, he chided, "No silly, I'm asking you to buckle up because you are important to me, and I want you safe."

"Well, since you put it that way, how could I not?" Tessa fastened her seat belt dramatically.

"That's my girl!" he said with a wink while starting the truck and putting it in gear. He draped his right arm over the back of the seat and turned to look out the back window as he reversed. She couldn't help but smile at the intensity on his face. Her safety-conscious, serious Dylan.

"So, what's this pit stop?" Tessa sounded intrigued.

"It's a surprise, just chill," he fired back, grinning.

"Seriously, you are telling me to chill? Mr. Always Serious?"

Dylan chuckled, "Just give me about 20 minutes, and you will see. We are stopping by my house."

"Your house?"

"Yes, that's where the pit stop is," he explained.

Tessa tossed her hands up. "Well alright then, guess I'm along for the ride. Besides, I trust you."

Dylan looked at her with a crooked grin and winked again, "That's my girl."

Taking in her surroundings, Tessa cocked her head and asked, "So, tell me, with this big fancy truck, do the ladies throw themselves at you?"

"Not really," he replied, looking sheepish, "but I do get a lot of women checking out the truck. I guess you could say it's a chick magnet."

"Is that right? Well, they obviously don't know you like I do, or it would be you they were after, not the truck." She looked at him, as the silence stretched a beat.

"If you say so," he finally replied quietly, rolling his eyes.

"I do." Tessa's voice left no room for argument. Then she turned the conversation back to the question at hand. "Did you forget something? At your house?"

"No, Ms. Nosy. I have something I want to show you," he hinted.

"Really? And it must be something you couldn't bring with you... Or are you just planning to get me alone in your house so you can have your way with me?" she countered, suggestively.

"I won't lie. That thought did cross my mind. But I think you know me better than that." He gave her a stern look to emphasize the point.

"I do, and you know I was kidding. Dylan, you are ever the gentleman, and I thank you for that. It shows how much you respect me."

His mischievous grin was back. "It wasn't easy then, and it won't be easy tonight, either."

"Oh, I have faith in you," she said with a single nod.

Just then, they pulled into his drive, and suddenly, Tessa could barely breathe. "This is your house?"

"Yes, ma'am." He said with a quiet pride.

"Dylan, this place is beautiful. I'm not trying to scare you off or anything, but this is the kind of house I have always dreamed of," she gushed.

Dylan grinned and exited his seat, walking around to her side to open her door. Tessa kept her eyes trained on the house, awestruck. As he opened her door, the step extended, slow and silent. Still captivated, Tessa didn't notice. A jolt of energy surged through her as he gently took her hand to help her step down. Dylan fastened his eyes on hers, the charged lightening in their depths showing her that he'd felt it, too. Time stood still for them both. When Tessa finally stepped onto the concrete, she withdrew her hand, shaking it as if she had been shocked. Dylan flashed a crooked grin, as if he could read her mind. "Right this way, my lady. I give you my word I will not drag you into the house kicking and screaming to have my way with you," he promised, voice laced with mischief.

Tessa's nudged him with an elbow, and replied, "Well, I can't promise the same. We'll just have to wait and see how the night goes."

Dylan threw his head back and laughed.

As they approached the front of the house, she admired the porch that wrapped around both sides of the house. She turned, taking it all in. "Oh, Dylan, I love this porch. It's just like the one I've dreamed of since I was a little girl." She ran a finger across the cottage chic white wicker chairs flanking the matching glass-topped table. A lovely bouquet of fresh-cut flowers added splashes of color and sweetened the air. Just beyond the door, a wicker love seat and coffee table completed the set. Planters under the windows offered more fragrant flowers in fresh turned earth. "Oh my God, Dylan, did you build these?" she asked, pointing to the planters.

Dylan watched her, mouth upturned, eyes sparkling. "Yes, ma'am, I sure did. Just this week as a matter of fact. When you told me about your dream porch, I knew this would speak to you."

"Seriously? You built these this week while I was in Florida?" she asked, surprised.

Dylan flushed, "I did. I knew it would make you smile."

Tessa threw her arms around his neck. "Dylan, I'm blown away. Do you hang on my every word?"

Dylan stood with her arms looped around him, his hands on her waist, and looked down at his boots. "I wouldn't say I hang on your every word, but I try to pay attention. You said you always wanted window planters, so I built some."

Touched, her voice softened from surprise to a quieter feeling settling in her heart. "You didn't have to do that. This isn't even my house." She turned slowly, absorbing it all again.

"I know, and I'm not trying to push you into anything," he reassured her. "But I didn't think it was a good idea to sneak over to your house to build them there. This seemed like a safer option for staying off your neighbors' radar and out of jail. I figured this was the next best thing."

"Oh my, you are full of surprises," she said, standing on tiptoe to plant a soft kiss on his cheek, "but then again, you always were a generous man. You're always thing about others first. This is beautiful."

Dylan steadied himself, grasping the wicker chair as if a little dizzy. "I'm glad you like it. If you're ready, we can go to dinner now."

"Hell, no!" she protested. "I want to see what's around the corner. This place is breathtaking!" She turned on heel and followed the porch around, finding that it continued all the way down the side, planters brimming with flowers under each window. She melted a bit more as she passed each one. Approaching the back of the house, she discovered three steps leading to the left then down to an expansive back deck, featuring a fire pit and cozy seating all around. An above ground pool and surrounding deck waited to the left of the open seating area.

Dylan trailed behind her as she ventured farther to the large backyard housing a swing set. Her heart fluttered as she realized that he'd created this area for his grandkids to have a place to play. A shop building beckoned from the back corner, opposite a detached garage on the other side, close to the pool. "How much land do you have here?" she asked, still dazed.

"Just a little over two acres. I remodeled the house before moving in. I added the shop not long after. I loved the house, but remodeling was a must. It was a mess. I knew exactly what I wanted," he said.

"Well, before I can be completely impressed, I need to see your work." Tessa stood, looking all business with her hands on her hips.

"You have seen it," Dylan said. "I built the planters and the shop and reconstructed the deck."

"I meant inside, goober," she said, gesturing toward the door.

Dylan shook his head slowly. "Not yet, we need to get to dinner."

Tessa stood her ground. "Is the pizza palace so fancy now that you needed to make reservations?"

"No, but the house is a mess right now, and I don't want you to see it." He had moved between Tessa and the door.

"Well okay, I guess I can let it slide this time," she teased, shaking her finger at him.

"You are so kind," he replied, offering his arm at her.

Linking her arm in his, she allowed him to lead her back up toward the front porch. As they passed the first window planter, she chuckled, then said, "You are something else."

"Why do you say that?" he asked her.

Beaming at him, she answered, "First the bracelet, then the window planters. You are too sweet for your own good. Always were."

Fifteen minutes of small talk later, they arrived at Pizza Palace. Eager to see just how much had changed over the years, they made their way through the doors to find that it was nice, but nothing looked the same. They waited at the hostess stand until a tiny woman asked how many. Dylan held up two fingers, then grabbed Tessa's hand and followed the hostess to a table tucked away in the corner. The small candle flickering in the center cast a romantic glow in the dim light. As they opened their menus, the server left to get Tessa's sweet tea and a glass of water with lemon for Dylan. Settling on fettuccine alfredo and salad over pizza, they placed their order, then turned their attentions back on each other.

Dylan propped one elbow on the table, resting his head in his hand, and smiled dreamily at Tessa. "You really are as beautiful as I remember. I'm so glad you sent me that message. I've been in a good mood all week. My son asked me why I was so happy yesterday."

"My daughter did, too. I told her that it must be all the sea air from my trip to Florida and I'm ready to go back. I'm not sure how to explain all this yet."

Dylan looked wounded, "You mean you didn't tell her you had a hot date?"

Tessa laughed. "I wanted to see how it went before I mentioned it. Of course, she's been bugging me for years to start dating again. Said she hates seeing me alone and sitting at home doing nothing."

Dylan squared his shoulders, quickly replying, "I'll take care of that—if you let me. I really hope we can see each other more."

"Right now, I don't see any reason why not." Tessa felt the blush creeping into her cheeks and was glad the restaurant was dark.

"Right now?" he said, incredulously. "Are you expecting something to change?"

"Hell no. Just not looking to jinx anything either." Tessa knocked on the table twice.

"It would take a lot to run me off," he promised.

Tessa took a sip of her tea. "Yeah, you say that now. let's just see how it goes, and in the meantime call it 'so far, so good.'"

The salad and bread arrived, cutting their banter short. Dylan picked up a piece of bread, tore half of it off, and offered it to her. "You share," she said, digging into her salad. "That's a plus." She pointed her fork at him and smiled.

As they ate, they discussed forty years of moments, catching each other up on their lives. Tessa noticed that Dylan listened intently, as if there was going to be a test. He asked questions, prompting to share more about various times in her life. She talked about the challenges of dating, with children, after loss. Tessa listened to Dylan as he described the life she'd missed. He was so different, yet he was the same Dylan she'd loved. Time and experience had marked them. They had both endured hardships. Dylan carried the weight of a bad first marriage, and she had led the lonely life of a young widow.

As Tessa told a story about one of the cruises she'd taken with Laura, she noticed that Dylan seemed to be daydreaming. He was looking at her but the faraway look in his eyes told her he'd stopped listening. Tessa snapped her fingers in front of his face. "Hello, you still with me?"

He blinked. "Sorry, I was lost in thought. What did you say?"

Unsure if she should be worried or amused, she replied, "I asked if you were OK."

Dylan ran his hand through his hair and sat up taller in his seat. "Yes, yes I'm fine. I was just… trying to remember if your eyes were always that color?"

Without missing a beat, she answered calmly, "No, they weren't. I had them enhanced." She brought her glass to her mouth to hide her smile.

Dylan's forehead crinkled while he considered this bit of news. "Seriously? You can do that?"

Tessa laughed, trying not to lose the sip of tea she'd just taken. "NO! I was being funny. Or at least trying to."

"Not funny," he complained dramatically.

"I think it is." She bit her bottom lip in an effort to stifle her laugh.

The main course arrived, saving Tessa from Dylan's response. Placing plates of cheesy pasta on the table, the waiter asked if they needed anything else. In unison, both replied,

"No, thank you," then spontaneously shared a laugh. The server left them to their meal. Tessa rolled some fettuccine onto her fork then raised it to her lips to blow on it. Dylan made a strangled noise and studied his plate.

A hush fell over the table, and Tessa worried that Dylan wasn't enjoying their date. He seemed distant and quiet. As they continued to eat in silence, she glanced around the restaurant, noticing that the stage was still there. She remembered that live bands used to perform on Friday and Saturday nights. Usually country artists played, but her dad's band had shared a song or two under this roof, as well. She thought about the weeknight visits, when they knew her parents wouldn't be there, and they dined to the tunes cranking out of the corner jukebox. Country music always brought her back to memories like these.

Dylan cleared his throat, snapping her back to the present. Tessa apologized then told him she'd been thinking about the songs her dad had performed there when she was young. "I remember thinking it was all so embarrassing."

"Why would it be embarrassing? I remember your parents spending weekends with his band. Oh, and didn't he play at that dance we went to? I'm not sure we actually heard them, though. I think we spent the entire time sitting at a picnic table outside, talking, holding hands... kissing." He said the last word softly, looking into her eyes.

Tessa blushed. "How could I have forgotten that?" She strained to remember where they had been that night. "Wait, was that the night my grandpa's fiddle was placed in the Hall of Fame downtown? He was the first person to appear live on tv in this area. He used to tell us stories about playing music with his band for the broadcast, between the local news report and the weather. Seems like ages ago."

"I just remember it had something to do with music and that your dad was there with the band. Of course, I was a little preoccupied, focusing on making music with you." He gave her a wink.

Tessa almost choked on her tea for the second time. "Sorry, you caught me off-guard there," she sputtered. Recovering, she asked him, "Is that what was distracting you?"

Dylan cocked his head. "Distracting me? When?"

"Just now. Right before I went down memory lane," she said with a smile

"Oh, that. I was thinking about those half-and-half pizzas we always ordered when we came here. Half my pepperoni, and half that nasty pineapple and ham you liked so much." The mischief was back, sparkling in his eyes.

Tessa laughed, "I remember that, too. Once you made a gagging noise just as I took my first bite. Of course, my taste buds have matured. I even like pepperoni now."

"Honestly, I wasn't exactly distracted…" he paused, as if deciding whether or not to continue. "When you blew on your pasta to cool it down, it… affected me. I can't tell you how much I have thought about those nights we spent in my car and bedroom since I got that first message from you. So many memories came flooding back." His voice grew husky as he talked.

"I know exactly what you mean. In Florida, I would start walking along the beach, and before I knew it, I would look up and be miles from my hotel."

"Seriously, Tessa? You could have ended up in the trunk of someone's car with a bag over your head! What were you thinking?" His voice held an edge and his eyes flashed.

Placing her hand on his, she looked him in the eyes, saying softly, "I was thinking about you, and all our crazy, memorable, hot make-out sessions." She gave his hand a gentle squeeze, reassuring him, "But I was fine, Dylan. It's safe there, plenty of people around. And besides, nobody would kidnap an old woman wandering around on the beach."

"Stop with that, you are not old!" He waved his hand dismissively.

"Still, the beach was overflowing with witnesses. Next time, you'll just have to come with me. I think you would like it there. Lots of hot women sunbathing." She broke off, taking another bite of fettuccini.

Dylan's voice still held traces of irritation. "I'm only interested in one hot woman, and she would be safer with me there."

"I'm not a child, Dylan," she said levelly.

"I know you are not a child, Tessa, but I would have been crushed if anything happened to you. We just found each other again," he pressed.

"And nothing happened to me. I am back safe. Drop it." Tessa sat her fork down firmly, then looked him in the eye.

Dylan sat quietly a moment, meeting her gaze. Softly, he responded, "Well, I see someone found her voice over the years"

"Yes, I did." She crossed her arms, keeping her glare trained on his face. "Is that what you liked about me? That I was a pushover?"

Dylan leaned forward, and reached his hand out across the table, palm upturned. "Tessa, I didn't mean that. You were so young and innocent, never fighting back when your brothers pushed you around. I'm glad you found your voice."

Tessa listened, and felt her anger draining, "I'm sorry. And you're right. I did let myself get pushed around. I thought it was easier not to argue. Obviously, that's one of those surprises we've been talking about."

"I can see that," he said with a smile. "But let's change the subject. Where do you want to go for our next date?" He cocked his head slightly, raising an eyebrow at her.

Tessa blushed. She allowed her gaze to roam over him, the hair that had turned a distinguished shade of silver, the eyes that still sparkled, and the smile she never had been able to resist.

"Are you blushing?" he asked her.

"Stop teasing me. You know I blush easy. You always did like it though." She considered his question, then nervously offered an idea, "As far as a second date, maybe you could come to the house. I could cook up some steaks?"

Her angst didn't last long. "That sounds like a plan. You came up with that pretty quick. Have you already been planning this?" He wore a comically inquisitive look.

"Not really. Sorry to disappoint. I'm just fast on my feet," she said, laughing.

They returned to the safety of small talk as they finished their meal, exchanging more stories about the kids and discussing what life had been like after Tessa lost Tom. Dylan shared the frustrations he'd felt after his divorce, and the pain of losing his second wife. The light of the candle faded, and Tessa and Dylan reluctantly called for the check.

Chapter 22

The drive back to Tessa's place measured out in memories. Together they laughed, reliving their original first date. Dylan confided that he'd never been as nervous as he was that night. None of the girls he had dated before held a candle to Tessa. He'd certainly never thought about getting any of them a ring. He even admitted to telling a friend after he dropped her off that night that Tessa was "the one." Tessa felt herself blushing and recounted how she went straight to her room after that date and wrote a letter to Laura. She reminded him about Laura's letter that he swiped out of her back pocket and swapped him playfully describing how she'd had to chase him around the house. He pointed out that it was that moment when Tess and Dylan began, when she had agreed to go out with him to get that letter back.

Pulling up to her house, they sat in her driveway talking, and it felt just like old times. Dylan reluctantly told her he needed to get home; he had an appointment with a new potential client in the morning. She assured him that she understood and automatically reached for her door handle. "Oh, no you don't," Dylan said gruffly. Coming around to open her door, he held his hand out to help her down from the truck. Looking up at him, she smiled at how he still towered over her. "You haven't grown much, have ya?" Dylan asked, confirming that he'd been thinking the same.

Tessa giggled. "Not really. Looks like I got my height from Mama. I passed her, but not by much!"

Tessa held his arm as he walked her to the front door, only releasing him to fish her keys out of her purse. "Dylan, I had a great time. Thank you so much for this," she said, beaming up at him.

"Are you kidding? It was my pleasure. Truly. I can't remember a time when I looked forward to a date this much." He slowly brushed her hair out of her face with a hand calloused from a lifetime of hard work, but still soft on her skin.

Her voice deepened from his touch. "You are so sweet. I was a nervous wreck. Excited nervous. But I really enjoyed this evening."

Dylan nodded, still looking down into her eyes. "Me, too. I can't wait to do it again. I almost lost a mouthful of coffee when I got that message from you. You made my day, my week." He leaned in to kiss her on the cheek, but Tessa turned, meeting his mouth with hers. Dylan kissed her lightly, safely. Tessa reached up, burying her fingers in his silver hair, deepening the kiss. Encouraged, Dylan wrapped both arms around her, pulling her against his body. Under the light of a bright moon, they stood transported, kissing like two teens, desperately not wanting the night to end.

The kiss grew longer, deeper, as his hands began to roam. She moaned as his hands moved lower, the sensation heightened by all of her memories of the things he'd done to her before. Tessa tried to talk herself into slowing down, to stop this before things got out of hand. As Dylan squeezed her, pulling into his body, she felt his reaction and knew she couldn't help herself. As she reached down, rubbing the proof of his arousal. His answering moan encouraged her, and she felt herself wanting more. Cupping her hand, she gently squeezed. Dylan ripped his mouth from hers, growling a warning, "Woman!" But he just as quickly moved to the nape of her neck, biting her there softly before moving slowly back to her hungry lips. She remembered what drove him crazy when they were younger, and quickly confirmed that things hadn't changed.

Needing air, Tessa pulled back with a mesmerized smile, eyes still closed. Dylan just watched her, waiting. When she opened her eyes, he looked into her eyes, the color of blue he'd found in their youth when things got passionate. He grinned, caressing the side of her face. "Yep, I still got it."

Tessa conceded, laughing, "Yeah, you've still got it. Now get out of here before I take it."

Dylan laughed with her, then pulled her in for a hug. "I said it then, and I will say it now, you are something else." He turned and walked back to his truck, waiting until she was safely in the house before pulling away.

Tessa closed and locked her door then leaned up against it. She wore a smile on her face that couldn't be slapped away. She thought again about their first "first kiss," how it made her feel, even though it seemed so fleeting at the time. But over the next year and a half there would be many, many more kisses, each and every one of them turning her to putty in his hands. Just like the one they shared tonight. Tessa wasn't as innocent now as she was back then. She had no parental pressures, no promises to keep. She admitted to herself, Dylan had always been the one. Still, she didn't want to rush it. They both had families to consider so they were going to have to take this slow, make sure nobody, including the kids, got hurt. Could they make it work this time? Time would tell, she decided. She shrugged, moving away from the door, heading into her room and switching off the lights along the way. As she sank onto her bed, her phone chimed.

I had a great time catching up this evening.

I did, too. Sorry I snapped at you at dinner.

Nothing to be sorry about. No complaints here, LOL. And I can't wait to see you again. By the way, I like my steak medium rare"

Awesome, that I can do. That's how I like mine as well.

Good deal.

Keep thinking about those kisses. You made me feel alive again. Something I haven't felt in years. Now get to bed. You have an appointment remember?

Yes ma'am. I might have a hard time getting to sleep tonight. Pun intended.

LOL, Sorry, not sorry.

Good night.

Good night, handsome. Sweet dreams.

The next morning, Tessa woke to the sound of her phone ringing. Looking at the clock, she realized she had slept in. It was almost 8 am! She picked up her phone and answered.

"Hello," she yawned.

"Tessa, are you okay? I didn't hear from you this morning and got worried," Dylan said, sounding concerned.

"I'm fine. Guess I overslept. Took me a while to get to sleep," she reassured him, stretching.

"So, I still have that effect on you, huh?" In his voice, she could hear the grin she couldn't see.

She confirmed, "Looks like you do. You are so funny. I will say, hearing your voice first thing in the morning makes me smile. Great start to the day. Now go to your appointment!"

"Still bossy, I see." Dylan didn't sound at all disappointed.

"ME? You've always been the bossy one," Tessa responded, adamantly.

Sounding distracted, Dylan admitted, "I get that way when it comes to someone I care about. But I'm almost to the house where my appointment is so I will catch you later. I just wanted to make sure you were ok and that nobody broke in after that display on your porch last night."

Tessa's face heated. "Shut up! Good luck at your appointment. I'm going to grab some coffee. Catch you later, turd," she said, heavy emphasis at the end.

"Don't call me a turd. Have a good day," he told her sternly, just before the line clicked.

Some things never change. When Dylan was done talking, he was done. He is a turd, she decided, shaking her head and smiling.

Tessa went into the kitchen and grabbed a cup of coffee. Passing through the living room, she turned on the tv for background noise, then went back into the master bedroom to get dressed, outlining her day as she went. With the impending arrival of spring, she wanted to decide on a plan for her garden. Dylan's window planters had inspired her. Maybe she should check the big box nursery. She had always taken pride in her flower beds and had several exotic plants that came up every year. She could fill in with some pansies or violas, something with bright colors. After her second cup of coffee and a muffin, Tessa decided to head out to see what she could find.

Tessa found the drive relaxing. On a whim, she stopped at the local coffee shop, splurging on a white chocolate mocha, then drove the short distance to the gardening store. She sat in her car for a few moments, savoring her mocha while it was hot. Just the smell alone was heaven. She thought, not for the first time, that the coffee shop should sell air fresheners featuring their signature coffee scents. Their coffee sales would undoubtedly soar through the roof.

Heading inside, Tessa bee-lined for the outdoor and garden center. She perused the varieties of flowers and plants currently set out on display, looking for just the right color pop. She thought to herself how nice it would be to bring Dylan and his newly discovered expert eye.

Strolling along, a tropical vine boasting beautiful dark pink flowers with small but vibrant purple centers caught her eye. She cocked her head, deciding where would be the best place to plant it. She'd want to erect a trellis, out front maybe, so the neighbors could enjoy seeing it, too. Reading the instructions for planting, she realized this plant needed full sun. The magnolia tree that dominated her front casted too much shade. She decided the back would be a better option, but it would have to wait. As she placed the plant back on the shelf, she was startled by the familiar voice behind her. "Now what would a pretty lady like you be doing all alone on a beautiful day like today?"

Realizing she wasn't imagining it, her heart quickened in panic. She'd been caught dressed in her comfortable gardening clothes and no makeup. Tessa turned, confirming her dread. Dylan stood, surveying her, and she felt a mess. She exhaled, responding, "I could ask you the same thing."

"Well, you could, but I'm not a pretty lady," Dylan teased with his signature grin.

"But you are quite the handsome dude," she countered, still trying to remember how to flirt in her panicked state.

"Dude? That's the best you could come up with?" Dylan's eyes danced with amusement.

They shared a laugh. Still feeling awkward, Tessa looked down at her outfit and admitted, "I didn't want you to see me looking like this, death frozen over."

"You look nice, Tessa. Sometimes girls put on too much makeup and worry about clothes, trying to hide imperfections. But you don't have any that I'm aware of," he offered sweetly.

"And you, sir, are too kind." Gesturing to the wall of flowers before them, she explained, "I was just looking for some new flowers for my beds. The weather is so nice today, and I wanted to take advantage of it."

"The weather is nice. Of course, seeing you warmed me up several degrees," Dylan said, watching her face.

"Oh, my goodness," Tessa fawned in an exaggeratedly feminine voice, "are you trying to pick me up, sir?"

"Why, yes ma'am. I believe I am," he drawled.

Tessa, becoming serious again, asked, "I thought you had an appointment today?"

Dylan waved his hand dismissively, "Already done. It went pretty good. All I need to do is work up a bid and get it to them Monday. They seem like a nice couple."

"After seeing what you did to your house, I'm sure you will get the job. Do you ever take clients to your place to see it?"

Dylan shook his head. "No, I have pictures of my work and a pretty a good reputation in this area. Most of my clients come through recommendations."

"So, if I need any work done, you're the guy to call?"

"Trust me. I'd work for you anytime," he answered with a wink. Turning his attention back to the rows of plants he asked her, "So what flowers have you decided on?"

"I'm not sure," she answered, looking around. "I came on an impulse, but I probably need to do a better evaluation of what I already have and go from there. I do know I want to pull some of the greenery out and add more color. Just don't know what yet," she trailed off with a shrug.

"I understand that," he agreed, "too many to choose from."

Ready to abandon her project for now, she focused on Dylan's shopping. "Well, what are you here for?"

"Getting ideas and pricing for the kitchen remodel. They want to take out a wall to make the room bigger and give her more cabinet space," he explained.

"Want a woman's point of view?" she offered.

"Might help," he said, pondering the idea. He pulled a few pictures up on his phone to show her what the room looked like now. On the way to that department, she asked questions about their design preferences. Together they selected cabinets, countertop, flooring, and appliances for the kitchen. Dylan took photos and grabbed some samples to bring back to the clients. Moving on to the living room renovations, he explained that it would be the easy part of the job. After moving the wall back a few feet, it would only require flooring and paint. Tessa suggested new light fixtures for both rooms and thought a new back door leading from the living room to the back porch would be a nice touch. Dylan took more photos of Tessa's ideas.

"You sure made my job easy. You have a great eye for this stuff," he complimented her.

"Thanks, I know it sounds silly, but I like looking at this kind of stuff and trying to see it in a house," she admitted shyly.

"Doesn't sound silly at all," he assured her with a smile.

She looked at him gratefully. "Glad someone thinks so. My son thinks I'm nuts because sometimes I stop by here just to look."

"Well, you know kids." He snapped the last few photos, then turned toward the front of the store. As they walked up the aisle toward the doors, Dylan asked if she would join him for lunch. Tessa agreed, and they both climbed into their own vehicles, deciding to meet at a steak house not too far from the big box store. He beat her there and waited at the front door. He opened the door for her and placed his hand on the small of her back, leading her inside. She felt a flood of warmth from the familiar habit he obviously hadn't forgotten. They didn't have to wait long to be seated. The waitress handed them menus and went to fetch their drinks.

As they both looked over the menu, Dylan asked, "So, what are your plans for today?"

"Didn't really have anything planned," Tessa said without looking up from her menu. "I woke up this morning and thought about the beautiful flowers I saw at your place yesterday. Which motivated me to come into town and see what was available to plant in my own flower beds. Nothing really caught my eye, though—at least until you showed up," she said with a crooked grin.

"So, I caught your eye, huh?" he teased her with a wink.

"Just a little. Don't go getting a big head, now." She said, tossing her hair.

The waitress brought their drinks and took their order. After the waitress left, Dylan quizzed Tessa about the salad she'd selected. "You didn't order much. Not hungry?"

"I don't always eat lunch, but I'll throw down on these rolls," she assured him, grabbing one and putting it on her plate.

"Throw down, huh?" he asked, laughing.

"Yep, big time. I will probably be good for the rest of the day after eating these rolls and the salad," she told him, taking a bite.

His mouth dropped open. "Then you don't eat enough. In fact, I think you weigh the same as you did when we were dating."

Tessa laughed, shaking her head. "Oh no, I definitely weigh more than I did back then. Three kids and many years have changed my metabolism. I don't burn off as much as I did then. Part of getting old I guess."

"We may have aged. But you haven't changed much," he countered.

"I have changed more than you think; you just haven't seen it yet," she warned.

"In what way?" He asked the question, then popped a bite of his own roll into his mouth.

Looking him straight in the eyes, she said, "Well, for starters, I'm not the innocent little girl I was then. I'm not as shy or quiet either." Catching sight of his unabashed grin, she felt the way she had the first night they met. She loved it when he smiled, the way his whole face lit up. This one seemed to be provoking her to prove her point.

Dylan maintained the eye contact, scratching his head. "You keep saying that, but all I have seen so far is the same shy little girl who stole my heart over forty years ago," he responded, taking a sip of his drink.

"That's because I'm being good. Maybe I just don't want to scare you off," she replied indignantly. Dylan threw his head back and laughed. "Keep laughing, buddy, you'll see one day," Tessa threatened.

"Oh, you think so? You think you can scare me off?" Dylan taunted gleefully.

"Anything is possible," she fired back. But then Tessa conceded, "however that's not my intent."

"Please tell me what has changed? Hell, I haven't seen anything to make me believe you have changed one bit." He seemed genuinely confused.

"Dylan, darling," she assured him with a sigh, "in time you will understand."

About that time, the waitress brought their lunch. Chatting as they ate, Dylan interrupted to feed her a piece of his steak. Tessa closed her eyes and moaned. His face twisted as if that moan was almost his undoing. As they paid the bill, Dylan suggested that she follow him to his house. He wanted her opinion on new flooring for his place now that he knew what a good eye she had for that sort of thing. He jokingly offered her a job providing design suggestions for future clients.

While driving to Dylan's house, Tessa once again lost herself in her thoughts. She thought about the crazy turn her life had taken. Forty years ago, she could never have dreamed how easy it would be to reconnect with someone with a device you could keep in your pocket. Now she was following him to his place. After the impressions the porch and backyard left, she couldn't wait to see the inside.

Pulling into his drive, she realized she must have followed him on auto pilot. She honestly didn't remember anything about the short drive over, which was so unlike her. She considered herself a diligent driver, prepared for the unexpected. You couldn't predict when someone might swerve in front of you or slam on their breaks. She pressed her palm over her face. Wouldn't that have been interesting to explain to Dylan, had she rear ended him? How do you word it when you're so busy daydreaming about the person in front of you that you don't notice their brake lights come on? That would go over just great. Dylan would laugh his ass off.

As she finished her inner dialogue, Dylan hopped out of his vehicle. Opening her door, she almost took him out with it. "Holy crap, how did you get over here so fast?" She laughed nervously.

Dylan chuckled, too, "I wasn't fast at all. You sat there like you were waiting for an invitation, so I figured I would come and invite you in."

He took her hand, and they walked up the front porch steps. Releasing her, Dylan inserted the key in the front door and twisted. As the door swung open, he stepped aside for her to enter.

Chapter 23

Tessa eagerly stepped through the doorway and was immediately overwhelmed with how beautifully everything was staged. Dylan had chosen vintage farmhouse decor. The furniture sat, comfortable and cozy, in the impeccably clean space. She could easily imagine a family sitting together here, talking about their day, warmed by a bright fire burning in the fireplace. Kids huddled around the large square coffee table in deep cherry, busy with coloring books, homework, or board games as their parents watched, quiet and content, from the matching cushioned chairs carved of reclaimed wood. She shook the visions away, noticing there actually were vases of vibrant flowers on the end tables and coffee table. Just beyond the armchairs, lay an antique couch with matching upholstery and varnish that looked plucked straight out of the civil war era. A broad fireplace dominated one wall, with a thick, wooden mantel holding pictures of Dylan and his children. She noticed that their mother didn't make an appearance in any of the photos. The wall on the other side of the room held a big screen tv. A small cabinet with doors and two drawers crouched just below, displaying a remote control and some additional photos. One framed picture depicted a beautiful woman whom she assumed was his late wife, surrounded by smiling kids in front of a waterfall. But no Dylan.

He sat, quietly watching her take in the surroundings for as long as he could stand it. He cleared his throat, choking out a husky, "That bad huh?"

She whirled to face him. "No! It's definitely not bad, not bad at all. Just not what I was expecting from a man living alone. It's so beautiful... and clean. Not that you ever were a pig or anything. Somehow I wasn't expecting this." She'd already begun surveying the room again.

"What were you expecting?" he asked her.

Tessa thought for a second. "Well, I guess I didn't really know what to expect. Not something out of Home and Gardens, though."

Dylan let out a snort. "Now that's funny."

"What's so funny about it? I'm serious. Your home is beautiful. I adore these tall ceilings," she cooed, staring straight up at the vaulted heights.

"Thanks. It's been a lot of work, but I think it's been worth it," he told her. She could hear the pride in his voice as he glanced around the room with a satisfied smile. He continued, "When we bought the house, it was pretty run down. It's old and had been through a few families. We did get a really good deal on it, and I went to work remodeling it. The ceilings were one of the features that attracted me to this place. I like how open and big it makes the house feel. I did add on some during the remodel. Most of the bedrooms were tiny and two of them didn't have closets. Come with me, I want to show you something."

Taking her hand, he led her through a dining area, then into the kitchen, each time finding more high ceilings, clean spaces, and tasteful décor. To the left, a small hallway pointed them toward a door. He opened it to expose a vast laundry room, almost as big as one of the bedrooms in her house. With wide eyes, Tessa exclaimed, "Wow! This is amazing. This room is huge." Off to the right she discovered a drop-down ironing board encased in a cabinet, with a narrow table nearby for a folding station. The room opened up to the left hosting a washer and dryer along one wall. Cabinets extended down the wall and above the units, offering storage for laundry detergent and such. Adjacent to the dryer, a hanging rack stood at the ready, providing space to hang clothes up, right out of the dryer.

Just beyond, a door beckoned. Noticing her gaze lingering there, Dylan opened the door for her to see what was inside. She discovered a sizable pantry, shelves teeming with what looked like at least one of everything from the local grocery store. Tessa took it all in, her mouth hanging open a bit wider with each discovery. "What the hell are you going to do with all this food?" she asked.

Dylan shrugged. "You never know when you might need something. I hate having to stop what I'm doing to run to the store for a can of this or jar of that. So, I try to stay stocked up."

"I see that," she stammered. "Don't tell me you are a master chef, too?"

Dylan laughed, but his eyes shimmered with confidence. "Well, I wouldn't go that far. But I do like to try out different recipes on company."

Tessa arched an eyebrow. "Company, huh? By company, do you mean women? As in, you use your cooking skills to impress women?"

He pretended to scoff. "No, actually that's not what I mean at all. The kids and their families come over most weekends. That pool isn't for me, ya know?"

Tessa bit her bottom lip, looking him over from head to toe. "Hmmm… really? Because looking at that physique, I'd guess you spend a fair amount of time in it," she finished with a nod.

He shook his head. "You'd be surprised how little time I actually spend in the pool. And, for your information, other than family, I've never had a woman in the house before today." He leaned against the door, looking relaxed and sexy.

Tessa looked dubious. "Are you serious? I figured you'd be hard pressed to keep the women away, especially with a beautiful house like this!"

He flashed his signature sarcastic grin. "Why do you think I don't bring them here?" He winked.

Tessa turned her attention back to the room. After shuffling out of the pantry and closing the door, she noticed another one on the other side of the room. Tessa looked to Dylan, asking with her eyes. He nodded once, and she quickly walked over, opening it to reveal a small washroom with just a toilet and sink. She was impressed when he explained the historical significance of the room. When the house was constructed in the late 1930's, this typical "bathroom" held a corrugated round tub filled with water heated at the fireplace. Traditionally, family members took turns bathing in the water, starting with the father, then the oldest son. Going down the line, the sons would take their turns, then the daughters, until finally the mother would bathe last, often with a baby in her arms. This particular bathing room held a special feature most didn't have, a hole in the floor with an aligned plug in the tub, allowing the water to drain underneath the house. This addition indicated the family who had originally owned the house was wealthy.

Unleashing her imagination again, Tessa tried to picture living in that time, easing into the shared bathwater. She shuddered. Nope, she couldn't do it.

"Someone is deep in thought," Dylan said, interrupting as her nose crinkled.

Tessa turned her gaze to meet his. "Oh, I was just thinking about how filthy that water would be by the time that poor Mama got to take a bath. That's pretty disgusting," she said, crinkling her nose again.

Dylan agreed, "Yes, it would be."

"Glad I wasn't around in those times," Tessa said, sounding relieved.

Dylan laughed. "You'd be surprised how much you could deal with, especially if you didn't know any different."

"Maybe," she considered, briefly, "but still." She shook her head.

"Come on," he coaxed. "I want to show you the master bedroom."

Teasing him had become so natural, the words were out before she gave them any real thought, "I bet you do."

"Oh, hush, silly," he replied, anxious to show off the rest of the house.

"Lead the way," she conceded. They wound back through the kitchen and front room, this time veering off to the right and pausing before another closed door. Dylan cracked it open, peering inside. Turning back to Tessa, he theatrically opened it the rest of the way for her to enter. She gasped, catching sight of the beautifully appointed room. A four-poster bed of glossy, dark cherry wood dominated the room, flanked by matching nightstands. The deep blue comforter provided a masculine feel, adorned with alternating blue and white pillows. To the right of the bed, a tall dresser stood, top bare, with the exception of a hat advertising his remodeling business. On the left wall, a mirrored dresser held four small top drawers, with three pairs of larger drawers extending down to the floor. The simple, wide mirror stretched the entire length of the dresser. Nearby, a chair and matching ottoman hid under some clothes tossed over one arm.

Looking up, she saw yet another door. Pointing, she asked what was behind it.

"The master bath," he replied.

"May I?" she asked him, already taking steps toward it.

"Of course. I can't promise it's clean, but be my guest," he offered.

Tessa slowly opened the door. Her breath hitched. "Oh, my word," she breathed, "what a beautiful claw foot tub!" She rushed over to feel the smooth porcelain under her hand.

Dylan smiled sadly, "You'd be surprised how long it took me to find that. My late wife wanted one so badly. I couldn't tell her no. But she was sick by the time we got to this room. And by the time it was done, she wasn't able to enjoy it. But she fell in love with it, just seeing it."

Tessa rested her hand on Dylan's shoulder. "What's not to love?" she said softly. "It's a shame she never got to enjoy it." She gave him a slight squeeze. She wanted to ask him about her, but knew it was important to let him take the lead on sharing that part of his life.

Walking deeper into the bathroom, Tessa found an open walk-in shower built into a tiled alcove. The space was huge, with two seating areas resting under three shower heads. The checkered black and white tile accentuated the clean look in the otherwise all-white bathroom. Once again, she was struck with how tidy Dylan was.

Gesturing around her, she told him, "This place is amazing. You do good work."

"Thanks," he replied, running a hand through his hair. "I worked for years getting it just the way I wanted it. The kids were little during the bulk of the work, and unfortunately, I missed a lot of time with them." He looked at his feet as the admission rolled out of his mouth.

Tessa lifted his chin. "I'm sure they understand."

He sighed. "They say they do. Once we found out she was sick, I was home more. I just wanted it to be perfect for them. I wanted her to enjoy it. In the end, I just... I wanted her to see it. And she did. We spent awhile here, together, before she passed."

Tessa's heart broke for him. She turned back to the shower so he wouldn't see the tears in her eyes.

"So, have you seen enough?" Dylan asked.

"Are you in a hurry?" she countered.

"Not really," he said, putting an arm around her. "But I was thinking we could sit out back awhile."

Tessa nodded her agreement. "That sounds great. But first, didn't you want my opinion on the kitchen floor?"

He pretended to think. "Did I?" He paused dramatically. "Or was it a ploy to get you into my lair so I could kidnap you and keep you forever?" he rushed with an evil laugh.

"Right..." Tessa drawled. "Ok, number 1, forever is a very long time. Might wanna think about that. And number 2, what made you think I'd have to be kidnapped?" she asked with a wink.

Still pretending to be introspective, he weighed her answer. "You have some good points. I think I like the way you think," he decided, leading her back to the kitchen. "Ok, here's my dilemma. I'm thinking about expanding the island to include a built-in stove and grill. To do that, I'd have to tear the flooring up and install a vent pipe leading under the house. Which isn't a problem, really, but if I'm going to do that, I might as well redo the entire floor because this tile could and probably would split when we cut it out for the new island anyway."

Looking for the least invasive solution first, she asked, "Can't you just cut out what you need for the pipe and build the island on top of the existing tile?"

"We could, maybe, but if the tile splits under the island, it could eventually work its way out," he explained.

Tessa scanned the ceiling, then down to the floor. "How big of a pipe are you talking about?"

Dylan held his hands apart, illustrating the approximate size needed. "Big enough for a vent. Nothing huge, just what's needed."

Tessa, deep in thought, widened her focus to view the kitchen as a whole. "You want to keep the old farmhouse vibe, right? Have you thought about a decorative vent hood that would hang from the ceiling and vent through the roof?"

Dylan considered her suggestion. "That's a good idea, actually, but I'd still need to replace the flooring." Tessa could see the wheels in his head turning. "It would be a bit more work, but it would be functional and appealing to the eye." Dylan worked through it out loud, talking to himself. "I'd need to get with a buddy of mine to see if he could make the hood and find out what material would be best." He paced as the picture formed in his head.

Tessa concentrated on the floors. "What about a tile that looks like weathered wood? It would look good with the floors throughout the rest of the house."

"Are you sure you're not a decorator?" Dylan praised.

"Ha-ha, nope this is me as an amateur!" Tessa responded. She glanced at the clock over the stove. "I hate to go, but I need to get back to the house. And I'm sure you have a busy day planned, too."

"Not really, I'm playing it by ear today. It will take me a bit to get that bid worked up, but after that I've got nothing on the agenda."

"Maybe you could come tour my house," Tessa offered. "I mean, it's not as nice as this one, but it's home to me."

Dylan perked up. "I think I could do that, maybe even bring some burgers or pizza?"

"No, sir. I owe you a steak dinner," she reminded him. "I may not be the best at cooking steak, but…. a deal's a deal!"

"You could leave the steaks to me," he suggested. "Can I bring anything?"

"Okay, you're on steaks. If you do want to bring anything, just make it Mexican." Tessa rubbed her hands together in anticipation.

"Sure thing, I'll run by that Mexican restaurant a few miles down the road and pick up some fajitas. How's that sound?" he asked.

"Wonderful," Tessa gushed, leaning over to give him a quick goodbye kiss on the cheek. Dylan diverted, intercepting her lips with his and turning her chaste peck into a long, hot exchange that made her knees go weak. Tessa wobbled on her feet as he released her. "If you keep kissing me like that, I'll never leave," she warned.

She lingered, wrapped in the comfort of his arms, watching the subtle smile tugging at his lips. As she stared, he lowered his head to kiss her again. Her arms reached around his neck automatically. It felt so very right. The kiss was urgent, but gentle as their tongues danced together and the kiss deepened. A groan pressed against her lips, and his arms tightened around her as he guided her backwards towards the living room. Before she knew it, they were sitting on the couch, kissing like two kids experimenting for the first time. She was taken back forty years, to all the nights they spent necking in his room or in the car. She felt his hand under her shirt but didn't make a move to stop him.

"Damn, Tessa, you still turn me on. I don't think I could ever get enough of you," He growled, leaning his head back on the couch. "I'm sorry. I didn't mean to let it go this far."

"Well, I'm not," she answered, placing a hand on his thigh. "I'm actually pretty turned on myself." She squeezed lightly. "But I think maybe I should go home before I do something I won't regret," she continued, laughing.

Dylan stood, readjusting. Watching him, Tessa suddenly had the urge to reach down and help. She physically shook the idea from her head; she was trying to be a lady. As if he'd read her mind, Dylan grabbed her hand and placed it over his arousal. Tessa's eyes widened in surprise. "See what you do to me… still?" Dylan said, not the least bit shy.

"That's all you. I was just going to give you a hug and a quick peck on the cheek," she protested.

Dylan flashed his quick grin. "I didn't say I was complaining. Having you in my arms takes me back. I like it," he said, wrapping her up again.

She leaned her head into the crook of his shoulder. "Sounded like a complaint to me," she whined, playfully.

Dylan ran his hands down her arms. "You know, it might be time to try something we never have before." He met her questioning gaze. "Making love."

Tessa's face felt hot. She stood, still leaning into him, silent. He continued, "You're not waiting for marriage anymore. You do know I always respected that about you, right? It showed me that you respected yourself."

Tessa was glad he couldn't see her face as it flushed deeper. "I always thought that was why we broke up," she admitted softly.

"Never, Tessa, just the opposite. You were so young, and you were saving yourself for marriage. I didn't want to mess that up for you. I honestly don't remember exactly why we broke up. We should have just run away and got married."

She chuckled. "That would've gone over just great with my parents. Although my mom did want us to get married, eventually."

Dylan spun Tessa to face him. "I knew there was a reason I liked your mom. Just wish someone would have told me," He said with a wink. He leaned down, kissing the top of her head, then released her again. "Maybe you should go before I do something you might not be ready for," he warned in a voice laced with regret.

Tessa lifted her chin defiantly. "What makes you think I'm not ready?"

"We will see, baby girl, but not now. Soon, I hope."

Tessa stretched up on her tiptoes, successfully giving him that kiss on the cheek. "Later, handsome. Don't forget the fajitas, ok? And make sure they send flour tortillas."

Dylan leaned in for a gentle goodbye kiss. Tessa closed her eyes and sighed. She felt him shudder. "Go, before I change my mind!" Dylan instructed, swatting her behind. Sashaying out the door, Tessa couldn't help but throw a mischievous grin over her shoulder.

Arriving home, Tessa walked in the front door, shut it, and lingered there. She could still smell his cologne and feel his soft lips on hers. Pulling herself out of her reverie, she turned her attention to getting things ready for dinner. As she tidied the house, she decided they would eat out back on the covered deck. While the space was large enough to fit approximately twelve guests, she had a nice bistro table for two. She wiped it down, along with the larger patio table on the other side, admiring the view. She enjoyed having the greenhouse, and of course, the covered hot tub right off the deck made a nice addition. The gardening maintenance was minimal because most of the flowers were out front. The riding lawn mower made that easy. And her son came by to put her weed eater to good use every two weeks like clockwork. She was blessed to have such loving children so committed to taking care of their Mama.

While there wasn't much tidying to do, Tessa set to work unloading the dishwasher and refilling it with the few dishes waiting in the sink. She ran a duster over the furniture and swept the floors. There were a few things out of place, but it didn't take long to remedy that. Moving into her room, she quickly made the bed and picked up a few clothes. When she was satisfied with the house, she jumped in the shower, then dressed in a pair of jeans and a t-shirt. She wanted to be comfortable but presentable. After fixing her hair, she pulled out her makeup. Selecting a soft lipstick, she ran it lightly over her lips, remembering the feel of Dylan's lips there. Tessa looked in the mirror, noticing the slight pink tint in her cheeks, which only made her blush more. She felt like a kid again. She didn't dislike it at all.

Tessa lost track of how many times she'd looked at her watch. Checking again, she surveyed the place one more time. She had set the bistro table with plates, silverware, and napkins. Dylan should arrive in about twenty minutes. She made one last trip to the bathroom to reapply her lipstick. Studying her image in the mirror, she started rethinking her eye makeup. She'd used her signature green eyeliner that made her blue eyes pop. She briefly wondered if she was overdoing it, then remembered that she'd worn the same eyeliner the night they went for Italian food. Perhaps it was good luck.

Dylan showed up right on time. She was expecting him, of course, but Tessa still jumped when the doorbell rang as she filled two glasses with ice. Working to calm her nerves, she made her way from the kitchen to the front door, pausing at the hall dresser in the entry way to check her appearance. Taking a deep breath, Tessa swung open the door to find Dylan standing there, clutching dinner, a bottle of wine, and a dozen roses. Struggling to catch her breath, she held the door open for him. "The kitchen is to the right. Keep walking, you can't miss it," she directed as she trailed behind him.

Dylan unloaded the food and the wine onto the counter as Tessa came up behind and, giving him a kiss on the cheek, took the roses from his hand. "Thank you for these!" she squealed, burying her face into the blooms and taking in a deep breath. "You didn't have to do this. I haven't had roses in years! Other than the ones I grow in my garden, of course," she clarified with a sheepish smile.

"Beauties for my beauty," Dylan said cheesily as he returned the kiss to her cheek.

Tessa felt her face heat up. "You are too kind, Dylan," she said, fetching a vase from the bottom of the cabinet to put the roses in. She added water, rearranging them for a moment, and set them on the table.

"I saw a blind man selling them on the corner and thought you would like them, and it would help him out. I knew he was blind because he thought they were a bag of oranges. I got them real cheap," he dead-panned.

Tessa looked at him with wide eyes and an incredulous expression. She opened her mouth to say something, then closed it again. Dylan started laughing. "You are so funny. I'm kidding, silly. I would never take advantage of a blind man."

She stammered, "I didn't think so. That's why I was so shocked. You just caught me off guard! Now that I've had a chance to process, it's obviously a joke. But... you got me," she admitted, holding up her hands in defeat.

Laughing, Dylan grabbed her, wrapping her in his arms. "You are still as gullible and adorable as you were when we were young," he accused.

Tessa protested, "I am not!"

"There's no point in arguing about it. You can't change my mind," Dylan insisted. "So, what can I do to help with dinner?"

Rolling her eyes, Tessa pointed to the door leading outside. "I have a table set up on the back deck," she said.

Dylan let out an audible gasp. "You want the neighbors to talk?" he teased, waggling his eyebrows.

"I'm not worried about the neighbors. They pretty much stay to themselves, anyway. Besides, it's none of their business," she assured him.

Together, they carried the dinner outside to the covered patio. Dylan surveyed the backyard as they set everything up on the bistro table. "Very nice," he said, looking around the porch and yard.

"Thanks," Tessa responded, brushing the hair out of her face. "The upkeep can be challenging during the summer months, but I enjoy it."

Still scanning, he paused. "Is that a hot tub?" he asked, gesturing toward the covered square off to the side.

"Yes, but I'm thinking about selling it. I don't use it much, and I want a fire pit there," she said.

"Well, if you do decide to sell it, let me know. I can build you a nice fire pit," he offered.

Tessa got excited, picturing the space as she'd dreamed it. "That's a great idea! I'll have to get back with you once the hot tub is gone." She turned her attention back to Dylan and their meal. "Would you like a beer in a cold mug? Nothing goes better with fajitas than beer!"

Dylan nodded his agreement. "That sounds perfect, thank you."

Tessa headed back into the kitchen and pulled two frosty mugs from the freezer. She filled them with beer, then took them outside. Settling in at the bistro table, they took a moment to appreciate the great weather. A light breeze tickled her wind chimes, emitting soft, magical music that always relaxed her. As they usually did, Tessa and Dylan fell into easy conversation, catching up on the kids and grandkids. They talked of travel, and while he only had a few experiences, she professed a love for exploring and meeting new people. She explained that her travels had tapered off after Laura had passed away.

Once the food disappeared from their plates, they carried them into the kitchen where he rinsed, while she loaded them into the dishwasher. Tessa wiped down the counters, urging Dylan to look through her movie collection. Dylan called, "Hey, Tess?"

She smiled tenderly at the shortened name she hadn't heard in years. "What's up?" she called back.

"Mind if I put a movie in?" he asked. "I'm not quite ready to go to that big ole house alone."

"Go ahead, the remote should be on the end table. I'm almost finished in here," she said as she tidied the last few surfaces.

Dylan found the remote just where she'd said it should be and turned on the tv. Meanwhile, Tessa stood just inside the doorway, composing herself. His presence still shook her up after all these years. The introductory music reached her, dispelling her nerves. He remembered! As she walked through the doorway, he smiled, patting the spot beside him on the couch. Tessa took it with a cheesy grin.

Voice dripping with faux innocence, he asked, "Why the grin?"

"Seriously? We watched this at the drive-in when we were dating." She fixed him with a pointed glare, "Don't tell me you don't remember."

Dylan laughed. "Oh, I remember. That's why I brought it from home. I think about you every time I see it."

Surprised, Tessa went to her video cabinet and looked inside. Sure enough, her copy was still there. She pulled it out, showing it to Dylan, and they both laughed. As Tessa settled in on the couch next to Dylan, she told him that her girls loved that movie so much, they'd almost worn it out watching it when they were young.

Familiar characters emerged on screen, pulling them into the story. Casually, Dylan placed his hand on her left thigh. Tessa felt a thrill go through her. He clearly still had the magic touch. She inched closer and closer to him until he finally slipped his arm around her and pulled her into him, kissing the top of her head. Tessa lost herself in the old memories and the resurging feelings. She was so mesmerized that she didn't pay much attention to the movie. As the movie ended, Dylan turned to her and asked, "Do you remember what I said to you that night?"

Tessa paused, gazing into his eyes. "Yes, I do."

"Tell me," He coaxed.

Tessa countered, "Don't you remember?"

Dylan leaned in slightly and smiled, "Oh, I remember. I'm just curious if you do."

"I said I do," she insisted.

"Tell me," Dylan repeated, keeping his eyes focused on hers.

Tess took a deep breath, then blurted out the memory. "That was the first time you told me you loved me. You took my face in your hands," she remembered, as Dylan reached up and cupped her face again. "And you told me you loved me. Then you gave me a gentle kiss that turned into much more."

Dylan softly kissed her lips, just the way he did that night. "I have never stopped loving you, Tessa," he whispered.

Tessa froze and stared at him as if he had suddenly sprouted a second head.

His brow furrowed. "Did I say something wrong?" he asked.

Tessa quickly reassured him. "No, not at all. You just caught me off guard...again." Her hands reached up to cover his, then slid down and lingered at his wrists. "I never stopped loving you either."

Dylan took her into his arms and kissed her deeply, the way he did when they were teens. Tessa moaned and leaned into his kiss. As his arms tightened around her, she swung a leg over his lap and straddled him. Without missing a beat, his hands wandered up her shirt and under her bra, quickly finding what they were looking for. She moaned louder, encouraging him not to stop. Carried away by her own response, she failed to notice that he had unbuttoned her jeans. Gazing into her big blue eyes, he slowly lowered the zipper, daring her to try to stop him.

Tessa teased, "You sure about this? Not that you have anything to worry about anymore."

Dylan cocked his head and smiled. "Are you saying that if I continue down this path, you won't stop me this time?"

Tessa's voice didn't waver. "That's exactly what I'm saying."

"So, after forty years, I finally get to make love to you?"

A rush of pink stained her cheeks as a quiver went through her entire body. "That's correct."

Dylan stood and pulled her up from the couch. Reaching out his hand, he said, "Then lead me to your room." And she did.

Chapter 24

Tessa held Dylan's hand as they started down the hallway. Along the way, they passed by pictures of Tessa's family throughout the years, mostly shots of her husband and kids. She paused at the door at the end of the hall, looking into his eyes as if making sure he really wanted to walk through.

"If you're not comfortable about this, I can go home," he offered.

Tessa scowled playfully. "The hell you will. I'm not letting you leave until you make love to me. I just want you to keep in mind," she paused, gathering a shaky breath, "it's been a long time since I have been with a man. So, just be patient and gentle. Pretend it's my first time."

Dylan laughed. "Sweetheart, I can't make any promises. This is something I have dreamed about many times over the years. But I can promise to try."

Tessa opened the door to her room. A queen-sized bed made of natural wood waited in the center of the average-sized room. A mirrored dresser graced one wall, and on the other, a desk hid under piles of papers she frequently planned to organize. An alcove just beyond the bed held a walk-in closet and bathroom. The room was clean and organized, except for the desk. Roses and butterflies flecked the light bedspread, swimming under a million pillows.

Tessa led him to the edge of the bed, let go of his hand, and laid down, patting the spot beside her. Dylan followed and took her into his arms. Lowering his mouth to hers, he whispered, "This will be a dream come true." Then he kissed her with a passion she had never known. As his kisses deepened, their hands roamed. She held one hand to the back of his head, fingers fisted in his hair, keeping their mouths locked as his tongue invited hers to dance. Her other hand slowly moved behind him, drifting down to his ass.

Dylan broke the kiss and raised her shirt, kissing his way to her bra. He unhooked it, sliding it over her head with her shirt. She looked into his eyes, anxious to see his reaction to the scars that marked her torso. "What is that from?" he asked, continuing to trail gentle kisses from her scars to the still undone jeans below. Tessa hissed as his lips dipped below the denim. "It's from the accident. Damn, please don't stop," she sighed.

"Not on your life," Dylan responded. He got up on his knees and grabbed the waist of her jeans and the panties underneath, pulling them both off in one tug. They went flying across the room and hit the floor. He stared as she lay naked in front of him. This had never happened before. She watched him, holding her breath, waiting to see the inevitable disgust at her scarred body. His gaze wandered every inch before he finally broke the silence. "You are more beautiful than I remember."

Tessa's eyes teared up. "You say the sweetest things," she murmured, as she pulled him in for more kisses. His hands roamed, exploring south. She squirmed under him. Suddenly, he stood up, stripping off his clothes, giving her a chance to admire him. He was still fit and in good shape. That didn't surprise her. He was always a hard worker–truthfully, he worked more hours than any one man should.

Dylan suddenly seemed awkward, suddenly laying back down beside her. "Not as buff as I used to be," he mumbled.

"You look pretty darn good to me," she said, "now shut up and kiss me."

Dylan grinned. "Someone is getting sassy."

Tessa pulled him in for a kiss. "I'll show you sassy," she said as she rolled over on top of him, giving in to her burning desire to kiss him again.

Between feathery soft kisses along her neck and across her cheeks he whispered, "I have to slow down if I'm going to survive this."

Tessa raised her head sharply. "What do you mean? I thought you wanted this?"

Dylan toyed with her hair. "Trust me, I do. But I want it to be a magical night for you, for both of us. We have both thought about this for so long. I don't want it to be over too soon, if you know what I mean. I want to take my time and make love to you, the same way I wanted to all those years ago, Tessa. I don't want a quickie, as the kids say."

Tessa felt her cheeks blushing. Dylan smiled up at her knowing that she understood exactly what he meant. He stretched out beside her, trailing his finger down her arm. "Tessa, I don't want this to be a meaningless fuck, you know? I want to build on this. I want to try to get back what we had back then. I respected you then, and I respect you now. Let's take this slow, and if ever I start down a direction you're uncomfortable with, promise to tell me, and I will do the same. Deal?"

"Deal," Tessa replied. "I know I got a little carried away. Number one, because it's you. Obviously. Number two, because... well, honestly, because I really need this." They both laughed, then Dylan rose up on one elbow and brushed her hair out of her eyes. He slowly leaned in for another kiss, clinging to her like a man starving. It was sweet, gentle, and very erotic. She could feel herself melting into this man. She knew she was falling for him all over again. She kept telling herself to slow down, but she had little to no self-control when it came to Dylan. She never did.

As the kissing intensified, their hands resumed their wandering. They were touching each other the way they did when they were young, but this time without any clothing or any concerns about getting caught standing in their way. Tessa traced his biceps, thinking he had grown into a beautiful specimen of a man. She let her hands rove across his chiseled chest and stomach. Dylan rolled on top of her, allowing her hands to move to his back, then down to his ass. Damn, he had a tight ass. Probably thanks to all that walking and climbing on ladders he did during the day. She cupped both cheeks in her hands and squeezed.

Dylan raised his head. "Hey, that's not fair. I can't get my hands on your ass. You know I'm an ass man," reminded her with a cheesy grin.

"I remember," Tessa taunted with a wicked glint in her eye. "But it's my turn."

"If you insist," Dylan relented. "That just leaves me free to explore other fronts. I love these, too, you know," he said, glancing down hungrily.

"You are free to explore any part of me you wish," she offered, raising her head for another kiss. Dylan gave it to her, though it was short and sweet, cut off as he quickly lowered his head to make good on his promise. Tessa almost came undone. Moaning, she gripped the back of his head, a hand full of hair keeping him in place on the left, as his hand lavished attention on the right.

"They taste like honey," he murmured, "so sweet and so rich." She blushed but pushed his head back down. She could feel his laughter on her skin, and it was magic.

He moved lower, his fingers playing her like a finely tuned instrument. She gasped at the feel of the invasion, relaxing as he trailed kisses from her swollen lips down her body. His mouth felt soft and silky, charging her with a little nibble here and there. He made his way to the ultimate destination and lingered, fingers and mouth working magic together. She hadn't been touched by a man like this in years. She could feel the pressure building, release not far behind. "Dylan, you need to stop; I'm not going to last much longer."

"That's okay," he said with a wicked grin, "there's plenty of night left, and I want to taste you." She knew he meant every word of it, too.

Lost in building heat, she cried out, "Oh, Dylan, damn you are good at that. Keep it up, and I won't let you go home." He stopped. Her mind raced, thinking she must have said something wrong. He didn't move, so she raised her head to look at him. He found him gazing down at her with that cocky grin on his face.

"I will go home eventually. But not until you are completely satisfied and spent," he promised before returning his attention to the center of the throbbing that consumed her. She thought she would pass out if he didn't stop, but instead, he pushed her over the edge as she exploded from within. He kissed his way back up her body to her mouth as she calmed. When she finally opened her eyes, he was smiling at her. "That's the look I waited to see on my baby girl's face."

Tessa blushed. "That was incredible. You are a man of many talents," she sighed contentedly.

Dylan grinned back, "You haven't seen anything yet."

They both laughed as he moved back in, trailing kisses below her neck, feasting on her skin until she was breathless. As he moved back on top of her, she felt a nudge, then sucked in a breath as he entered her. She closed her eyes and smiled. "Finally, my sweet Dylan," she whispered.

"Tessa, open your eyes," he demanded. "I want to look into those blue eyes as we finally make love." She couldn't think of any time she'd felt as alive as she right did then, one with Dylan. She had always loved him. She had found paradise, and it was just as beautiful as she always thought it would be.

Her eyes fluttered open, lazy smile lingering, and he drove deeper into her. It was like the fourth of July of the past–all fireworks, but without parents coming home, without boundaries for them to push. Tessa felt complete, whole, and young again. She closed her eyes and made a small sound.

He paused. "Tessa, keep your eyes open," Dylan pleaded. She opened them again, but this time he noticed redness around the edges. "Baby, what's wrong? Do you want me to stop?"

"You do, and I will scream," she replied thickly, squirming to get him to continue.

Concerned, Dylan ignored her teasing. "Why are you crying?"

"Oh, I'm not really crying. I'm just a little overwhelmed. You feel so right here."

Dylan smiled down at her. "You mean I'm not the only one who dreamed of this?"

"No, silly, you are definitely not the only one. I have thought about this so many times," she assured him, "and it's much better than I could have ever imagined. Please don't stop."

Dylan lifted her chin, then bent to plant another soft kiss on her lips. Locking his gaze on hers, he began moving again. Tessa could feel the pressure building inside her again, and her breathing became irregular. Dylan broke their gaze with a shake of his head. "Not yet, my love. I plan on dragging this out for a while." He withdrew slowly, then returned. He was torturing her, and she knew just how to get him back. As he began to withdraw again, she tightened around him. He growled and chuckled, surprised at her little ploy. "Looks like you have a few tricks of your own."

They spent most of the night making love. Tessa counted five orgasms. When she couldn't take anymore, she rolled over and said, "Give me a minute to catch my breath. Then we can reenact Valentine's Day, in the car, at the lake."

Dylan rose up on one elbow and looked down at her. "Tessa, you're tired. You don't have to do that tonight. But I would like a rain check if that's okay?

Tessa sighed, completely relaxed, and getting sleepy. "Okay, you let me know when." She curled up next to him. "You are amazing, you know that? I don't think I have ever flown that high before. I would say it was worth the wait, but I have dreamed of this day since you first kissed me and that's a pretty long wait."

Dylan laughed and smoothed her hair.

Tessa looked him straight in the eye. "You don't believe me?" she whined, faking hurt with a pout.

Dylan laughed again. "You better take care of that bottom lip before you try to walk, you might trip on it."

Her eyes felt heavy. "Mmmhmmm," she mumbled contentedly.

The next thing she knew, birds were singing, and she felt the warmth of sunlight on her face. Coming fully awake, she looked around–no Dylan. Sometime during the night, he had covered her with a blanket, left a note on the back of a piece of paper that had measurements scrawled on it and slipped soundlessly out the door.

Tessa,

I hate to leave you alone after such an incredible night. It far surpassed anything I could ever dream of, and you look so beautiful when you sleep. But I have an appointment at 8:00 and I need to get home and shower. I will call you later.

XOXO,

Dylan

Chapter 25

Tessa read the note for a third time, then slid out of bed and went to her bathroom to shower. As she was getting undressed, she noticed a few hickeys on her breast and smiled, realizing he, too, remembered how he'd made efforts to keep them from view when they were teenagers. Just before she stepped into a steamy shower, she received a notification on her phone. She opened the message from Dylan.

Hey beautiful. Hope you slept well. Sorry I had to leave so early this morning. I had forgotten about my appointment with a couple here in town. I'm just glad I'd set an alarm to remind me an hour before. Barely had time to get to the house and take a quick shower. I'm working up the bid now. See you soon.

She smiled again as she closed the message and climbed into the shower. The steaming water felt good on her sore muscles. Dylan had her turned every which way but loose last night. She relaxed, allowing the hot water to soothe her until it began to flow cooler. Reluctantly, she turned off the faucet, and stepped out, drying off. She pulled on a pair of cutoff jeans and a t-shirt, intending to pull weeds from her garden, then go flower shopping. She determined that this time she was not leaving the store without anything to plant. She stepped out her door just as Dylan pulled up in his truck. He quickly hopped out and made a show of looking her over, head to toe. "And just where are you going looking like a teenager headed for trouble?" he asked.

Tessa glanced down at her outfit and rolled her eyes. "Right... Have you lost your mind?"

"As a matter of fact, I did. Just last night to be exact," he told her, flashing his signature grin. "And it was amazing!"

She tossed him a skeptical glance. "Well, something ain't right because I certainly don't look like a teenager. But if planting flowers is your idea of trouble, then I guess I'm guilty."

"I just dropped by to see if you've had lunch. I would love to be seen out with a pretty gal today," he said, hopefully.

Tessa didn't have to think about it. "I actually haven't had lunch and would love to join you. What did you have in mind?"

"I've got some steaks in my truck. We could go to my house and grill them. I have something I want to show you, anyway," Dylan offered.

Tessa nodded dramatically. "Oh, I saw that last night. And I admit, I'm impressed."

Dylan's face flushed red. "Woman, answer my question. Lunch or not?"

"On the condition that you'll take me flower shopping after," she answered, gesturing to one of her flower beds.

"It's a deal," he promised.

Tessa turned and locked the door behind her as Dylan opened the passenger-side door of his truck. As soon as she got close enough, he leaned in for a kiss. "I love how your eyes sparkle in the sunlight," he murmured as he pulled back.

"Why sir, you say the sweetest things," she returned in her best southern drawl as he helped her into the truck. As he walked around to get in, she automatically fastened her seat belt. He slid in behind the wheel, turned, and patted the middle seat. Once she'd scooted, Dylan backed out of her driveway, placing his right hand on her knee, just like old times.

Over the twenty-minute drive to his house, Dylan told her about the new job he'd acquired that morning. He explained that it would be a few months before he could start, but he hoped she would go with him to select flooring and light fixtures soon. Once they arrived, Dylan left Tessa in the kitchen and went outside to fire up the grill. She noticed an unopened box in the living room picturing a drop-in cooktop and grill with a copper hood. Dylan reappeared. "Oh, I see you noticed my new purchase. I picked them up this morning. The more I thought about your idea, the more I liked it. And it'll be a little easier than running it through the floor, too. The copper really caught my eye. It'll go great with the lighter colored cabinets and new granite."

Tessa was flattered and a little speechless. She was no interior decorator, by any means. And yet, he saw value in her ideas. What a rush. "Well, I'm no expert," she started tentatively, "but I've seen similar ideas in magazines, and I thought it might work well for this space. Can't wait to see it finished."

Dylan cautioned her, "It could be a while. I have several jobs lined up to oversee. And I used to work weekends, but that was before I found something better to do."

"Oh, what's that?" Tessa asked.

"The same thing I did last night," he said with a leering grin and a wink.

She shook her head, holding herself back. The urge to take him in her arms and declare her love for him tugged at her, but it was too soon for that. Besides, after last night, she wasn't sure she could trust her grasp on self-control.

"Want to throw together a salad?" he suggested. "Everything we need is in the refrigerator."

She nodded, and as Dylan went to check the grill, Tessa opened the refrigerator door, placing the ingredients on the counter. One at a time, she opened cabinets until she found a bowl to hold the small salad. She began prepping the produce, and Dylan returned just as she finished. They engaged in friendly conversation while they finished preparing the meal. Before she knew it, they were sitting at the kitchen table, plates dressed with perfectly cooked steaks, seasoned fries, and salad. They remained at the table, chatting, long after the food had disappeared. Suddenly, Tessa heard a voice from the front room. "Dad, you home?"

Dylan called back, "In here son."

Tessa stood up to clear the table, but Dylan urged her to sit back down; they would get to the dishes later. Dylan's son strode quickly into the kitchen, then came to an abrupt stop as he saw Tessa sitting there. "Oh. Dad, am I interrupting something?"

"Not at all, son. I'd like for you to meet an old friend of mine. Tessa, this is my son Tommy; Tommy, this is Tessa. Her parents were friends with your grandparents when we were much younger."

With a few steps, Tommy closed the gap from where he'd halted to Tessa, offering his hand and a curious hello. Tessa responded, shaking his hand, as Dylan pointed to one of the empty chairs. Tommy took the seat. "I just came by to check on you. You were supposed to call me this morning, but I guess I can see why you didn't," he explained, flashing a grin very reminiscent of his father's.

Dylan laughed. "Tessa here is helping me with that job I bid on the other day. I ran into her at the store, and she picked out the flooring, cabinets, and lighting. And the couple loved all of her ideas."

Tommy nodded, "I see." He looked from his dad, to Tessa, then down at the mostly empty plates on the table. "Looks like I interrupted lunch," he said.

Tessa responded quickly, "Actually, we're finished, and I was just getting up to take care of this mess."

Dylan threw her a stern glance. "No, you are not. I told you we'll get it later." He turned to Tommy, asking, "so son, you came to check on me because…?"

Tommy reminded him pointedly, "As I said, you were supposed to call me this morning, and I called you three times. No answer. I left two voice messages."

Dylan pulled his phone from his back pocket and checked. Sure enough, he had several notifications for missed calls and voice mail. "Sorry, son. I met with a couple this morning about designing a new house for them. Then we had lunch," he said gesturing at the plates before them. "And later, Tessa and I are going to get some flowers to plant at her place and I want to look at new counter tops for in here."

Tessa broke in, "You're replacing the counter tops too?"

Dylan shrugged, glancing around the kitchen. "Might as well, everything else will be new."

Tommy followed his dad's gaze, settling on the new appliances pushed against the wall. "Those are a good choice, Dad. They'll look great in here," Tommy praised. Then, holding up his hands, he continued, "Just don't ask me to help. You're such a perfectionist, drives me crazy. I can only imagine how must worse it'll be working on your own house."

Tessa let out a loud laugh. "I guess some things never change."

Dylan looked from one to the other, rolling his eyes at their matching grins. "That's what makes a stellar reputation, son. How do you think I land all these jobs?"

Tommy's eye held a familiar gleam as he countered, "That would be thanks to me. I do all the heavy lifting. You always seem to be running an errand or preparing another bid."

"That's what keeps you working, son," Dylan pointed out.

"I guess it does," Tommy admitted. "Well, I see you are busy. Now that I know you are all right, I'll leave you two alone," he said as he pushed back from the table.

Tessa stood, too, protesting, "You don't have to go on my account. Sit down, visit. I'm just going to clean up a little bit."

Dylan interrupted sternly, waving for her to sit back down. "No. You're not. I told you we will get to that later."

Tessa stood her ground, arms crossed. "Why are you so stubborn?" she demanded.

Tommy laughed, looking from one to the other. "Tessa, you might as well give up on that. Dad's always been this way."

"Oh, I know," she said, fixing Dylan with a pointed look. "Your Daddy's been acting like this a long time, since we were young."

Tommy raised an eyebrow. "Oh? Dad, is there something I need to know?"

Dylan answered his son, keeping his eyes trained on Tessa. "Tessa and I dated forty years ago."

Tommy's face registered surprise. "You dated her before you were married to Mom?"

Minutes stretched as the three sat around the table, Tommy asking questions, slowly unravelling the story of Tessa and Dylan. Tessa told him about how she once had a friendship with his mom, too. Dylan filled him in on the day they met. Together, they explained that they didn't really remember why they broke up. Then Tommy asked how they came to find one another again.

Neither spoke for a moment. They exchanged glances and Tessa flushed. Dylan laughed at her reaction, then with a look, urged her to spill.

Tessa picked up her long-neglected fork and inspected it. Placing it back down, she answered, "I looked your dad up on social media." She paused, then looked up at Dylan as she continued, "I was thinking about all the good times we had and just wanted to catch up."

Tommy looked from one to the other. He thought he saw a spark in his dad's eyes but didn't know Tessa well enough to read her face. They held each other's gaze in the weighted silence. Tommy cleared his throat. "Well, now that I know you're okay, Dad, I'm going to head home. Tessa, it was nice meeting you." The silence stretched. Tommy stood up and pushed in his chair. "You kids behave," he quipped and turned to leave.

Tommy's movement broke the trance they'd fallen into. Tessa told Tommy goodbye, saying how good it was to meet him. Dylan offered to walk him out. By the time he returned to the kitchen, Tessa had cleaned up the mess and she giving the counter tops a final wipe down.

"I told you to leave that," Dylan announced as he entered the room.

Tessa returned the sponge to the sink. "I know, but I had to do something with all this nervous energy. Did I say too much?"

Dylan laughed, then moved behind her to massage her shoulders. "Nope, as a matter of fact, he said you seemed real nice. Said he could tell we had chemistry, too, and he approves. I guess me being single and alone for so long has turned him into a bit of a worrywart. He said with you in the picture he won't have to worry so much."

Tessa sighed with relief. "I got started talking and couldn't shut up. And he's probably going to start telling everyone. You'll be getting hassled with questions about us now."

Dylan continued to work the tension out of her shoulders. "Probably. And Donny works for me, so he'll have plenty of access. He always did like you. Said I married the wrong woman."

Tessa leaned back. "I always did think that Donny was a smart guy," she drawled with a grin in her voice.

Dylan turned Tessa around to face him. "Maybe Donny was onto something," he said huskily, lifting her chin as he leaned down to kiss her until her knees went weak.

When the kiss ended, Tessa groaned. "Man, I missed those melt your legs kisses," she said with a sigh.

"Is that right?" Dylan asked, pulling her back into his arms and kissing her until she thought her legs really had melted. A kiss so steamy, she couldn't stand under the weight of it, just like those she remembered from forty years ago.

Dylan broke the kiss, taking a step back as they looked at each other in the lingering silence. Then, without a word, he took her hand and led her into his bedroom, gently laying her down on top of the comforter. Moving over her, his lips found her neck like they first had decades ago. His lips trailed fire on Tessa's skin. She couldn't believe she was there with him again.

"Last night wasn't enough," he whispered between kisses, "Now I'm going to take my time. Explore every inch of your gorgeous body."

Making good on his promise, Dylan started slow, placing tender kisses on her forehead, cheeks, and lips. Pausing at her neck, he planted kisses with his lips. His hands found the hem of her shirt, lifting it to press against the smoothness of her stomach. Slowly they inched higher, finding her bra and slipping underneath. Tessa thrust her hands in his hair, pulling slightly as she groaned with pleasure. In a swift motion, her shirt and bra hit the floor, and Dylan's mouth had replaced them, driving her mad. But he didn't let up, returning his mouth to hers and moving his hands to the button of her jeans. Her hands fisted into his hair, holding his lips to hers. She didn't think she could ever get enough of this man. As his hand dove beyond her zipper, his fingers found her ready. He moaned into her mouth. The fire built in her eyes, this touch scorching her with pleasant heat. Her hips raised instinctively as she began frantically tugging at her jeans.

Dylan stilled her hands, taking over, tossing the rest of her clothes to the floor, too. He stood, watching lust darken her eyes to a deep blue. He began to remove his own clothes, making her laugh by doing a silly strip tease. Watching, she reached down to touch herself, but he playfully slapped her hand away. "Oh no you don't," he chided, "that's mine now." Lowering his head, he kissed her belly, branding her with desire. Rejoining her on the bed, Tessa leaned up on her elbow, taking hold of him now. Mouth and hands working in tandem, they drove each other crazy until Dylan shuddered with impending release. "Tessa, I want this to last. If you don't stop right now it won't be long," he whispered thickly.

Tessa stopped and smiled up at him. "Then I guess we will need to slow down because I want to do this all day."

Chuckling, Dylan ran a finger down her jawline. "Baby girl, normally I would say that's not going to happen, but with you, anything is possible."

Tessa caressed his arm with a finger, up, around, down. "Dylan, lay down beside me. I want to feel your body next to mine."

He didn't hesitate. He stretched out next to her, molding his body to hers. He took her into his arms, holding her, kissing her. Tessa could feel her heart swelling in her chest. As the temperature began to heat again, Dylan whispered to her, causing her heart to beat wildly in anticipation. Taking his time, Dylan kissed her eyes closed, drifting down the sides of her face, off her jawline to Tessa's sweet spot, just below her ear. She moaned, melting into a puddle of bliss. With her hands twisted in his hair, he moved on, nibbling down her neck and body, taking a pit stop at her breasts as her hands guided him from one to the other. She finally pushed him lower. Slowly, his lips burned a path down every inch of her waist and belly. Stopping, he stuck his tongue in her belly button, making her giggle again. His magic hands moved lower, invading her. With her eyes closed, Tessa arched her back, hissing, "yesssssss" as he strummed her. His tongue followed the path his fingers had forged, and she moaned louder, "Oh, my Dylan. You know what I like."

"Oh yes, I remember," he murmured, lowering his head back down, fingers and tongue working wicked magic. Her head thrashed back and forth on the bed. She begged him to stop the teasing, to join them. He didn't, allowing the exquisite torture to build. Finally, she came apart with a loud moan, riding his hand until she was drained. He kissed his way back up her body, charging her again. When she opened her eyes, she found him gazing at her, his hand possessively claiming the soft of her belly. "I love the way you come apart for me," he said, slowly, deliberately.

"Anytime," she beathed distractedly, already moving toward his obvious arousal. Stroking again, she wanted him in her mouth. Taking charge, she got up on her knees, pushing him down onto the bed. She ravaged his mouth until she was drunk with lust, then lowering her head to take him in, teasing with her tongue first. Her body became so in tune with Dylan's, she could feel him getting close. Pulling back, she sat, allowing her eyes to rove over him. His eyes followed hers as they blazed their trail, shuddering as she smiled, remaining still. Suddenly she became a blur of movement, climbing on top of him, and swiftly aligning their bodies, impaling herself completely. Dylan held her still, for a beat, then two, as they shuddered together, as one. She shifted, and he hissed, "Tessa, you are driving me crazy here."

Smiling, she looked down with a wicked glint in her eyes. "Good," she whispered, biting her lip, as her hips began to rise and fall in a slow rhythm. Pulling his hands from her hips, Tessa placed them above his head, holding them in place as she rocked slowly. Watching his eyes as she rode, she could see them change, growing darker, pupils dilating. Then, he begged for release, and she gave it to him, sitting up and increasing her pace. She actually felt him let go, something she had never experienced before, and still joined, they shuddered together, listening to the sound of rapid breathing and racing pulses punctuate the stillness. Spent, she moved to lie next to him, head on his chest as they both tried to catch their breath.

"Holy smoke, Tessa. Is this what I've been missing all these years?" he asked, jaggedly.

Tessa remained quiet. "Tessa?" Dylan whispered, "are you okay?"

Long seconds passed with no response. "Tessa?" he said, louder, concern in his voice. "Baby girl, are you okay?" He sat up, angling to catch a glimpse of her face.

Tessa's eyes were closed, a lazy smile painted on her face. She felt heavy, relaxed, and utterly incapable of moving. "That," she finally answered, dramatically, "was amazing. I think I need a nap now."

Dylan laughed, curling up behind her and drawing the comforter over them both. They fell asleep in no time, wrapped in the comfort of one another.

Chapter 26

Disoriented in a strange room, Tessa awoke, immediately feeling the presence of someone with her. She felt movement next to her, but remained still, trying to get her bearings. As her consciousness came more fully awake, her heart leapt, remembering she was at Dylan's house, in his bed. He stretched beside her, then rolled over and whispered in her ear, "Well, hello, baby girl." She smiled, glancing back over her shoulder to see his handsome face.

Catching a glance at the clock, she asked sheepishly, "Why did you let me sleep so long?" She rolled onto her back and looked into Dylan's sparkling eyes.

Dylan watched her, propped on one elbow. "I didn't have the heart to wake you up," he explained with a kiss on her shoulder. "You fell asleep on my chest, then I curled up behind you. I wasn't in any hurry for you to move."

"Mmmmm, I remember," she said, stretching before snuggling back into him. "I just wanted to make sure my memory wasn't playing tricks on me. You might want to be careful, Mister. You may have awakened the beast."

"You promise?" he responded, eyes flashing. "I'd happily take a million more days just like this. Of course, I warned you. Remember? Back when we were dating, I told you when we grew old together, we would be kissing. Just. Like. This," he said leaning forward, curling his lips over his teeth and pressing a toothless kiss to her waiting lips.

Tessa let out a high-pitched giggle and playfully swatted at him. "I can't believe you remember that!"

Dylan settled back onto his pillow beside her. "It came to me last night, after you dozed off. Funny how the mind works, isn't it?"

"So," Tessa said, "Looks like I'm not the only one with a good memory."

He smiled up at the ceiling. "Mine isn't as good as yours, but I do have many fond memories of us," he said, reaching down to take her hand.

Snuggling up to him again, Tessa ran her finger slowly up and down his bicep. As he turned toward her, she kissed his chest, sliding her arm around him to grab a handful of him from behind. "I've always loved this ass," she said, giving him a slight squeeze. "A lot of memories snuck up on me these past few weeks, too. But this? Today? This memory is etched into my mind forever. Trust me when I say, I don't mind."

Dylan softly kissed her forehead. He whispered, "I will never forget it either. It's been better than I ever imagined."

Tessa returned her hand to his, saying, "So, you have imagined us making love?"

"More times than I can count, Tessa," he replied softly. "I can't tell you how excited I was, receiving that first message you sent. I was counting down the seconds until you returned from Florida, checking my phone every few minutes to see if you'd sent something new. Pretty sure Tommy thought something was up because I was always checking my phone," he admitted with a laugh.

Tessa blushed. "Well, I almost fainted when you sent me the proof that you were the Dylan I was looking for. It was hard to tell from your profile picture. Plus, I couldn't stop thinking about that fourth of July in my parent's driveway," Tessa trailed off.

Dylan laughed. "That's one memory I will never forget."

"I thought my mom was going to kill me. Good thing she didn't see everything, but I think she saw enough to figure out what was about to happen," Tessa admitted, blushing.

Dylan turned, looking at her profile lying next to him. "Are you telling me that if they hadn't shown up when they did, I might have not had to wait over forty years?" Dylan asked, incredulously.

Tessa flashed a grin. "Let's just say… I was extremely excited. There's no telling what might have happened."

Training his eyes back on the ceiling, he responded, "Damn, I bet we would have had an amazing life. After the last few days, I have zero doubt about that."

Tessa stretched her naked body, got up, and said as she headed to the bathroom, "I don't doubt that either. But then we wouldn't have the kids we have now, and I don't know about you, but I think mine are pretty awesome."

"Mmmm, good point. But, then again, we wouldn't know the difference," he countered. "We'd have kids with your eyes and my smile. They'd be beautiful. Not that they aren't now," he admitted.

Tessa called from the bathroom, changing the subject, "I hear ya. Hey, how about we go get my flowers, unless you have something else to do. I need to get my flowerbeds finished."

"Actually, I do have an appointment and a few errands to run," he said, reluctantly. He sat up, swinging his feet off the side of the bed, offering, "How about I call you later, and we work out a plan for this evening?"

Tessa walked out of the bathroom, shaking her head. "This evening isn't going to work for me. I already have plans," she explained as she picked up her clothes and began to dress.

Dylan's brow went up. "Oh? A date?"

Tessa paused, arms in the sleeves of the shirt she hadn't pulled over her head yet. She looked over, catching his eyes with hers. "No silly, not a date. An old friend of Tom's is going to be in town this week for a family function. He wants to come by the house and catch up."

"A friend of Tom's, huh? Sure he doesn't want to do more than catch up?" he baited.

Tessa rolled her eyes, pulling the shirt over her head and smoothing it at the waist. "I'm positive. His mom is celebrating her 85th birthday. I'm sure his wife will be with him. Besides, I'm a bit smitten with someone else anyway," she said, playfully.

Dylan, still perched on the side of the bed, flashed his signature grin. "Is that right? Do I need to be worried about this someone else?"

"Maybe," she shot back before making her way to where he was sitting. She reached down, cupping his face in her hands. "But if it makes you feel any better, that someone else is you, silly." She leaned down, and Dylan met her halfway, completing a goodbye kiss that melted Tessa to her core. "After a kiss like that, you have nothing to worry about. If I didn't feel the need to shower, I would have jumped you just now," she warned, moving in close again, then pulling back to stand up straight.

Dylan stood and grabbed her wrist, pulling her back toward him. "Well darling, jump away."

Tessa placed her palm on his chest. "Ha-ha. As I said I've got to get a shower and I really need an iced caramel mocha. Besides," she said, moving in closer and poking him in the chest, "you, sir, have an appointment, remember? Call me tomorrow, and we will make plans. But right now, I am headed to the coffee shop. Then I'm going to buy flowers and head home to plant said flowers before I hit the shower." She stood on her tip toes and gave Dylan one last peck on the lips before turning to head out the door.

Driving into town, she couldn't help but smile. It was amazing how much could change in a few short weeks. She couldn't help but wonder where things with Dylan would lead. Feeling herself heading back into daydream-land, she checked the dash clock. Steve would be stopping by around 7:00 or 8:00. She needed to focus on what she had to accomplish. Pulling away from the coffee shop drive-thru with an iced coffee and a sandwich, she drove the short mile and a half to the local nursery. As she pulled into the parking lot, she realized she couldn't remember the short drive. Pay attention! she chided herself. But that was hard to do after the magic of last night and this afternoon, not to mention all the hot memories flowing back from the past. Finding herself among rows of flowers, she shook her head, trying to clear it. She selected three flowers that she thought would add vibrant color and texture to her gardens. Loading them into the car, she noticed how sore she felt from the unusual strenuous activity. On the drive back home, thoughts of him folded around her again like a soft, warm blanket. He made her feel things she had yet to sort out. All she knew is she definitely wanted to do that with him again.

Tessa arrived home and unloaded the flowers onto the grass near her garden beds. She popped inside quickly to change into cut-off shorts and a tank top, then grabbed her tools and started planting. An hour and a half later, the flowers were all planted and watered. She stood back, evaluating the full view. The new plantings filled in the gaps, providing the depth of color and shape she was looking for. Pleased, she went inside and started tidying the house. Picking up after one didn't take long. With floors swept and mopped and shelves dusted, she headed back to her room to shower. She allowed herself time to savor the hot water on sore muscles and the feel of thick, soft soap lathering on her skin. Afterward, she quickly dried her hair, then dressed in a pair of capris and a blue button-down top. Moving to the kitchen, Tessa poured a glass of tea and took it to the patio, admiring her yard. She decided the vegetable garden would be her next project. Only two tomato plants this year, she had them running out of her ears last season. And maybe this was the year to try her hand at cantaloupes.

Finishing the tea, she grabbed the bag of shoes and clothes she'd previously purged from her closet to donate to the rummage sale her daughter's church was hosting next week to raise money to send kids to church camp. She dropped the bag off at her daughter's house, then stopped by the store for a few things on the way home. When she turned onto her street, she noticed an unfamiliar car in her driveway. As she got closer, she saw Steve sitting in the driver's seat. She parked on the street, then walked up behind the car and knocked on his window, startling him. He jumped out of the car and wrapped her up in a big embrace, lifting her off her feet. "I was just sending you a text letting you know I got in early," he exclaimed.

Tessa smiled as he set her back down. "No need to hit send now," she pointed out. "Come on in. I ran a few quick errands and I need to get the milk in the fridge."

Steve followed her inside, then looked around the house while Tessa put away her few groceries. He moved through the main areas, from frame to frame, looking at all the pictures of his old friend and the kids as they were growing up. Tessa emerged into the living room, and Steve glanced up at her, gushing, "You haven't changed a bit over the last few years. The house looks great. I love what you've done with the flower beds."

Tessa leaned against the door frame. "Thanks, I actually just planted those. I'm trying to get a head start on summer."

"Well, you did a good job. And you seem to have settled in here. I know you said you were selling the other house because it was too big for just one," he said, glancing around again.

Tessa thought a minute, then answered, "It was, and there were just too many memories there. I couldn't move on with my life."

Steve nodded, thoughtfully. "I understand that. I think that's how Tom would have wanted it."

Tessa wore a sad smile as Steve moved to sit, then continued, "We actually talked about it. You know, about if anything happened to him. He brought it up not long before he passed. It was kind of creepy, as if he knew something was going to happen." The silence filled in again. "I promised him I would look after you. But then I moved away. Not too good at keeping promises, I guess," he said, brokenly, with a guilty shrug.

Tessa waved her hand, as she moved the rest of the way into the room and took a seat. "Nonsense, Steve. You had your own life to live. You always sent the kids cards for their birthdays and presents for Christmas. They remember their Uncle Steve, fondly. Just wait 'til I tell them I saw you again. They'll be so excited."

He rubbed his palms together, a nervous tic. "That's nice of you to say. But I should have come and visited more. You know how it is… Time goes so fast, and it just gets away from you."

Tessa nodded. "That's so true. It's crazy. Seems like just yesterday the kids were little, playing ball, in gymnastics. Looking back, I don't know how I managed to do all the running we use to do then. I couldn't do it now to save my soul," she said with a chuckle.

They decided to sit outside on the deck. Tessa grabbed a couple of beers on the way out, then they sat and talked for hours. Tessa asked about his family and discovered that he had married a woman with two kids and was living in Arizona now. His mom was doing well and didn't look a day over sixty. His sister had remarried and moved back to Oklahoma, and his brother was teaching in California now. She told him all about her kids, too. As the light faded, Steve said he needed to go, so Tessa walked him out to his car. Another twenty minutes passed as they stood outside his car, talking about Tessa visiting the family in Arizona in the fall. Before retreating behind the wheel, Steve embraced her, holding her there as he told her all the things he knew his old friend would want her to know. He said that Tom would be proud of the kids and of the amazing job she did raising them. He told her she was a strong, beautiful woman, that he admired the life she had made, and that he knew Tom would have, too. Pulling away, he ducked quickly into the driver's seat. Tessa stood in the drive and waved as he drove off, both with tears in their eyes.

Chapter 21

From two houses down, Dylan sat, frozen where he'd stopped his truck in disbelief, watching Tessa wrapped in another man's arms. He hadn't intended to spy on her. She'd been running through his mind all day, and he couldn't wait to see her again. He had just wanted to surprise her with a dozen red roses, to make her feel special, like the first time he gave her flowers. But when he saw that man embrace his Tessa, he felt stung, and like a passerby at a train wreck, he couldn't turn away. His heart shattered as she lingered in arms, and a hum of anger began thrumming behind his temples, growing as he watched them say their goodbyes and she stood, waving, as the man drove away.

Dylan drove away, too, blind with pain and rage. Somewhere along the drive to his house, he threw the flowers out of the window with a primal yell. He was so mad he could spit nails. How could she lead him on after all these years? Why didn't she tell him that she was seeing someone? How could he be so blind? He knew. He knew she could have practically any guy falling at her feet. But damn, she lied to him. An old friend, right. He felt like a fool.

When he got home, he went inside and didn't even bother turning on any lights. He walked straight to the back deck and just stood there, looking off into the distance. He couldn't believe this was happening. She was everything he dreamed she would be and more. Except he didn't take her for a liar. She had fooled him. Furious, he pulled his phone out of his pocket and stabbed at the buttons, deleting her messages. He didn't want anything else to do with her. Crushed, he sank down to the smooth wooden planks and stared off into space. He tried to shut his mind off, to erase her like he had their messages, but to no avail. He could still feel her kisses and smelled her perfume. He was haunted by the feel of her under him, coming apart in his arms as he made love to her. There had to be a way to make those memories disappear or he would go mad.

Chapter 28

Tessa glanced at her phone. She was surprised she hadn't heard from Dylan. After Steve had left, she'd sent him a message asking how his appointment had gone. She thought he would've answered by now. He'd never left her on read before, but the last few days had been glorious, and she wouldn't ruin that by reading too much into this. Surfing through channels, she finally settled on a light sitcom for background noise while she attempted to unwind before bed. She was tired, and as she allowed her mind to wander, it took her back forty years again.

September, 1980

Dylan pulled up in her driveway. She ran outside, hugged and kissed him. He felt stiff under her touch, but she dismissed it. September still clung to the August-fueled heat, so she invited him in where it would be cooler. A strange look passed over Dylan's face. "I'd rather you come with me to my house and talk," he said. Tessa got a sick feeling in her gut. It wasn't the words, she realized, but the empty way he voiced them.

"Why? What's going on?" she insisted.

Dylan's face didn't change. "Just ask your mom if we can run to my house for about an hour."

On shaky legs, Tessa went inside and found her mom in the laundry room hanging up clothes. Taking a deep breath, she asked if she could go with Dylan to his dad's house, explaining that he wanted to talk to her, and she didn't have a good feeling about it. Mama granted permission, promising to be waiting when she returned in case she needed to talk. After a reassuring hug, Tessa headed out the door.

When she got to the car, she found Dylan already inside, behind the wheel. Opening the passenger side door, she noticed the arm rest was down. She climbed in, and for the first time, didn't slide to the middle. Dylan didn't look at her as she got in the truck, or during the quiet ride to his house. When they pulled up into the driveway, all the lights in the house were on. Dylan sat silently, eyes fixed straight ahead, not making a move to open his door. Tessa knew what was coming but waited, staring out her window, hoping she was wrong.

Dylan finally spoke up, breaking the heavy silence. "Remember my friend, Troy, and his girlfriend, Rebecca?"

Tessa turned to face him. "Yes. Are they ok?"

His gaze stayed on the house, through the windshield. "Yeah, they're ok as. I mean, they are not hurt or sick or anything like that. But she's pregnant. Her mom is pressing them to get married. So, that's kind of what I needed to talk to you about. Troy doesn't have a job, and he can't afford a ring. I said I'd ask you if they could use the promise ring I gave you last Christmas for the small ceremony at her mom's."

Tessa paused, not sure what to say. "Well, how long would they need to use it before they get their own and I get it back?"

Dylan didn't answer, didn't blink, just continued staring out the windshield. She waited. Finally, he continued coldly, "Well, that's the thing. You won't get it back. I think we should break up."

Tessa sat in shock, tears building in her eyes. "Why?" she whispered.

She could hear him breathing in the silence but couldn't bring herself to look his way. She wouldn't let him see the tears. Long minutes passed, then he said simply, emotionlessly, "Things have changed. I just don't want to be tied down."

"Are you seeing someone else?" Tessa asked through the tears that had escaped her control.

"No. You know I wouldn't do that. But Tessa, we are both too young to be tied down. I'm the first guy you've dated. What if there is someone else out there you like better than me? You need to go out with other guys. You are old enough now, and you need to know what else is out there." His reasoning sounded as empty as his voice had from the moment he showed up to her house.

"I don't understand," she said softly. "This is all I've ever needed."

"Tessa, I'm almost twenty, you're sixteen, in high school. You're still a little girl. This just isn't working anymore."

Tessa sat, shaking. The finality in his voice silenced her. She kept her eyes cast down to her lap where she twisted the ring around and around her finger. She finally slid it off, setting it on the seat next to her. She needed to get away before the dam broke. She fumbled with the door handle, pushing it open, then slid off the seat and started walking home.

Dylan ran to her and grabbed her arm. "Tessa, get in the truck. I will take you home." She pulled her arm free and kept walking. "Tessa!" Dylan called after her, but she didn't turn around.

About that time, their friend, Darla, pulled into his driveway. "Hey, lovebirds!" she called, "Going for an evening stroll?"

Dylan turned to her, gesturing toward Tessa as she continued walking, and requested urgently, "Can you take her home please?"

Darla pulled her car up next to Tessa and asked if she wanted to get in. Tessa swore she saw the remnants of a grin disappear from Darla's face as she looked up. Ignoring that, she climbed in. She just needed to get home. Dylan stood in the street, looking lost in the rear-view mirror as they drove away.

That was a night Tessa never wanted to think about again. Darla had gotten pregnant and married her Dylan just three short years later, and that's when Tessa closed the door firmly on those memories. She wasn't sure why it reared its ugly head now. Spending time getting close

187

to Dylan again must have reopened the door. But things were going well now. She wouldn't spend her time thinking about their darkest days, and she didn't want to jinx it, either.

She decided to call it an early night and go to bed. After putting on her pajamas, brushing her teeth and making sure the house was locked up, she climbed into bed. Pulling the covers up, she reached over and picked up her phone. Several hours had passed since her last message to Dylan, but he hadn't even seen it yet. She sent another short message.

Guess you've been busy. I'm going to bed.
Sweet dreams, handsome.

A familiar sick feeling crept into her stomach as she set her phone aside. Ignoring it, she switched off the light. After tossing and turning for several hours, sleep finally found her. A few hours later, she woke with a start. Thinking she must have heard something, Tessa got up, heart pounding, and checked all the doors and windows. Finding nothing out of sorts, she went back to bed. Impulsively, she decided to check for a response from Dylan. Once again, she saw that her messages had not been read. Her mind raced with possibilities. What if Dylan had been in an accident? She spiraled through countless scenarios, finally dozing off again as she repeatedly reassured herself that he had gotten busy and just hadn't read his messages. He would read them in the morning.

Tessa awoke the next morning to birds singing outside her window. She knew the forecast called for rain, but apparently it would be later in the day. Her body felt leaden, as if she'd been beaten in her sleep. Something was off, but she didn't know what. With a groan, she forced herself up and out of bed, woodenly getting dressed and dragging herself into the kitchen for coffee. The kitchen clock informed her that it was already after 9:00 am. Stumbling back into her bedroom, she sat, picking up her phone. Checking her messages again, she realized Dylan was no longer on her friends list. Searching for his profile page, she discovered it had been set to private, and she could no longer access it. The sick feeling returned. Something was wrong. She called his number, only to reach a recording informing her that the number had been changed or was no longer in use. Clicking the disconnect button, she decided to drive to his house. It was Sunday. He should be there. Pulling her hair back, she grabbed her keys, jumped in her car and headed his way.

When she arrived, his truck was gone. She waited, trying to decide what to do next. Finally, she left a note on his door saying they needed to talk. She drove the twenty minutes back home wondering what the hell was going on and hoping he'd call soon.

Back home, Tessa tried channeling her frustration into deep cleaning, hoping for distraction. It didn't work. Upset turned to anger as she moved through the events of the last few days, making love to each other, all the feelings and memories returning to surface. And now... just nothing? Damn it, if she did or said something to upset him, she couldn't figure out what it was. And if she had, why hadn't he said anything or talked to her about it? Typical Dylan. Run from everything. Stubborn was an understatement when it came to him. No communication, just close up and act like an ass.

Exhausted from all the cleaning, Tessa collapsed on the couch, watching old romantic comedies that usually made her laugh and cry. Tonight, she only cried. All the scenes that she normally found funny couldn't reach her now. She compulsively checked her phone. Still no word from Dylan. When the 10:00 news came on, she switched her tv off and headed to bed; this time she had no trouble getting to sleep. Between the lack of sleep the night before and the emotional drain of the day, she fell into a deep, tortured sleep in no time.

Tessa found herself alone, walking down a long, seemingly endless hallway. It felt as if she walked forever when she finally came to a door on her right. A plaque inscribed, "Past Life" intrigued her, so she slowly turned the knob, pushing the door open.

Inside, she saw her parents sitting in Dylan's childhood house, talking with his dad. The scene flickered periodically, as if projected, like an old movie. Just past the parents, she saw young Dylan, trading stolen glances with a fifteen-year-old Tessa.

The room flickered to black briefly, then they appeared again, sitting together in her parent's driveway, kissing as if their lives depended on it. Another flicker, and she watched young Dylan slide her promise ring onto an excited young Tessa's hand. The next flash took her back to his truck, as a broken young Tessa set the ring on the seat next to him. Tessa could feel the intensity of the emotions as the scenes flashed through the high and low points of their lives together.

The next flicker of darkness lasted an extra beat, and when the scene resumed, she watched other-Tessa walking down the aisle to marry Tom. Only when she got to the altar, he turned, and it was Dylan standing there, not Tom. Other-Tessa looked up at him in confusion. He eyed her unhappily, then both fled the church in different vehicles, Tessa in tears and Dylan stomping mad. No wedding, no ring. Then darkness.

As the next scene emerged, she saw herself on vacation with Tom and the kids. Their last vacation, the one they took a year before he died. She watched them, sprawled on the beach in Hawaii, watching the twins build a sandcastle while her son played tag football with his new friends nearby. She eavesdropped as other-Tessa and Tom declared how lucky they were to have each other and dreamed aloud about the future and not so distant family plans.

When the next flicker of darkness broke, other-Tessa wandered another beach. As she sipped her Upside-Down Pineapple Paradise, Tessa realized this was her Florida vacation from just a few weeks ago. Other-Tessa seemed content, all alone, happy. Until she clasped her stomach, the familiar sick feeling overwhelming her again.

Tessa startled awake, sitting bolt upright in bed. Just as she had the night before, she assumed she must have heard something. Heart thudding, she dialed 911 on her phone, but didn't hit call. She crept out of bed, slowly and methodically checking all the doors. They were locked. Heading back to her bedroom, she heard a car door shut, then a vehicle started and drove by. Keeping her phone at the ready, she slowly cracked open the front door, finding a note taped to her storm door. She poked her head out the door, surveying the porch and yard, then stepped outside to remove the note. Back inside, Tessa locked the door again before setting down her phone and unfolding the piece of paper. It was a note from Dylan.

> *I saw you. I know he isn't just a friend. I can't do this. Don't call me and don't come to my house.*
>
> *Dylan*

Tessa tore into her bedroom, throwing on the clothes she'd worn the day before. It was after 2:00 am, but she didn't care. She was driving to his house to have this out here and now. How dare he make assumptions like that? She grabbed her purse and keys and ran to the garage, unlocking her car and jabbing the button on the garage door opener. Settle down, she cautioned herself. She didn't need to get into an accident or end up saddled with a speeding ticket. It's not like he was far ahead of her.

Pulling into his driveway, she congratulated herself for staying calm. She noticed that his truck was still running. Stepping out of her car, she marched up to the driver-side door. He was slumped over in his seat, asleep. She wrenched the door open, startling him awake.

"What the hell do you want?" he bellowed.

Tessa was too angry to back down. "Have you been drinking?"

Dylan bobbled, as if blown about by the wind. "Maybe I have. Maybe I haven't. That's none of your damn business."

"Well, I'm making it my business. What the hell is going on with you? And why were you driving when you've obviously been drinking?" she snapped.

"As I said, that's none of your damn business. Get in your little car and go back to your boyfriend," he slurred, pointing absently toward the direction of her car.

Tessa blinked, confused. "Boyfriend? What are you talking about?"

Dylan began to sink into his seat. "Don't act like I'm stupid!" he raved, faltering as he continued in a quieter voice, "I saw you in his arms when I drove by your place. Maybe I am stupid. It was obviously stupid to think you still loved me. Well, I'm not blind anymore."

Tessa, realizing he must be talking about Steve, tried to reason with him. "Dylan, you are not making any sense. Let's go inside and talk this out," she said, reaching for his hand.

He jerked his hand away as if burned. "No, thank you. There is nothing to talk about. Now, if you will excuse me, I am going to go to bed. I have work tomorrow. Drive safe and leave me the hell alone."

Tessa stood her ground. "If you think for one minute, I am leaving here without discussing this, you are wrong. You saw an innocent goodbye between two old friends, that's it. Nothing more and nothing less."

"It sure the hell didn't look that innocent to me," he grumbled.

"Well, maybe that's because you don't trust anybody. I don't know who hurt you. I do know it wasn't me. You're the one who broke my heart. Always so stubborn. Fine, go inside. Get some sleep. When you sober up and come to your senses, you know where I am. And don't worry, I'm not childish enough to block your number from my phone. But keep this in mind, Dylan Wilson, I will not wait on you forever. I told you I still loved you, even after you broke my heart, and I meant every word. But I know my worth, and I will not be treated like a child because some drunken moron is jealous over nothing."

Tessa turned on her heel, storming back to her car. Tears welled up in her eyes as she started having second thoughts. Did she make a mistake? She hadn't felt much like a woman since her Tom died. Being in Dylan's arms had awakened stirrings she thought were long gone. Dylan's agitated voice coming up behind her interrupted her thoughts.

"Who the hell do you think you are, coming to my house at 2:30 in the morning, calling me a drunken moron?" he roared.

Whirling to face him, she countered, "Who do I think I am? I'm the woman who never stopped thinking about you, Dylan. I'm the woman, who for the past few weeks, has been floating on cloud nine because the love of her life was back. And I'm the woman who would love nothing more than to slap the shit out of you right now and wake you the hell up. Because you're about to ruin a good thing. Now before you say anything else, you better chose your words wisely. I am right on the edge of knocking your ass out and leaving you lying in your driveway."

Dylan stopped moving as if he'd lost his fire. "Well, don't you sound tough? Go home. Leave me the hell alone," he muttered.

"Consider me gone," Tessa said, thrusting her arms in the air. "You are such an ass when you're drinking. Now I know why you are still single."

Wobbling, he slung back, "I'm still single because women aren't worth the hassle."

Tessa just shook her head. "Tell me that when you're sober, and I just might believe you." She paused, and Dylan studied the ground in silence. Turning back toward her car, Tessa had the last word, "Goodbye, Dylan. Have a nice life."

Tessa managed to get to the end of his street before the tears came. Once they did, they came with a vengeance. She pulled into an empty parking lot, giving over to the flood until she could pull herself together and drive home. As she lowered the garage door, the clock read 3:45 am. She sat in her car, numbly trying to process what had taken place. She had no idea what she was going to do now. She'd talked a big game but knew Dylan would always have her heart. She needed him like her lungs needed air; she couldn't stop loving him.

Chapter 29

ylan woke the next morning with a pounding headache. He strained to remember the events of the previous night but could only come up with bits and pieces. How he wished he could so easily forget the sight of Tessa in that man's arms. That was crystal clear; it was everything that came after that was enveloped in fog. He knew he had been drinking. Way too much, in fact, and he couldn't remember how he got home from the bar he'd stopped at some time after hurling roses onto the highway. He couldn't believe he drove home drunk. He concentrated on the bar and vaguely remembered a pretty, somewhat aggressive woman at the bar asking him to buy her a drink. Upset about Tessa and not wanting to be alone, he accommodated her, buying her several drinks while barely accommodating her chit chat. She'd asked for his phone number, which had prompted him to leave, belligerently informing her that no woman would ever sink her hooks into him again so she might as well give that up.

He kept hearing echoes of conversation. Goodbye, Dylan. Have a nice life. Where was that coming from? He thought harder. He did see Tessa again after leaving her house. They'd argued. Had she come to his house?

Rubbing his temples, he decided to venture out of bed for coffee. Stumbling into the kitchen, he found Tommy sitting at the table with a smug look on his face. "Hey son, what are you doing here?" he greeted him.

Tommy eyed him carefully. "When you didn't show up at the job, I came to check on you. I found your truck parked haphazardly, door still open, and empty beer cans strewn everywhere. Care to tell me what's going on?"

"Not really, but I guess I will," he grumped. "You remember Tessa? I drove by her house and saw her all wrapped up with another man. She claims he's just a friend of her late husband, but I don't believe her."

Tommy cocked his head, and asked calmly, "And why don't you believe her?"

Dylan exploded. "What is this, Twenty Questions? I saw what I saw. And it upset me, so I had a few drinks. So, sue me."

"Dad, cut the crap. This is serious. You don't drink and drive." Dylan started to speak, but Tommy held up his hand, cutting him off. "Now, before you argue with me about it, let me remind you that your truck door was wide open and you had more than a few empty cans everywhere. You also left your phone and your wallet in plain sight in your open truck. You never go anywhere without your phone, you missed work, and you didn't answer my calls, though I guess now I know why. So, do you want to try again?"

Dylan crossed his arms, defiantly. "Oh, so now you're going to give me crap too?"

Tommy looked lost. "Too? Who else gave you crap?"

"Tessa," Dylan said, sounding more deflated as he said her name. "I went by her place late last night and left a note on her door telling her I saw them and to not contact me anymore. I guess it woke her, I don't know. But she must have followed me home. It's fuzzy, but it's starting to come back to me. We had a fight."

"You must not have been too drunk if you remember all that," Tommy mused.

Dylan sank into a chair next to his son. "No, I was drunk. It really feels like a dream, I can only grasp pieces, but here you are, telling me about the mess I left, so it obviously wasn't a dream." He took a long swallow of coffee.

Tommy watched his father, then said, "So now, I assume you owe her an apology?"

Dylan set his coffee cup down on the table in front of him, hard. "I don't owe her shit," he blustered, "The way she talked to me tells me she has a red-hot temper, and I don't need that."

Tommy laughed. "Oh, so she's stubborn like you are?"

"Why do people keep saying that?" Dylan complained, "I am not stubborn. I just don't listen to bullshit."

"Dad," Tommy started after letting that last proclamation sit in the silence for a moment, "you got drunk and left a note on her door in the middle of the night, probably waking her up with those loud-ass pipes you put on that truck. And now she is stubborn just because she wanted to explain her side of what you think you saw?"

"No thinking to it," Dylan said, flippantly. "I was on my way to her house to give her a dozen roses and caught them mid-embrace."

"Where did you see them?" Tommy drilled him.

"In her driveway, next to his car. Clinging to each other."

"Or maybe she was hugging an old friend goodbye. Did you know he was going to stop by and see her?"

"Well yes," Dylan admitted, "she told me. This guy was her late husband's college roommate, I think. And he was in town and planned to stop by to see her."

"In town, as in, doesn't even live in this area?" Tommy asked, incredulously.

Dylan was packing sarcasm with heat. "That's what 'in town' means right?"

"But you don't believe her?" Tommy asked, gently.

This time, Dylan took a breath before answering. He knew his son wanted to help. "No, son, I don't believe her. I'm not stupid. I know what a great catch she is. Any man would be a fool not to fall for her."

"So that's really what this is all about? You fell for her, saw her hugging an old friend, and got jealous?"

"I am not jealous," he insisted.

"You are fooling yourself, Dad. I saw how you guys looked at each other."

"I'm not going to argue with you about it anymore, son," Dylan said, signaling that the conversation was over.

Tommy held up his hands in defeat. "Fine. Go shower, and then we'll get to work. I have the crew stripping up the old floor in the house you wanted to start on today. and I need you to look at the plans and explain something to me."

Still fiery, Dylan challenged him, "I'm not a baby, Tommy. I don't need you to take me to work."

"Actually, you kinda do. You left your lights on when you left the door open. Battery's dead. You go shower, and I'll hook up the trickle charger. We can leave it to charge for a bit, then I'll swing you back by at lunch to get your truck. Good thing the jobsite is only a few miles from here. Hurry up. You're burning daylight."

Dylan slunk to the shower. His head was still pounding, and he kept hearing Tessa's words over and over in his head. Goodbye, Dylan. Have a nice life. He was pissed, but the words still scared him. Struggling to remember what had prompted to say them, he focused on what he knew. He had driven to her house, left a note on her door. They argued in his driveway in the early morning hours. And she was beyond angry. He'd never seen her like that.

He realized, as he rinsed the soap off his body that he still had no idea what time it was. Hurrying, he finished his shower and dried off. He walked glancing at the clock on his nightstand. 9:43 am. Holy smoke, no wonder Tommy's so concerned. He was usually up way before now. He quickly dressed in work jeans and a t-shirt, then re-entered the kitchen to make a cup of coffee to go and put on his socks and boots at the now vacant table. Tommy returned, informing him that his truck was charging. He'd called to check in on the job, and everything was right on schedule. As Dylan pulled his pant legs over the tops of his boots, Tommy offered to stop and grab something for breakfast on the way. Dylan turned a faint green and admitted that he probably shouldn't attempt eating just yet. He swore he was never drinking that much again.

As the day wore on, Dylan continued to have flashbacks, revealing snip-its from his blackout. Did he really cuss at her? Did she really give him as good as she got? He'd never heard her talk that way before. She accused him of driving drunk. Then remembered, shame flooding, her husband had been killed by a drunk driver. She said he broke her heart, that she still loved him. Was Tommy right? Was he jealous for no reason? Maybe he had been unreasonable, let a knee-jerk reaction spin out of control. Dylan knew he was a proud man, and he had every reason to be. He was a straight shooter but tried to be respectful of other people's feelings and time. He always took people at their word. So why didn't he take Tessa at hers? The job site didn't help. They were working on the house that Tessa had chosen floors, appliances, and light fixtures for. Everywhere he looked he thought of her, the fun times they had in the store together, the awe he felt as he discovered hidden new talents, like her knack for decorating. Dylan doubled down, concentrating on sketching out the plans for the renovation. Tommy's crew picked up on the shift in his demeanor and gave him a wide berth.

A little after one that afternoon, Tommy delivered his dad back to his house to pick up the truck. More flashbacks rocked Dylan. Guilt was beginning to really set in about a few of things he'd said to her. He didn't know what to do from here. Call her and try to talk things out? Or go on with his life without her in it?

Chapter 30

Tessa was exhausted when she arrived home after the fight but didn't go back to bed. Instead, she curled up on the couch, replaying everything in her head. She was surprised at some of the things she'd said to Dylan but didn't regret them at all. He was a stubborn fool if he was willing to throw everything away without a real conversation. She missed exchanging messages with him during the day, the way he made her laugh. But she also had her pride. He had clearly awoken feelings in her she thought she would never have again, but she'd be damned if she was going to crawl back to him now. Especially when she wasn't wrong, and he obviously wouldn't listen to her to anyway. He'd always been stubborn. She felt that some part of her always knew that one day they would be together again. She just thought it would be forever, not a few weeks.

Spent, she called off her plans for a girls' lunch, rescheduling for the following week. The headache used as her excuse was certainly no lie. She just opted not to explain where the headache had come from. She wasn't ready to let them in on that part of her life just yet. She still needed to sort it out herself.

At 2:00 in the afternoon, she finally gave in to her body's need for a quick nap. She needed to be refreshed before running a few errands later that evening. Sinking into sleep, she found new dreams waiting for her.

Other-Tessa was in Florida again, but this time, Dylan was with her. They stood on the open-air roof of the hotel she'd stayed in before, surrounded by both of their families. Tessa wore a pale blue tea-length dress with baby's breath in her hair and a bouquet in her hand. Dylan stood beside her, handsome in new a pair of jeans and pearl snap shirt, the exact same shade of blue as Tessa's dress. They stood before a preacher, kids and grandkids pressed in close, as they exchanged vows. It had finally happened. She was Mrs. Dylan Wilson.

Kids and grandkids posed for pictures with the happy couple. Laughter rippled across the roof. The excitement was electrifying, as they all mingled, becoming one family.

The couple dodged bird seed while running for the elevator that would take them to the main dining room where their reception dinner awaited them. Other-Tessa glowed with happiness and Dylan beamed beside her.

After dinner had been served, and the cake had been cut and devoured, the newlyweds went to their honeymoon suite while the rest of the family headed for the beach, chatting about the charter fishing tour they'd be enjoying all together while Dylan and Tessa boarded a plane to Miami for the honeymoon cruise the kids had surprised them with. They were happier than they had ever been.

Chapter 31

Despite the rough day she'd left behind, Tessa woke with a smile on her face thanks to her dream. The reality of their situation set in, causing the joy of the dream to fade sharply. She swept her sadness aside, determined to press on, then readied herself for a day of errands. The most important item on the list: a bottle of wine.

She arrived back home after a productive day around 7:00 that evening. Parking her car in the garage, she grabbed her grocery bag, her dinner, and a new pair of flip flops out of the backseat, then went inside to wolf down a good old fashion burger and fries at her breakfast bar. It was not exactly the 5-star dinner she had dreamed about earlier, but it was just what she needed now.

Tossing the wrappers in the trash, she pulled a book from her shelf that she had been intending to read for a while, then refilled her glass of wine and stepped outside in the evening air. She could tell it was going to be a hot summer because it was already humid. Settling in at her bistro table, she set her glass down, opened her book and quickly lost herself in her reading. Three chapters in, she heard her phone ring. Setting her book aside, she headed inside and picked up the still-ringing phone. She didn't recognize the number. Shrugging, she silenced it and went back to her book.

A bottle of wine later, she looked up and noticed it was starting to get dark out, so she decided to get ready for bed. No doubt she would sleep well tonight. She couldn't remember the last time she felt this tired. She locked up, tossed the empty bottle into the trash, then headed to her room. While plugging in her phone, Tessa noticed she had two other missed calls from the same number she hadn't recognized earlier–and a voicemail. Curious, she wondered who it could be. Probably another auto warranty scam. Prepare to be blocked! But three calls in a row seemed extra determined, even for those pests. She decided to listen to the message. What she heard after she hit play stopped her in her tracks.

Tessa, this is Dylan. Would you please answer the phone? This is my new number. I guess I changed my number yesterday when I was so mad. You were right. I was drunk. And I had no right to talk to you the way I did. Please call me. Please. I know I have some major kissing up to do…

I don't know where this will lead or if you will even listen to it. Tessa, I do love you. I've missed hearing your voice today. I miss your messages. I'm sorry, Tessa. Please forgive me.

Listen, if you decide to never talk to me again, I'll understand. But, Tessa, please don't make your decision without giving me a chance to say how sorry I am in person. Today has been awful. I've lived my life without you for too long already.

I can't believe I acted like that. I was so drunk, Tessa. I left my phone in the truck, the door wide open. Left the lights on and killed the battery. Tommy came over this morning and set me straight on a few things. And he was right, Tessa. And you were right.

Please, don't shut me out, baby girl. If I don't hear back from you, I'll get the message. I'll leave you alone. But it would be easier if you would just let me know what you want. It's killing me, not knowing. I love you. I never stopped loving you. I didn't know it, but I need you in my life. You make me a better man, Tessa.

I'll wait. I'll wait to hear from you. Just think about it, ok? If I don't hear from you this week, I will get the message and leave you alone. I love you, Tessa. I'm sorry.

Tessa dressed for bed, then listened to the message twice more, thinking about what he said. They had history, made each other laugh, and when they were good together, they were so good together, but was it enough? Maybe. Maybe not. She needed time to think. Tessa switched off her light and burrowed under the covers. Her thoughts scattered in a million directions. Were they even compatible long term?

He was so stubborn when they dated all those years ago and was only more hard-headed now. She wanted to do things her own way, and he was used to being the boss. But she didn't need a boss, damn it. What she needed was another glass of wine. The bottle wouldn't hold answers, but it would help her sleep. She could think about this tomorrow. Tessa felt like Scarlett O'Hara, she heard the words in her head, dripping with southern drama, tomorrow is another day.

Tessa opened a second bottle, a small, individual size, and poured it into her glass. Sitting back down on the bed, she shook her head. This jealousy was out of control. She had other guy friends, too, and as sure as she's breathing, Dylan would have a problem with that. It had been a few years since she'd last seen Laura's husband, Mark, but he remained an important part of her life. When Tessa lost her Tom, Laura and Mark were there for her, offering support. Laura would take her shopping while Mark helped with repairs around the house. Then Laura died, and they became even closer in their shared grief. He still called her from time to time when he was missing Laura. Now that he was retired, he spent most of his time sailing to exotic locations. Every once in a while, a postcard would arrive from him, showing some exciting corner of the world. They were actually planning a visit soon, when he stopped in Texas next month to stay with his son and new daughter-in-law. After what happened with Steve, she could only imagine how Dylan would react to that.

Tessa felt just tipsy enough to help her sleep. Switching off her light, she snuggled into her covers. As expected, she fell asleep instantly.

Chapter 32

Dylan sat at his kitchen table, phone in hand, willing Tessa to call. It had only been an hour since he'd left her the voicemail. He knew he screwed up. He could only hope his apology and rambling declaration of love would be enough. He opened the social app and checked her page for new posts. Nothing. One of her daughters had tagged her in a random share and a few friends had liked a picture she posted a few weeks ago. Other than that, her page hadn't changed. Absentmindedly, he scrolled through his feed, seeing nothing. He didn't know what he would do if she didn't call. He tried to tell himself that he would just move on, but he knew better. He had to get her back.

He waited another hour then went to bed where he tossed and turned. Sleep wasn't in the cards for him tonight. He couldn't stop thinking about the few short weeks they had spent together. It hadn't been enough time for him. Hell, forever wouldn't be enough time for him. He knew as soon as he saw her after her beach vacation that he was totally smitten again. They slipped so easily back into their relationship, as if it never really ended all those years ago. He thought about her all day, every day since receiving the message that set everything back in motion. He'd already become a happier person. His crew, the kids, everyone had noticed a change in him. Sleep finally caught up with him around 2:00 am. Tortured sleep, but maybe better than none.

Chapter 33

Tessa awoke, feeling like someone had taken a hammer to her head while she slept. Hampered by the pain, it took her a few minutes to remember drinking the whole bottle of wine. And then she remembered why, and suddenly it felt like someone took a hammer to her heart. His voicemail had snapped her out of denial. How could Dylan talk to her like that? And did he seriously think she was playing the field, playing him? She still couldn't understand why Dylan had behaved like such a jealous asshole. She remembered how possessive he could be whenever he even thought another guy had looked her way. He should have grown out of that by now. She definitely hadn't missed that dynamic of their relationship. But she had to admit, jealousy drew a thin line. It was funny how too much and too little both felt wrong. Tom had trusted her always–with anyone, at any time. It made her happy to be trusted, but sometimes, it hurt, too. She sometimes found herself wondering if he just didn't think anyone else would want her, or if it just didn't matter much to him. Cognitively, she knew that wasn't true, but it didn't stop the sting sometimes when irrational fears became a little too loud.

She still wasn't sure what she should do. And, she decided, it might do Dylan some good to sulk a little longer. Determined again to seize the day, she cleaned the house, ran to the store for a few groceries, and visited a friend who was recovering from chemo treatments in her battle against uterine cancer. Her friend was having a good day, so they spent hours together chatting, and Tessa insisted on helping with a few of her household chores. As her friend tired, Tessa reluctantly got into her car to go home. She took her time driving home, opting for the side roads that wound their way through a lifetime of memories.

She passed the pool where she and her brothers used to swim as kids. It was the same pool where Shelley had worked, and she and Dylan had met at when she was grounded. Stopped at the light, she gazed at the property. It had clearly been closed and abandoned for a while. Wild shrubs invaded, and weeds thrived in the large cracks in the pavement. It was heartbreaking to see. As the light turned green, she turned right, into the dilapidated parking lot. She pulled into a space, then sat, allowing memories of her childhood to swim through her mind. Once when she was in the third grade, a boy she liked had pushed her into the deep end of the pool. Caught off guard, she struggled and thought she might drown until Rex, the cute lifeguard all the girls fawned over, had jumped in and saved her. Tessa smiled, remembering Laura insisting that she should have let Rex give her mouth to mouth. This place made her think of Shelly, too. She thought about sitting at the picnic tables with her on her 3:00 pm breaks, talking endlessly about Dylan and Cal. Tessa wondered what had happened to them. She knew they'd married, had a daughter, then divorced. She never knew why.

Feeling nostalgic now, Tessa pulled out of the parking lot and pointed her car down the street to the house she had lived in before she met Dylan. She sat by the curb, gazing out through the driver's side window, seeing the old house she had once shared with her family. She pictured the three small bedrooms, arranged in a split-master layout, wood floors running between them, connecting them with the small sitting room and kitchen. She remembered venturing into the large garage with the memorable dirt floor. She blinked, now really seeing the new build where her old home once stood.

Putting the car back in drive, she moved on to her school, finding it, too, had been demolished and rebuilt. At least they kept the name. She didn't linger there but drove to the park nearby where she and Dylan used to walk, hand-in-hand. She closed her eyes, visualizing the fireworks they'd watched there together, before getting caught making out in her driveway.

Exhausted, Tessa her car toward home. She pulled into her drive and sat in her car considering what to do about Dylan. Could she forgive him? She knew she could. But it shouldn't be that easy. They would definitely have to discuss his jealous temper, set boundaries. She shook her head and sighed aloud. You can't teach an old dog new tricks, she thought sadly. His words still stung. He had never talked to her like that. But, she had also never seen him drunk. She leaned forward, knocking her forehead lightly against the steering wheel. What to do?

Getting out of the car, she moved to the kitchen table, trying to order her thoughts. She listened to his voicemail again. And again. Confusion bubbled up with tears in her eyes. She longed to call him, to tell him he was forgiven and settle back into his arms again. She knew she needed to wait. He had to understand that he couldn't just apologize and magically make everything ok. She decided she would hold off another day or two, then send him a message. But first, she needed to decide what she was going to say.

Chapter 34

ylan threw himself into his kitchen remodel. He needed to keep busy, to try to keep his mind off Tessa, or he would go crazy. Tommy helped him cut a hole through the ceiling over the island and he had already run the pipe up through the attic and roof. While Dylan ripped up the old flooring for the new tile install booked for the next day, Tommy perched on the roof, flashing the pipe and installing the cap. Dylan couldn't wait for it to be finished so he could show Tessa. If she ever decided to talk to him again. Once the flooring was removed and swept away, he met Tommy outside with a glass of tea. They sat on the front porch discussing the remodel and the other jobs lined up, kicking off the next week. After they finished their tea, Tommy headed home.

Dylan walked back inside, surveying the mess in his kitchen. He grabbed the broom and set to work. Before long, the kitchen had been restored somewhat, still obviously under construction, but orderly, with all his tools put away. His growling stomach demanded his attention, then he immediately thought of Tessa again. He debated with himself, then decided to test the waters, sending her a message inviting her to join him at the local burger shop to talk. After the prolonged radio silence, he was surprised when it didn't take long for her to respond.

I've already eaten, but thanks for the invite.
Enjoy your burger.

Dylan read the message again, trying to decide where they stood. She said no, and quickly. But she was polite, almost friendly. He buried his face in his hands He didn't know what to think. Maybe she was still upset about the fight. Be patient, he reminded himself. He wasn't sure how much patience he had to give. "I think I'm having withdrawals," he said out loud to himself. He drove the short distance to the burger place and ordered his usual burger plus a shake. While waiting for his food, thoughts of Tessa continued to haunt him. Feeling defeated, he slumped over, resting his head on the driver-side window. When would he learn not to blow up before getting all the facts first?

Arriving home, he grabbed his food and headed inside. Somehow, after all these years of living alone in that big house, it suddenly felt too big and too empty. Sitting at the table, he picked at his food. He could hear Tessa now in his mind, asking him to make love to her. He shoved the thoughts away, deciding to go to bed. Tomorrow, Tommy's crew was starting a new job, so he needed to be on his game. He ignored the inner voice that interrupted, warning him how impossible that would be without Tessa.

Chapter 35

His morning sucked. From the moment he opened his eyes, he felt like someone had beaten him in his sleep. And he had overslept, which gave them more time, he supposed. Forcing himself to move quickly, he swung his feet out of bed, and went straight to the kitchen to make coffee. When he heard his phone ringing, he ran to his room, hoping it was Tessa. Stubbing his little toe on the door jam, he cussed and continued, limping now to the nightstand. He grabbed his phone and looked at the display. It was Tommy.

"Dad, turn on the tv! Channel 12. Some idiot wasn't paying attention while driving and hit Tessa's car. They said she's in critical condition." Dylan felt a chill flush throughout his body as he grabbed the remote off of the nightstand and switched on the tv. Two newscasters chatted about the weather. Damn, he missed the story.

He turned his attention back to Tommy. "How do you know it was Tessa?" he asked, hoping his son was wrong.

"They showed her driver's license picture. Dad, I'm sorry. I thought you should know," Tommy rambled.

Dylan's heart dropped. "Where? Where did it happen?" he asked, cutting in.

"Apparently she was pulling out of the coffee shop not far from your house. Guy crossed the center line and hit her head on. They said he was texting."

Dylan's hand clenched. "Holy shit, did they arrest the bastard?"

"He was transported to the hospital, too," Tommy explained. "They are taking them both to Salem Hospital, downtown."

Dylan snatched his keys off the counter. "I'm going to head that way. Can you get everyone started at the job?"

"Yes, sir," Tommy assured him forcefully. Softly, he added, "Keep me updated? She seems like a real nice lady, Dad. Did you guys work things out?"

"No," Dylan answered, brokenly. "I left her a voice message, but she never called me back. I am such an ass."

"It's okay, Dad. We can worry about all that later. And she seemed to really like you. Just go to the hospital. And don't worry about work. We've got it handled. I'm here if you need me," he said, soothingly.

"Thanks son," Dylan grunted while pulling on his boots. "I might need you. Keep your phone on you please and call me if you have any problems."

"Will do, Dad. Be careful. Don't drive like an idiot. You won't be any good to her or anyone else if you get in an accident, too," he warned.

Dylan took his son's words to heart and drew a deep breath, trying to calm down. "I promise, son. Thanks."

As the call disconnected, Dylan poured coffee into his tumbler and headed to the hospital. He blinked rapidly, trying to keep the tears at bay so he could see to drive. The entire drive, he berated himself up for being such a jealous ass. Why hadn't Tessa called him back? If she survived this, he would make it all up to her. He had no idea how just yet, but he was willing to spend the rest of his life trying to find a way.

Approaching the entrance, Dylan noticed two distraught women huddling together outside, both looked just like Tessa. Pacing toward them, then away again, he debated before he awkwardly approached them to ask if they were there for Tessa Edwards. One woman was talking animatedly on a cell phone clutched so tightly her knuckles were white. The other practically vibrated as she paced back and forth.

As Dylan spoke, the one on the phone turned away, while the other stopped pacing and turned, looking him up and down. "Tessa's our mother. Who are you?"

Dylan extended his hand. "Sorry, my name is Dylan Wilson. I'm an old friend of your mom's. I heard about the accident on the news and had to see if she's ok. Is there anything you need?"

The young woman took his hand, shaking it as she exclaimed, "At last we meet! I know who you are, Dylan. You were Mama's first boyfriend. I'm Kendra, her daughter." Tossing a look over her shoulder at the doorway that separated patients and doctors from frantic loved ones, Kendra explained that the doctors were working on Tessa, but so far, were optimistic.

A voice interrupted, "Did I hear right? You're Dylan?" Kendra's twin stood, studying Dylan's face, her now forgotten cell phone dormant in her hand.

"Yes ma'am. I'm sorry we are meeting under these circumstances," he said, offering her a hand as well.

"I'm Sandra," she explained as she accepted the handshake. "I guess my sister told you they are working on Mom?"

Dylan ran a shaky hand through his hair. "Yes, she did. Do you know anything yet?"

The girls shook their head in unison as Sandra spoke up, "Nothing yet. We were here when they unloaded her from the ambulance. She was awake then, aware of what was going on. They had her on a back board because they weren't sure about the extent of her injuries. She let us know that it hurt like hell." Sandra paused, smiling sadly at her Mama's spunk.

Kendra continued, "The police are supposed to come out and talk to us once they get everyone's statement. They talked to four witnesses at the scene, and it sounds like this guy was on his phone."

Dylan's voice held an edge as he asked, "So, he's here too?"

Kendra sounded angry, too. "Oh yeah, he was brought in first. Crying like a little bitch because he lost his damn phone." She started pacing again, adding nervously, "Sorry about the language. Mama would threaten to wash my mouth out with soap."

Dylan gave a chuckle. "I bet she would. Don't worry, your secret is safe with me. Do you two need anything? Breakfast, coffee, a hammer to beat that idiot with? I have a bunch of them in the back of my truck," he offered.

Before the girls could respond, their brother, Justin, came barreling through the ER door. "Girls, they are taking Mama in for surgery. She's bleeding internally, and they said that's the most important thing to get under control right now. She also has three broken ribs and a broken arm."

As one, the three siblings headed back, with Dylan close behind. As the doors closed behind them, an attendant wheeled Tessa out into the hall. The doctor stopped up to the group, asking if they were family. Kendra spoke up, confirming their relationships. The doctor looked Dylan over, then decided not to press the issue. He explained the need to find the source of Tessa's internal bleeding and get it stopped. They would also be setting her broken bones. He warned them that Tessa would have a rough recovery ahead of her but assured them that the prognosis was good. He gave them a moment with Tessa but encouraged them to make it quick. The nurse assured them that Tessa could hear them, even unconscious. As a group, her children surged toward her, pouring declarations of love. Each gave her a kiss as they left her side.

Dylan approached next, whispering in her ear, "Tessa, I'm here baby girl. I love you. Please be ok. I need you in my life; we all do." Then he pressed a tender kiss to her lips. She felt cold, lifeless under his touch. It was more than he could handle. He stepped back, standing numb as they wheeled her away. Her children turned from the empty hallway to watch him as he stared down the hallway. They didn't know what to make of this man. The girls wandered back to the waiting room. Justin slowly approached Dylan.

Justin stood beside him until Dylan turned, emerging from his trance. "I'm Justin, Tessa's son."

Dylan heard him, but stood, looking at him in silence for a minute. He finally spoke quietly, voice low and broken, "I'm Dylan. Your mother and I dated forty years ago." He paused and took a shuddering breath. As he resumed, the words began to pour out, unstemmed, "We recently found each other through social media. We talk all the time, every day. We went on a few dates again, amazing dates. I own my own remodeling business and Tessa started helping me with design choices, picking out tile, counter tops. Your mom really has an eye for decorating." Then he stopped abruptly, as if the faucet had been shut off. He wasn't sure why he shared that much information. He stood stock still, numb and confused.

Justin eyed him, warily, "Are you the one who got jealous because you saw her hugging our father's friend?"

Dylan looked up, startled, "Yes. She told you about that?"

"She did. She told me about that and the next morning when she showed up at your house. I know all about the fight you guys had," Justin spoke dispassionately, deliberately.

Dylan looked at his boots, then returned Justin's gaze. "I never meant to hurt your mother. I really don't know what came over me."

Justin paused, weighing Dylan's words. "Funny thing is, I talked to her this morning before she headed to get that coffee. I don't think hurt is the right word anymore. She was pissed. You were always the jealous type, she said, but you still surprised her. But then you left her that voicemail message. And she decided to go pick you up a coffee and show up at your house so you two could talk this out."

Dylan's mouth opened, but no sound came out as understanding dawned. Justin put a hand on his shoulder, "I'm sure everything will be alright. Now we just have to hurry up and wait. The doctor told me it could be a couple of hours. How about we go get some coffee?"

Knowing that Tessa was on her way to see him when that man had slammed his car into hers left him elated and devastated, all at the same time. He looked at Justin gratefully, choking out, "That would be great. I'm buying."

"Yeah, you are," Justin agreed with a nod and a smile.

Stopping to get the girls, they found the hospital coffee shop. As the ordered, Dylan had to laugh when both of the girls proclaimed their signature drinks to be the same hot caramel mocha that their mother loved so much. Justin took his coffee black, just like Dylan. Gathered around the table in the coffee shop, they quietly sipped their brews, each lost in thoughts about Tessa. Dylan felt worse knowing Tessa was on that road because she'd been headed to see him. He fantasized about getting his hands on the ass that hit her but banished the idea. He needed to focus on his Tessa.

Dylan's phone rang, shattering the stillness. He excused himself and walked away to answer his phone. It was Tommy.

"Hey Dad, any news yet?"

Dylan paced the lobby as he relayed the news. "She's bleeding internally so they took her back to surgery. She also has a few broken ribs and a broken arm. I did get to see her briefly when they were wheeling her into surgery. She doesn't look good at all, Tommy. She has several cuts on her face, and she was unconscious and very pale." He fell silent, taking shaky breaths before continuing, "Tommy, she was at that coffee shop getting coffee to come see me."

"Wow, Dad. I'm so sorry," he said. "Can I do anything?"

"Maybe. I don't know. Her kids are here with me. I guess I could use some moral support. Is everything lined up there?" he asked, hesitantly.

"Yeah, it's covered. All the guys know what's going on." Tommy's voice took on a teasing tone, "Oh, and Uncle Donny said he has a bone to pick with you. He's pretty upset that you didn't tell him you and Tessa were back together. He said she was always good for you. He always liked her."

"We're not together. But I plan on changing that as soon as I can." Dylan sounded determined.

"I will head that way. Do you need me to bring you anything?" Tommy offered.

Dylan thought for a moment, then answered, "Nothing that I can think of right now. Thanks for understanding, son."

"She seems great, Dad. I'm sure she'll pull through this." The line went quiet. "Dad, you there?"

Dylan answered this time, "Sorry son, I'm here. I think I need to call the phone company and get my old number back. I hope none of our clients have been trying to get a hold of me."

"A few of them have called me already," Tommy admitted. "Oh, and I called the phone company. They said they can change the number back, but you have to call them."

Dylan felt a rush of pride over his son. Tommy was reliable, kind, and smart. He was truly fortunate to have Tommy handling things. "Thanks, son. I'll do that now. See you in a bit?"

"Yes, sir. I will head that way."

Ending the call, Dylan headed back to the coffee shop. Kendra stood as he approached, wanting to get back to the waiting room in case the medical team came out to talk to them. They all agreed that was a good idea and headed that way together. Dylan sent a message to his Tommy, letting him know where to meet, then put his phone on silent and slid it in his pocket.

They all walked silently to the waiting room. Minutes that felt like hours passed in the stillness before finally, Sandra spoke. "What was Mom like, when you guys were first dating?"

He grinned, "Your mom was a spit fire," he said, laughing. "She was so ornery, loved pulling pranks on people. And talking, my goodness that girl could talk!" He eyed the girls who were drinking in all the details about their mother. "You know, Tessa looks like her Mama, and you two look like her." He smiled as they looked at each other with expressions almost painfully familiar to him.

Justin chimed in, "She's still ornery. She likes to tell the same old corny jokes to anyone who will listen. And it makes her so happy, we just laugh like we haven't heard them a million times." His voice broke a little, but he paused and resumed, sounding stronger, "But man can she cook. Christmastime has always been her favorite. She loves to decorate every room in the house. When we were little, she would always bake Christmas cookies and let us decorate them. I mean, those were some ugly cookies, but she would never admit that. She'd just gush about what a good job we did and how pretty they were."

The girls agreed, laughing tearfully. Sandra added, "We really need to talk her into doing those with us again this year."

Kendra nodded, supplying more memories. "She always made such a big deal out of our birthdays. Huge parties, pretty cakes. I remember one year she hired a clown. We loved it."

Justin interjected, "I was lucky. My birthday is in July and we had a pool, so I got to have swimming parties." He sounded young and excited again as he described them.

Dylan just sat back, listening, letting them spill out their stories. He could picture it all in his mind. It was no surprise that Tessa was a good mom to her kids, but it was touching to hear how much it meant to them. Time sped up as they told story after story until the doctor came out. A curtain of silence fell, and they all stood, trying to prepare for the worst.

"She came through with flying colors," the doctor said, smiling. "Her ribs were just fractured, so we got lucky there. The internal bleeding resulted from a tiny rupture in her small intestine. We were able to repair it. We set her left arm and will re-evaluate it tomorrow for swelling. It has to go down before we can put a cast on it. But honestly, she's done remarkably well. Is she right-handed or left-handed?"

Kendra took over, "Mom's right-handed." She filled the doctor in on the care-giving plan. They had already set up a rotating schedule to stay with her until they were satisfied that she could do things on her own. Dylan interjected, offering to help in any way he could. The doctor remarked that Tessa was lucky to have so much support, then said they could visit her room, but only two at a time until she was moved to another unit. He assured them that Tessa should be able to go home in a few days. They just wanted to keep a precautionary eye on her. The girls decided to check back in with their jobs, then take turns sitting with her overnight. That left Justin and Dylan to sit with her; Justin led the way.

The room was dimly lit, but they could see her form lying on the bed, a chair on each side. Monitors and machinery beeped and hissed in the otherwise quiet room. Justin bent down, kissing his Mama on the cheek. He hovered, whispering to her, assuring her that he was there, and she was going to be ok. Dylan sank into one of the bedside chairs, propping his elbows on the bed and holding her hand. An IV impaled her perfect skin, providing fluids and medication. His heart broke, seeing her this way. He knew what a fool he had been. The doctor had warned that she would be drowsy the rest of the day, but he couldn't help watching her beautiful face, wishing she would open her eyes. A long cut marked her forehead and several smaller cuts scattered across her face and hands. He noticed a larger gash on her shoulder that had been stitched closed.

His throat clenched and felt raw as he surveyed her injuries. She was on her way to see him. To discuss the fight caused by his jealousy. He sat, watching her for a long time, frustrated, tormented by helplessness. How could he just sit idly by? He had so much to make up to her. He stood up abruptly, telling Justin he had to go. Bending down, he whispered in her ear "I'm so sorry I hurt you, baby girl. I promise to make this up to you." He pressed a soft kiss to her forehead, then left her with her son. On the way out, he called Tommy with an update and telling him that he didn't need to come to the hospital after all. Tessa was going to be okay.

Chapter 36

Dylan and Tommy stood in Tessa's back yard, squinting at the newly vacant space where the hot tub had been. She would be home from the hospital in the next day or two, and there was a lot to be done. With her kids' permission, he'd set to work on giving her the firepit she wanted as a welcome home surprise. He felt lucky to have Tommy's expert help.

Kendra and Sandra pitched in, too, keeping her plants watered to help ease Tessa's worry. They filled the fridge and cabinets with groceries and changed the sheets on her bed. As Dylan worked next to his son, he overheard the girls discussing the plan once more. Kendra would head to the hospital tomorrow and stay with her the first night. Sandra would tag in the next day. Everyone hoped she'd be coming home then.

Two days later, Dylan returned to the hospital just after lunch. Sandra had spent the night and was looking disheveled. He found Tessa awake, just finishing a few bites of her lunch. "Hey," she said in a shaky voice.

"Hey, yourself," he responded quietly, glancing at Sandra who had just dozed off. "You look better than the last time I saw you. You have the color back in your cheeks, and I can see those pretty blue eyes."

Sandra startled them both, interrupting, "Oh my goodness, just tell her how worried you were and stop with the sappy stuff."

They shared a laugh as Sandra excused herself to go get a cup of coffee.

Dylan sat on a chair beside her bed and took her hand in his. "Baby girl, I'm so sorry. I should have trusted you."

Tessa smiled. "I forgive you. You were cheated on. I understand how that could make you apprehensive about what was going on when you saw your girl hugging someone else."

Dylan looked at her, hopefully. "So, are you still my girl?"

Tessa paused, looking away. "I honestly don't know what to say. Right now, I just want to go home."

He gave her hand a gentle squeeze. "I understand. I want you concentrating on getting better. And I'll respect your space, but I would like to stop by and see you, if that's okay?"

"I think that would be okay. But until I'm back to my old self, I would like to put the discussion on hold."

"Nothing would please me more," Dylan said with a smile. "May I kiss you?"

Tessa blushed and nodded. He moved in gently and touched his lips to hers. She gave a low moan, then felt his lips slowly rise in a smile. Taking a few steps back, he gazed down at her. He spoke softly, "You know, when I saw you in that bed after you came out of surgery, my heart fell. Facing the idea of never seeing you again, I knew how royally I'd screwed up."

"The sad part is that it took this accident to bring you to your senses!" Tessa responded.

"You are going to hold this against me, aren't you?" he asked, running his hands down the length of his jeans.

"Maybe for a little bit. Dylan, it hurts that you didn't trust me. I meant it when I said I understand your fears, but you didn't even give me a chance to explain. If you had stopped that day, I would have introduced you to Steve. You would have seen the wedding ring on his finger, and heard how much he loves his wife, just listening to how he talks about her."

Dylan cast his eyes down, studying the cracks in the hospital tile floor. "I know. I meant what I said before. I have a lot of kissing up to do. And I really, really am sorry. The thought of losing you again is too much to bear."

Tessa pressed on. "Dylan, I am not one of your wives. I have never given you reason not to trust me. And the way you talked to me that morning when I showed up at your house and you were passed out in your truck… My God, Dylan, you know how I feel about drunk driving. If we can't communicate with each other, I just see no reason to carry on." Tessa turned away, sad but firm.

Dylan stood frozen for a few seconds, as if deciding what to say. He mumbled, "I'm going to run downstairs and grab something to eat. Do you want anything?"

Tessa's eyes flashed fire. "There you go, deflecting again."

Dylan shook. "I'm not deflecting Tess. I need time to sort out what I'm feeling. I have been in love before, but I've never felt this way about anyone else and yes, those demons are still there. I need to figure out what it all means."

Tessa watched him a moment, then said calmly, "Go. Sort out your feelings. Let me know when you are ready to talk because if we are going to work, a lot of talking needs to take place. As a matter of fact, until you know what you want, and where I fit into your life, just keep your distance. Let me heal, physically and emotionally before you break my heart again. I'm not sure I have another forty years to invest."

Dylan stood to leave, took a step forward, then stopped. He watched the tears welling up in her eyes. He cleared his throat, "As you wish. I have my old phone number back, in case you need me. But for the record, I do know what I want. And I don't plan to stop until I get it."

Tessa turned on the television as he left the room, trying to distract herself from thinking about him. It didn't work, but still, she felt she'd made the right decision. At this point in her life, she didn't need any drama. She loved him and that would never change. She knew he loved her, too, despite his impossibly stubborn nature. She was taking a chance of losing the love of her life by taking this stand, but she had to do it. Life was too short to live in distrust. She didn't need that.

Chapter 31

ylan walked down the hall with his head down so nobody would notice the tears streaming down his face. He went straight to the gift shop and paid for two dozen roses to be sent to her room, then headed to his truck, feeling lost. Would she ever take him back? He loved her; he would do anything for her. He needed to talk. Dylan pulled up to Tessa's house where Tommy was working on the fire pit, just in time to catch Justin leaving. Seeing Dylan arrive, Justin killed his truck and met him on the front walk.

"Hello again," he said, reaching out for another handshake, "the fire pit looks amazing. Mom is going to love it. Tommy was finishing it up right as I got here."

Dylan smiled, hoping Justin was right. He wanted to make her happy. "Your mom mentioned to me that she wanted a fire pit when she sold the hot tub. I thought this would be a nice surprise and a good place to relax during recovery."

"She is going to love it. She has talked about selling that hot tub for years." He looked in the back of Dylan's truck, catching sight of the chairs and fire tools he'd brought to complete the effect. "Those will look amazing around the pit. Did you buy them for her?"

Dylan smiled. "I did. I guess I'm still trying to kiss up. It might take a while," he admitted. Justin helped Dylan unload the six chairs, and together they set them up around the fire pit. They chatted as they worked, and Dylan learned that Tessa talked constantly about her trip to Florida. He hadn't realized just how much she loved that hotel. Justin also casually mentioned that Tessa had talked to him about

Dylan and their past. He didn't provide details, and Dylan didn't want to ask. He would find out later. If there was a later.

Justin, Tommy, and Dylan stood around the firepit, admiring their work, and visiting for a short time until Justin said he was headed to the hospital. As they said their goodbyes, Dylan promised to be finished with cleanup and gone before dinner time. He overheard Tommy and Justin promising to get together for a few games of pool soon. Dylan smiled, thinking how easy all of this could have been, then turned his attention to helping Tommy clean up the site. When they finished, each climbed into their trucks and headed their separate ways. On the way home, a plan hatched in Dylan's mind, growing from something Justin had said. It would only work if Tessa gave him another chance, but he'd have to worry about that later. For now, he had details to work through. And whistling, he felt hopefully and happy for the first time in days.

Chapter 38

The doctor came in early morning. Tessa glanced at the window; it was still dark outside. She hadn't slept well that night. She hoped he would release her today. She couldn't wait to sleep in her own bed without the constant beeping driving her mad, and the steady interruptions to check blood pressure or temperature. The girls planned on taking turns staying with her for a bit, and she was okay with that, especially once they agreed that she would be the one to decide when she could take care of herself. The doctor, however, had different ideas. She fell just short of the goal to be fever free for twenty-four hours. One more night, he had said cheerfully as he left the room. One more night, her mind echoed, but she felt depressed. She rolled over, trying to get more sleep, but that didn't happen either.

Sandra arrived promptly at 7:15 with a caramel mocha and blueberry muffin. Tessa was still disappointed, but the coffee and muffin definitely brightened her day. After taking the first, life-affirming sip of sweet caffeine, she took a nibble of her muffin, then shared the bad news with Sandra, stressing how ridiculous she found the extended stay. Sandra shook her head, backing up the doctor. "Seriously, Mom, you were in a pretty serious accident. It wouldn't bother me if they kept you at least a week. Besides, I know you. You'll go home and overdo it. You always do. You're always so focused on trying to take care of everyone else. It's time to let others take care of you." Sandra took a breath, but continued, "Mom, you know I love you, but you need to slow down. Focus on you."

Tessa knew her daughter expected her to argue, but she just grinned. "Well, for your information, smarty pants, I have slowed down. I've started taking better care of me since I got back from Florida. And I'm ready to get back to that. Honey, I really appreciate you worrying about me, seriously I do. But…"

Tessa stopped and thought about what she was about to admit to her daughter. But being honest about the situation was exactly what she needed. She plunged ahead, "But since Dylan has started taking up so much of my time, I've realized how much I missed out on because I don't think about myself, too. He really has made me feel alive again. I don't know what is going to happen. I don't know where any of this is going. But the one thing I am sure of is that I have the best kids a girl could ask for."

She paused again, but felt like it was time to let go, let it all out. She looked at Sandra and said, "I'm doing things I've wanted to for years but never had the time because I gave it all away. I've learned to say yes to me and what I want in life. Hopefully, I have a lot of life left. I plan on making the best of every minute I do have. I want to travel again. I haven't been on a cruise in years, and I started thinking a solo cruise could be cool. Or, who knows, maybe I'll find a handsome man who steals my heart."

Sandra cocked an eyebrow and smirked, "I think you already have."

Tessa sighed, waving away the idea. "Let's not go there. I mean, we talked, but I'm not sure we settled anything. He's just so stubborn," she breathed. Tessa leaned back and closed her eyes, then plunged ahead again, "He knew Steve was a friend of your dad's, yet he still got mad jealous over a goodbye hug. I don't know. The man I saw slumped over in that truck is not the man I fell for over forty years ago. He says he loves me, but love doesn't talk that way. I don't think it's something I can just get over. I have always cared for Dylan, but I don't like the man I saw that night. I feel so derailed. I was on my way to talk to him. I knew exactly what I was going to say. Now, I just don't know."

Sandra looked at her mom sadly, "Mom, how long did ya'll date and why did you break up?"

Tessa opened her eyes again, staring at the ceiling. She took a deep breath and spoke with a clear voice. She started at the beginning, explaining how they met when she was only fifteen years old, coming together because their parents used to be neighbors. She spoke tenderly of how sweet and protective he was, how in love she felt. Her voice hardened when she told her daughter that he broke her heart with no real explanation. Then sharper as she mentioned Darla, and softer again, steadier as she described running into each other periodically over the years. Her tone changed again, became light, joyful as she told her about getting back in touch with him, messaging him during her trip to Florida, and all the time she's spent with him since her return, only growing sad again as she trailed off with a broken, "and now…"

Sandra sat in silence for a few short minutes. Her eyes shone with tears as she took Tessa's hand, tugging to get her to look at her as she spoke. "Mom, don't you see? He's your true love. I know you loved Dad. But Dylan was your first love, the one who showed you what true love could be."

Tessa laughed, incredulously, "My what?"

"Your true love, Mom," Sandra insisted. "He's the one you've been waiting on. I don't remember much about our lives with dad, but I do remember it wasn't perfect. We all love him, and I remember how you cried when he died, but I don't remember you ever looking at Dad the way you look at Dylan when he was in here."

Tessa sat silent, stunned by what Sandra had to say. But Sandra wasn't finished. "You know, I realize the fight you guys had, well, it was an ugly one. But overall, Dylan seems like a nice guy. He was so worried, literally pacing the floor when they brought you in. I really think he genuinely cares for you. Give him a chance, Mom. Just listen to what he has to say."

Sandra's words worked on her heart, but Tessa wasn't quite sure she was ready to expose it again. She told her daughter, "We are definitely going to talk, trust me. But as far as anything more, I just don't know. I won't lie, he holds a special place in my heart, and he probably always will, but I can't, I won't deal with this kind of jealously."

Sandra nodded. "So, don't tell me, tell Dylan."

"Oh, I plan on it," Tessa agreed.

A knock on the door interrupted their conversation. The gift shop attendant strode in, delivering two dozen roses, one yellow bouquet signifying friendship, and one red for love. Tessa's eyes widened. "Wow," she exclaimed, "those are beautiful. Who are they from?"

Sandra walked over, removing the cards. "Let's find out," she said opening the card from the red roses first, knowing they were probably from Dylan. She slid the card out of the tiny envelope, unfolding it with dramatic flourish. "I love you. Please don't shut me out. Dylan," she read aloud with a knowing smile.

"Wipe that smile off your face," Tessa said, trying to hide the fact that her heart melted just a wee bit. "Ok, who are the yellow ones from?"

Sandra already had the note open and had a head start on Tessa. Looking up at her mother, she tried to keep her face neutral, then began reading again, this time out loud. "So many memories over the last 40 years make me smile. You are forever in my heart. Dylan" Sandra looked a bit like she was melting, too.

Tessa wasn't ready to give up her fire. "Wow, I guess he remembers all those years when we were still kind to each other."

"Mom," Sandra protested, "seems to me like he's pretty serious about you. Being a friend is just as important in a relationship as love. If you have both, then you have all you need."

Tessa rolled her eyes but couldn't hide her smile. "Have you thought about writing for Hallmark?"

Sandra laughed. "There she is," she said, "that's the mom I have been waiting for."

Chapter 39

Tessa smiled at the feeling of the warmth of the nearby fire on her skin. Sitting outside by the fire pit with Dylan, she found herself memorized by the flames. It was the first burn, and she was still thrilled that he'd surprised her with it when she arrived home.

Dylan looked nervous, but handsome in the flickering light. "Tess, thank you for the chance to talk. First, I want you to know that I trust you. I know that hug was innocent, and I'm so sorry for everything–what I said to you, all the trouble I caused. More than anything, I'm sorry about the accident. If I hadn't been such an ass, it wouldn't have happened. Not to you."

Tessa leaned forward, looking into the dancing flames. "Don't bet on it. There's a reason it happened the way it did. I have no idea what that is right now. But at least we're talking about it. Dylan, I would never do anything to hurt you. Never do anything to drive you away."

"I know that now. I was such a fool and it almost cost me the love of my life," Dylan said softly.

"Well, we got lucky this time. In a lot of ways, real lucky. But if anything like this happens again, you have to promise me we will talk, without the hateful words. If you are too mad to talk, then voice that. Let me know that you are upset and need time to process or whatever." She watched him, saw the light come back into his eyes as she spoke of their future.

"I promise," he said, revealing the classic Dylan grin she'd missed so much. "Now get over here where you belong and let me hold you."

Tessa smiled, holding up a single finger. "On one condition. Dylan Wilson, I know you are keeping something from me. I keep catching you looking at me with a cat that ate the canary look on your face. Not to mention all the suspicious texting. You're not sneaky, by the way. What do you have up your sleeve?"

Dylan raised his arm and looked into his sleeve. "Hmmm, looks like it's just my smelly arm pit. Want to smell for yourself?" he said with a wink.

Tessa shook her head, chuckling, "Nah, but thanks for the offer."

Tessa moved over by Dylan and snuggled in close as they shared a laugh, the heat from the fire, memories from yesteryear, and dreams unharnessed until the fire had burned down to glowing embers and it was time for Dylan to go home. She knew he had a busy day and needed to get some sleep. Tommy's crew was scheduled to finish the first kitchen remodel Tessa had helped him with, and she was excited to see her ideas implemented. She promised to drop by after her hair appointment. Not wanting the night to end, they discussed a few more details for their newly made plans for a trip to Florida. She couldn't wait to show him all the things she fell in love with while she was really falling back in love with him.

He finally kissed her good night, driving off into the night with a smile on his face as she headed inside to bed. Walking on air, she got ready for bed, then curled up under the covers, eagerly anticipating dreams of him. Everything was finally as it should be.

Epilogue

One year from the day that Tessa boarded her flight to Florida, she entered the airport again, this time with Dylan. She couldn't wait to show him why she loved it so much. Careful to stress why this should remain a vacation destination, she started with a cons list that she relayed to him while parking: too much sand everywhere, the consuming humidity, not to mention all the tourists. She knew they would enjoy their time there, and that they would be ready to go home when it was over. After checking their bags, they settled in at the bar to have a drink while waiting for their flight, the usual White Russian for Tessa, and a beer for Dylan. Tessa pulled up her tablet and they read through the messages they had exchanged over the last year, laughing about how nervous they both felt at the time.

Tessa had convinced Dylan first class was the way to go, and as he sank into the seat and stretched his legs, he agreed. Dylan had flown before, but years ago. To pass the time, they quietly planned their itinerary. Her niece and family had moved to Alaska, so the two lovebirds were pretty much on their own. They made plans to go to the same area Liz had taken her to for shopping.

Dylan grew quiet, constantly checking his phone. Tessa thought he might be nervous, but he assured her that he wasn't. He was just checking in with Tommy to make sure everything was going okay. Dylan smiled apologetically and switched his phone to airplane mode. He cracked a joke about the drunk sunbather, causing Tessa to erupt into giggles. As the pilot taxied out to the runway, Tessa put her phone on airplane mode, too, and they both sat back in their seats, ready for takeoff. Tessa turned to peer out her window, gazing at the clouds as they passed through them. Dylan squirmed in the aisle seat before closing his eyes, resting with a silly grin on his face. They held hands as the plane took off, spiriting them away to the beach vacation he had sprung on her just a week before.

The relatively uneventful flight offered small snacks and lively conversation about dating in the 70's and how much times have changed. They agreed that this generation of kids were missing out on drive-in movies, getting drinks from an actual car hop, and making out at the lake in the rain. When the in-flight movie was announced, they laughed in disbelief and talked of kismet, then she rested her head on his shoulder as they prepared to watch the movie from their first date. As the opening credits rolled, Tessa accused him of arranging it. Dylan denied it with a shake of his head, telling her he wouldn't mind actually seeing the movie this time. She blushed, reminded of what happened last time the movie had played.

As the plane bumped down the runway in Pensacola, Tessa swapped her shoes for the flip flops she'd packed in her carry-on again, starting to feel a little giddy about the week ahead. Dylan projected the calm and cool demeanor he always did, but she knew he was ready to make memories they'd never forget. The limo Dylan arranged as a surprise arrived to pick them up from the airport. Tessa clapped her hands as Dylan told the driver to take the long way to the hotel so they could enjoy the champagne he'd ordered.

Driving along the beach, Tessa sipped champagne and watched the people out her window. She noticed new shops and restaurants. For a girl who loved the beach, she was surprisingly unimpressed by seafood, but knew Dylan loved it. She made a mental note of the new choices where she could dine on chicken or steak. She made heroic efforts not to oooohh and aaaaahh at the sights, sure that would set Dylan on a mission to secure every wonder for her. In the reflection of the window, Tessa saw Dylan typing on his phone. After ignoring it the first few times, she finally sighed, instructing, "Dylan! Put that down and enjoy our vacation. Work will still be there when you get back."

"I will baby girl," he promised, "one more second. It is work stuff, but Tommy has it under control. He just had a quick question."

Finishing his text, Dylan switched the phone off, sliding it into his pocket.

Thirty minutes later, they were pulling up to the hotel. As the driver unloaded their luggage, a bell boy arrived, and they were quickly off to their room. Abandoning the luggage for later, Dylan and Tessa emerged onto their third-floor balcony. The sun shone high in the sky and the beaches were crowded with people. Dylan stood behind her, arms wrapped around her and rested his chin on top of her head. "I see why you love it so much," he murmured, "it's beautiful here."

She rested her hands on his forearms, reinforcing his hold. "Just wait until you see the sunset tonight. Or the sunrise in the morning. They are breathtaking."

He nuzzled her neck. "Baby girl, nothing is as breathtaking as you are right now."

Ignoring the feeling of her flush, Tessa turned in his arms, looking up into his peaceful gaze. "Do you realize this will be the first night we spend together?"

Dylan teased, "Are you trying to warn me that you hog the covers? Or that your morning breath will take the paint off the walls? Wait, do you look like Medusa in the morning?"

Tessa rolled her eyes. "No silly. It just took us so long to get here. I'm excited about waking up next to you in the morning. I might have to creep into the bathroom and run a brush over my teeth. You're not too far off about my morning breath." She leaned into him, tilting her face up.

Dylan laughed and kissed her on the tip of her nose. "Tomorrow will be amazing. I promise. I have the day all planned."

"I know. You told me not to make any plans for our first or last day here. And I didn't. As long as I get my coffee in the morning, we can do whatever you want," she promised.

Dylan chuckled and shook his head. "Don't worry. You'll get your coffee; then we are going shopping. You'll need a fancy dress for our last vacation dinner."

Tessa bounced up and down on her toes. "So that's tomorrow's plan? Because I saw some nice shops when I was here with Liz. I'm not usually big on shopping, really. But there were a few things I had my eye on last time."

"And why didn't you get them? I told you I would send you money if you needed any. Do I need to turn you over my knee?" Dylan reprimanded, playfully.

Tessa threw her head back and laughed, "No dummy. I didn't have a reason to buy one before. But if you are taking me to a nice dinner, I have a reason now. But don't go getting any ideas. You will not be paying for it." Tessa crossed her arms and the look she shot him dared him to argue.

Dylan held up his hands in concession. He'd already known she would argue with him about letting him pay, so he had given Sandra money along with detailed instructions to deposit it into Tessa's account the morning of their shopping trip.

Dylan didn't have swim trunks, so they went to the gift shop to purchase something suitable for lounging on the beach. Tessa could already taste the Pineapple Upside-Down Delight she planned to order at the bar the moment she arrived. With Dylan appropriately attired in bright shorts that showed off his ultra-white legs, they left the room and headed downstairs. Tessa couldn't resist teasing him, saying how thankful she was for the sunglasses and sunscreen she'd packed.

Despite the crowds they'd noticed earlier, they found a nice spot on the beach with a cheerful umbrella to shield them from the bright rays warming the sand. A figure approached, and as he neared, Tessa sprang up to give her favorite server a hug. She quickly introduced him to Dylan. With a quick smile, Dylan offered his hand, saying, "I remember that face from our... interesting video chat. Good to meet you in person, Sam. Thanks for looking out for my gal last year." Sam accepted his hand and they shook. Dylan clapped him on the shoulder, and once Sam brought their conversation back to business, ordered a Pineapple Upside-Down Paradise for Tessa, and a cold beer for himself. Sam left to get their drinks, and Dylan eyed Tessa, commenting, "I think that young man is smitten with you." Tessa waved him off with a laugh.

As their drinks arrived, they sat in a comfortable silence, listening to the waves. The next few days passed by in a blur of happiness. Tessa and Dylan shared a couples massage that she booked–in their hotel room, taking pains to avoid ending up at the salon she'd visited before. They shopped, and Tessa picked out a pretty tea length dress in light peach. Dylan encouraged her to finish the look with matching sandals. They spent days exploring the area, visiting most of the restaurants, and Tessa even managed to sell him on a couple's pedicure. Tessa emerged from the salon with fingers and toes tipped in the perfect peach to match her new dinner dress, while Dylan's clear polish gave him a nice natural shine. One afternoon, they took in an excursion on a fishing boat where Dylan caught a huge Marlin. His contact photo in Tessa's phone was quickly updated to show a proud Dylan, grinning from ear to ear, and holding up his prize. Evenings belonged to the almost deserted beach where the lovers walked hand-in-hand, sometimes in animated conversation, and other times wrapped in the quiet presence of togetherness. After they eventually retired to their room, they spent their nights making love until they fell asleep in one another's arms. Mornings began with contented smiles, ignored morning breath, and shared showers, washing each other's bodies until they needed washing again. Tessa was in heaven. She didn't want the week to end.

But time marched on. On the morning of their final day, Tessa noticed that Dylan seemed preoccupied with his phone. She busied herself, sending their laundry out to be cleaned and preparing to pack for their return trip home. Dylan wanted to spend time in the room together for their last full day of vacation. They ordered breakfast from room service and dined on the balcony. They snapped selfies with their incredible view behind them until Dylan decided to lie down for a bit and invited her to join him. She lay quiet and still in his arms, her head nestled into his chest. After a few moments of heavy silence, Dylan asked her if something was wrong. Assuring him that nothing was wrong, she admitted that she was a little sad that the week had passed so quickly. Dylan caressed her cheek, then gathered her more tightly in his arms. He spoke low, his breath caressing her ear, "You are going to love what I have planned for dinner. It will probably be a long night, though, so you should get some rest."

Tessa's mind raced, wondering what he could possibly have up his sleeve. Listening to his heart beating rhythmically beneath her head, she drifted. Before she knew it, he was rousing her with a kiss on her temple, and they were up and taking a shower together. Dylan adjusted the water to the perfect temperature, then told her to step under the stream to wet her hair. Wordlessly, she did, and soon felt his hands working up a lather of shampoo in her hair. With her head back and her eyes closed she enjoyed the feel of his hands in her hair, then felt them move down to her breasts. After exploring her wet, soapy skin, he returned to her hair, rinsing out the shampoo. As the suds swirled around the drain, he guided her gently against the wall she was facing, rubbing her back. Soon, his hot wet body pressed against her. His hands reached back around, continuing the work they'd begun. She could feel the pressure building, just as he reached down to briefly stoke the fire there. Aware of his fullness at her entrance, she sighed. Dylan moaned and dove deeply. Bracing herself against the wall, she offered all that he wanted, and he didn't waste any time taking it.

They finished the shower, and Tessa slipped into her new peach dress. She wore her hair up in a bun with loose curls around her face. Dylan looked handsome in his finest clothes as they headed out into the hall. She had a feeling something was up but wasn't sure what it could be. As they neared the elevator, Dylan pushed the up button. Thinking he'd made a mistake, Tessa pointed out, "You pushed the wrong button."

Dylan responded with a nonchalant, "nope," keeping his eyes trained on the elevator doors until they slid open. Confused, Tessa stepped inside with him, and they rode silently to the top floor of the hotel. When the doors opened again, Dylan took her hand, leading her up the last flight of stairs to the rooftop. A soft gasp escaped her mouth as it dropped open once the door swung open into the evening light. Several strands of clear lights twinkled, casting a magical light across the rooftop. And there, in the center, both of their families stood, all dressed up, with teary expressions and broad smiles.

Stunned now, Tessa looked at Dylan, stammering, "What's going on? Did you arrange all this?"

Dylan turned to face her, holding both of her hands in his. Smiling, he looked her in the eyes, took a deep breath, then announced, "Tessa, if you will have me, I want tonight to be the night you finally become my wife. Will you?"

Speechless, Tessa surveyed the rooftop, noticing violin players at the ready, and an arch draped in white netting with a man standing patiently underneath. Justin stepped up, handing her a gorgeous bouquet of flowers. Kendra and Sandra wore matching dresses, each holding smaller versions of the bouquet she was nervously clutching in her hands. "You… all of you kids knew about this?"

Kendra smiled, eyes sparkling with joy for her mother, and said, "Yes, mom, we did. We actually helped arrange it. Now I believe the man asked you a question and you have yet to answer. Is tonight the night you become his wife?"

Glancing around once more at the beautiful scene, tears welled up in her eyes. She turned back to Dylan. "Of course, I will," she answered quietly. Dylan caressed her cheek, then turned, striding to the arch where their sons waited, his and hers. His daughter cued the violin players and the wedding march flowed from their instruments. Her heart thundered. She couldn't believe she was actually marrying Dylan, her Dylan. The man who drove her crazy and gave her an almost permanent blush. He wanted to be hers.

She floated up the aisle, finding it was Sam, her cabana boy, who'd been patiently waiting there, throughout her proposal, to perform the ceremony. Noticing the surprised look in her eye, he assured her, "Don't worry. I do this often. I'm ordained to perform weddings." Tessa threw her head back, laughing with abandon. Composing herself, she turned her attention back to Dylan. Her gaze caressed his face, studied the smile that had driven her mad for decades, then settled into the eyes that flamed every time he saw her. Taking his hand in hers, she whispered, "What took you so long?"

After the short ceremony, the newly united family adjourned to the hotel restaurant where a decadent buffet waited in a private room for their reception. They laughed, cried, toasted, and shared stories over dinner, until the couple retired to their room.

The next morning, Mr. and Mrs. Wilson returned to the restaurant for breakfast with their kids. The sunrise painted a beautiful morning for them and sharing it with their families made the occasion perfect. Over mimosas, Dylan presented Tessa with tickets for their honeymoon trip; he had booked four glorious days on a cruise ship in the Bahamas. Tessa never felt so alive. She was excited to spend the rest of her days with Dylan, reliving old memories and making new ones. The clinking of a spoon against glass pulled the newlyweds' gazes from one another long enough to hear the exciting news that Tessa would be a grandma in seven short months. Excitement erupted across the dining room, and Dylan whispered to Tessa that there couldn't be a more perfect ending to their Florida trip. Tessa agreed.

As the kids loaded into the shuttle that would take them back to the airport, Tessa's eyes filled with tears. She promised piles of pictures, assured them all she would miss them terribly, and vowed to prepare a big meal for them all once she returned from her honeymoon. She waved as they pulled away, Dylan beside her arm wrapped around her waist. Tessa looked at him and smiled. She kept pinching herself to make sure she wasn't dreaming. Looking down at the beautiful ring Dylan slipped on her hand. Then she remembered, she'd had this dream before. Now it seemed her dream had finally come true.

About The Author

Born and raised in the Midwest, Terrie lives with her "Superman" husband. They have 4 grown kids all of whom are cherished and loved. They were left with an empty nest, so they adopted one dog, one cat and five goats. They both enjoy traveling and do it as much as possible. When not traveling they also enjoy gardening and sitting on the back patio just chilling together or you can find Terrie sitting in her beach-themed she-shed writing. Terrie was the second of four kids growing up. Reading has always been her favorite pastime. Writing and publishing books is a dream come true.

Stay in touch...

T Edwards Barks

T Edwards Barks

author_tedwardsbarks

tedwardsbarks.com

Printed in the USA
CPSIA information can be obtained
at www.ICGtesting.com
LVHW040510061123
762866LV00054B/1238